COLD IN THE SOUL

A PULSATING SERIAL KILLER THRILLER

DEREK FEE

MIST MEDIA

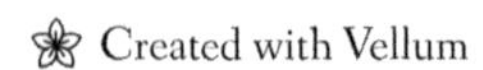
Created with Vellum

Publisher's Note: This is a work of fiction. Names, characters, places, and incidents are a product of the author's imagination. Locales and public names are sometimes used for atmospheric purposes. Any resemblance to actual people, living or dead, or to businesses, companies, events, institutions, or locales is completely coincidental.

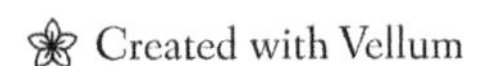

For Aine, Bobbie and Sean

PROLOGUE

He whistled as he dug. He had selected an area where the ground was loose and the digging was easy. Progress had been better than he'd expected. A hole three feet deep should do the job. Six feet long by two feet wide by three feet deep was the ideal in his experience. No inquisitive dog would ever stumble on a grave he had dug. He stopped digging and leaned on his shovel. The whistling had been unconscious. He recognised the tune as 'You are my sunshine'. Where the hell had that come from? Was he ever anyone's sunshine? Did he ever make anyone happy? He wasn't about 'happy'; he was about hate and about pain. He thought people should be able to see the hate in his face, but they didn't seem to and that was to his advantage. He laughed at the body in the wheelbarrow. I'm certainly not going to make you happy. Or perhaps I did for a while. But it was always going to end like this. He wiped the sweat from his brow with the back of his hand and then returned to digging, changing the whistling to humming and singing a few words in between. The hole was taking shape. The evening was still bright and the air was still heavy after a day of blazing sunshine.

He had contemplated using a chainsaw to cut the bodies

up and had even purchased a plastic jacket and trouser combination for the task. Then a police officer on a reality television show had said that murderers who use a chainsaw are stupid. Sawing the body simply spreads blood spatter all over the place and leaves lots of forensic evidence. He had reluctantly reconsidered his plans, realising it was better to be safe than sorry. His safety was always the primary consideration.

Ten minutes later he stuck the shovel into the loose earth he had piled up beside the hole and went over to the body. A pair of startled eyes stared back at him. The eyes could see and the brain could register, but the drug had paralysed the body. He saw a tiny movement and wondered what was happening behind those staring eyes. There was certainly fear, but there would also be horror at the prospect of being interred while still alive. He felt exultation. It was the feeling he lived for. No stimulant he had taken had ever come anywhere close to the feeling he got from taking a life.

Eager to finish, he began to dig with more gusto and a louder hum. It reminded him of the way black members of the chain gangs in the films sang to establish the rhythm of their work. Small droplets of sweat fell from his face into the hole. Another couple of inches and it would be perfect. He looked again at Browne's body. Bye bye, Rory, he whispered and blew a kiss.

UNTITLED

Two weeks earlier

CHAPTER ONE

Detective Superintendent Ian Wilson's eyelids fluttered and he forced himself to concentrate on what was happening around him. He was sitting in Chief Superintendent Yvonne Davis's office and enduring the weekly senior officers' meeting. It was an event he normally avoided like the plague, but he had run through his full list of excuses and was, therefore, obliged to spend a precious two hours of his life listening to the drivel spewed out by his colleagues. His own contribution had been the minimum acceptable. He had two active cases: the search for Sammy Rice, the former Shankill gang lord, and the ongoing investigation into the body found in a burned-out car in Helen's Bay. There was a third investigation, but that wasn't to be discussed, even with the senior officers. One of his detectives had proved that former political bigwig Jackie Carlisle had not died by suicide but had been sent to his maker with a hot shot administered by a Special Branch officer who was now missing. Davis and he had not informed HQ of the progress of that investigation. In the meantime, the colleague who established that murder had been committed, Peter Davidson, had retired and was sunning himself on a beach in Spain. Wilson glanced at his watch, hoping the officer speaking would take the hint. Davis looked as bored as him, but he supposed that she was responding to some edict from HQ saying she should meet with her senior staff once per week to prove that she had her finger on the pulse of her station. He pitied her.

Wilson came out of his reverie when he realised that everyone around the table except him was standing up. He thanked God under his breath and stood. He picked up one of the pads that had been left in front of every participant and slipped it into his jacket pocket. It was virginal and he didn't want to advertise the fact by leaving it behind him. He was a member of the management team as Davis called it, and members of the management team took notes.

'Ian, would you mind staying behind for a few minutes,' Davis said as she moved towards her desk.

The rest of the management team filed out and closed the door behind them. They cast envious glances at him before they left. He supposed he was developing a reputation as the chief super's pet.

'Have you seen Jack?' Davis sat behind her desk.

Wilson didn't have to ask which Jack she was referring to. DCI Jack Duane of the Garda Special Branch appeared to spend as much time in Belfast as he did in Dublin, particularly since he and Davis had become an item. Wilson sat in a visitor's chair. 'I haven't seen him in a week or so. Why do you ask?'

'He's been around for the past few days.'

Wilson had been surprised when Duane and Davis got together. Jack was a bit of a rough diamond, whereas she was a cool intellectual. Whatever the chemistry was between them, it was certainly working on Davis. When she had taken over as chief superintendent from Wilson's old mentor Donald Spence, she often dithered, but lately she exuded confidence. She had also adopted a decidedly more female look in her fashion choices. 'Is he here socially or on business?'

'Both.'

'And you're telling me because ... ?'

'There was a briefing at HQ yesterday from DCC Jennings. He slipped in a piece of intelligence from Dublin that a police officer's life is in danger. He made little of it by saying that the life of every police officer in the province is in danger. Then he cited the trouble in Derry. There was a smile on his face that I didn't like. Jack's sure it's you who is in danger. Do you keep your weapon handy?'

He opened his jacket to show there was no gun.

'That's downright stupid. Jack says the hitman is well-known to the Garda Síochána and he's the kind that over-weapons.'

'And that's why Jack's in town?'

'I think it's part of it. He likes you and I don't think he wants to see you dead; neither do I.'

She looked genuinely worried. 'Okay, if it makes you happy, I'll carry my gun.'

Her face creased in a smile. 'Good man, with a bit of luck you won't need it. I suppose the threat is linked to the Carlisle investigation. Davidson was getting too close to the real culprit and that's why he was assaulted.'

If she only knew who the real culprit was, maybe she wouldn't sleep so well at night, thought Wilson. 'I think you're right. He did a hell of a job. We wouldn't be where we are on the investigation if it wasn't for him. Thank God he didn't pay the ultimate price for his good work.'

'Any news from him?'

'Just a postcard, one of those where you send a photo to some digital company and they make up an individual card. It's a picture of him and Irene Carlisle sitting by a pool in Spain toasting us with cocktails. He looks pretty well recovered.' Wilson was glad Davidson was happy.

'It's an ill wind that blows nobody any good.'

'The pity is that Simon Jackson's in the wind. I'd like to give that bastard a taste of what he gave Peter.'

'No sign of him?'

'Disappeared off the face of the earth.'

'How are things downstairs? Is Moira McElvaney fitting in okay?'

'I don't think that DS Browne is happy with the new situation.'

'That I can imagine. How about the others?'

'Harry worked with her before, so there's no problem there. But Siobhan doesn't appear to be onside just yet.'

She glanced at the papers in her tray. 'Keep in touch, and the next time I see you I want to see a bulge in that jacket.'

He stood up. 'Your concern is both touching and appreciated.'

'You're too much, Ian. Get back to work.'

CHAPTER TWO

He heard the argument before he opened the door to the squad room. Detective Sergeants Moira McElvaney and Rory Browne were standing in front of a whiteboard shouting at each other. The other members of the squad, Detective Constables Harry Graham and Siobhan O'Neill, were spectating. It was not the best example of team spirit he'd ever seen. He knew that reintegrating Moira into the team that already had a sergeant might prove problematic, but to say that she and Browne hadn't exactly hit it off would be an understatement.

He marched up to the arguing couple. 'Enough! I could hear you two down the hall. We have a rule in this squad: arguing is okay but shouting isn't.'

'Sorry, boss,' Moira said. 'You asked me to take a look at the murder book on the body found in the boot at Helen's Bay. I was just pointing out some holes in the investigation and Rory took it as a personal slight.'

'She seems to believe that she can make much more progress than me,' Browne said. 'Maybe I should just quit and leave everything to her.'

Wilson had huge respect for Moira's ability as a detective

and was sure that she might well have done better than Browne, but he wasn't about to say that. 'We're a team, and if we perform well individually that means the team performs well collectively. So when we review our performance, it's with a view to doing better next time. We don't take offence. We move on.' If the argument had happened on the rugby field, the referee would have asked the participants to shake hands. However, Wilson wasn't ready to play referee in an argument between his sergeants. 'What's your point, Moira?'

'There was a giant conflagration on the edge of the sea and yet nobody at the café down the road saw anything. I don't buy it. Whoever set the fire must have left in that direction. I think we should interview the café staff again. There were also two patrons and we should check in with them again as well. Maybe they have remembered something in the meantime.'

'That's the argument?' Wilson said. 'If you have the time, it might not be a bad idea to have another word with them. If I were to hazard a guess as to who we're talking about, I'd say Eddie Hills. Moira hasn't met Eddie yet, so she's a fresh pair of eyes. Go talk to the people at the café and the patrons. It's worth a try. Rory, let's go to my office.'

Wilson motioned to Browne to close the door behind him. 'Take a seat. Look, I get it that Moira has ruffled your feathers a little, but we can't go on like this.' He saw Moira pick up her jacket and head for the door. She glanced into his office as she passed.

'She can be so bloody superior, boss. She thinks she knows everything.'

'That's not the picture I have of her. She's a first-class detective who gets results. And up to now, she's been a good colleague. She's not taking your job. She's taking Peter Davidson's place and we're lucky to have her. You two will have to get along sooner or later and I'd prefer if it was sooner.'

'Yes, boss.'

'Don't think of her as a threat, think of her as an opportunity. You're a smart guy and part of being smart is learning from others.' Browne was sitting with his head bent. 'And stop looking like an errant schoolboy. I want Moira to cast an eye over both the Sammy Rice murder and disappearance and the body in the burned-out BMW. You never know, fresh eyes might give us a lead.'

'I am sorry, boss.'

'There are two of you in it. I'll have a word with her as well when she gets back.'

Browne stood and left the office.

Wilson swivelled in his chair and took a small key from his pocket. He opened a locked steel box attached to the wall behind him, removed his PSNI issue Glock 17, two magazines and a shoulder holster, and laid them on the desk in front of him. He didn't like guns. Maybe it was because his father had put one into his mouth and blown the top of his head off. He moved the slide on the top of the pistol and verified that there was nothing in the chamber. He handled the gun and found that it still fitted his hand like a glove. As a trained athlete, he had excellent hand–eye coordination, and he was one of the best shots on the range. He removed a box of 9 mm shells and loaded each of the magazines with a full load, seventeen. Then he slapped a magazine into the gun and put it into the shoulder holster. It was a hell of a bind having to carry a gun on his person, but he had made a promise. He put the holster on and settled the gun underneath his left armpit. A fully loaded Glock 17 weighs about two pounds, so when people tell you you won't notice it when it's under your armpit, they're not exactly telling the truth. He knew he would get used to it; however, as far as he was concerned, it was an interim measure until they discovered that the whole hitman/assassination thing was a figment of someone's imagination. At that point, the Glock would be back in the box and could stay there as far as he was concerned. He slipped on his jacket and looked across at the glass door where Graham was looking in. He motioned for him to enter.

'What's up, boss?' Graham asked. 'I saw you tooling up. There must be something serious on the cards.'

'Nothing. It's just been a while since I wore the damn thing and I have to go to the range next week. I thought I'd get used to the feel.'

'That's why you loaded a full magazine?'

'Look, Harry, it doesn't concern you and it's on a need-to-know basis.'

'Peter reckoned he could remain safe and it almost cost him his life. What's going on, boss, maybe I can help?'

'It's probably nothing, but there's a threat against a PSNI officer and the chief super thinks it may be me. It's all a load of crap.'

'You got to be kidding me, boss. The people who put Jackie Carlisle in the ground know you're after them. They murdered one of the biggest politicians in the province, and you're not afraid of them? Those people would off you in a heartbeat. What if the chief super's right?'

'And what if she's wrong? All this is for nothing.'

'Holy shit, I thought after Peter that things couldn't get worse, but as long as you investigate Carlisle's death they will. Give it up, boss. Whoever killed him has the power and is not afraid to use it.'

'Don't involve yourself in this, Harry. You've got the kids to think about.' He stood up. 'I feel like Wyatt Earp walking around with this thing under my arm. Concentrate on giving the kids their tea and help them with their homework and stay lucky.'

CHAPTER THREE

Moira parked her fifteen-year-old Ford in the car park on Coastguard Avenue. Her finances had been decimated by her sabbatical and an old banger was all she could afford. She closed the driver's door carefully, feeling that if she slammed it, the door would simply give up the ghost and fall off. She walked towards the sea. It was a beautiful summer's day and the ocean ahead of her was a deep blue. She watched as two large ferries passed each other. She was carrying the murder book and, although the wreckage of the BMW had been removed, she wanted to see the exact spot where the car was left. Looking at a page with an A4-sized picture of the area in front of her, she could see that the BMW had been parked on a grass verge at the end of the road. She walked on until she reached the place where the car had stood. The burned grass had not grown back. Why had this place been chosen? The killer might have driven to any out of the way location and torched the car. She supposed the location must have some significance for the killer. Few enough people knew this place so presumably he had been here before. But for what reason? She walked around the area and then headed towards the café.

She was thankful to be back in the Murder Squad. It

hadn't been an easy return and she had learned a great truth as a result: you can never go back to how it was before you left. Somewhere at the back of her mind, she'd expected to just waltz back into her slot in the squad. She knew that she had been replaced, but she'd ignored that problem. Then there was her temporary appointment to Vice to cover some corrupt asshole who was on suspension. Her old flat had been let, no big surprise, and she had spent a week in a cheap hotel looking for something reasonable, and inexpensive. She had finally landed a studio in the University area. When the boss had called and told her that he had organised her back into the squad she almost jumped for joy. But the joy was short-lived when she heard that she would be replacing Peter Davidson.

A lot had changed since the time she had first joined the squad. Ronald McIver was in the nuthouse, Eric was shuffling paper at HQ and now Peter had retired. Good old Harry was still there, but she wasn't too sure about the newer colleagues. She'd heard that Rory Browne was a clever lad and a fast-track appointment. She'd expected some resistance from him, given that they both held the same rank, but she was frustrated that he appeared to take her interventions personally. If she cared to be strategic, she'd just keep her mouth shut – but that wouldn't be doing her job. She was more surprised at the frosty reception she had got from Siobhan O'Neill. She hadn't had time to work that young woman out yet, but most of what she'd learned about her didn't gel. She was a clever lass, maybe a bit too clever to be a copper and maybe a bit socially backward. Whatever the problem was, she regarded Siobhan as a work in progress. She pushed open the café door and went to the counter.

'How can I help you, love?' the lady behind the counter asked. She had a badge on her lapel identifying her as Hazel.

'A cup of coffee, please.'

Moira waited until she returned with the coffee to take out

her warrant card. 'Were you working here the day the car was torched at the end of the avenue?'

Hazel set the coffee on the counter and looked at the warrant card. 'Two pound fifty, love.' She held out her hand. 'There are no freebies for the police in this café.'

'None expected.' Moira passed over the money.

'I've already been interviewed by your lot.' Hazel deposited the cash in the till. 'I saw no one coming from that direction.'

'You have no CCTV?'

'No, love; they keep talking about it and it's getting cheaper, but we have no trouble with break-ins.'

'Have you spoken with any of the other staff or patrons about the incident?'

'Are you joking, love? We talked about nothing else for a week.'

'And did anything new occur to you?'

'Not really. Well one thing: your lot were going on about CCTV all the time but sometimes we have people flying drones around here. Maybe someone was flying a drone that day. Sometimes they come in here for a cup of tea and a scone when they're finished.'

'Anything else?'

'That's it, love.'

'Thanks.' Moira took her coffee and went to a table beside a window that looked out towards Carrickfergus across the lough. There was nothing in the murder book about drones flying in the area. It was always possible that those interviewed had mentioned it and it hadn't been followed up. That didn't mean that it wasn't worth following up now.

CHAPTER FOUR

The first thing Wilson did when he entered the apartment was to take off the holster and put it and the gun on the top shelf of the bookcase. If he had a lock box in the apartment, he might have stowed the gun there, but his aversion to firearms was so great that he had never kept a gun at home before. The statistics were clear: the existence of a gun in a home increases the odds of death for all the inhabitants. He did his best to conceal the gun by pushing it to the rear of the shelf.

'What the hell is that?'

He turned to see his partner, Stephanie Reid, standing in the living room. 'You're home early.'

'No deflection. What's a gun doing on the top shelf of the bookcase? I thought we were both agreed about no guns here.' She stopped for a second. 'Oh my God, it's that assassination attempt that Jack told you about isn't it? Tell me and hold nothing back.'

He poured himself a Jameson. 'It's nothing. There was a staff meeting today and the chief super mentioned that I should carry a gun until this assassination story proves to be a hoax.'

'And if it's not a hoax?'

'I'm sure it is.'

'Jack isn't so sure and I trust him to have your back more than some of your fellow officers.'

He wasn't about to argue with that. He sipped his own drink. 'What can I get you?'

'Nothing for the moment. I thought, given that the weather is so nice, we should eat out tonight.' She nodded at the shelf. 'I suppose that thing will have to go with us as well.'

'I promised Davis.' He took a larger sip. 'But only until the assassination threat blows over.'

'Are you and I living on the same planet? If I knew someone was out to kill me, I wouldn't be sitting around with my thumb up my ass. I'd be getting out of Dodge. You don't get paid enough to have someone want to kill you. What have you done to deserve someone putting a hit on you?'

'I have no idea.' He hoped she would buy the lie.

'I got a call from the hospital in LA today. I think they're getting a little fed up waiting for me. So why not go in tomorrow and hand in your resignation, and when they ask why, tell them that being dead doesn't appeal to you. Then give Jennings the two fingers. We could be on the next flight to LA.'

He walked over and went to put his arms around her. She pushed him away. Her eyes had a film of water on them. 'Not right now, Ian. Twenty minutes ago I was looking forward to having a nice dinner in the open air with the man I love. Now I'm afraid to sit outside because someone might walk over and shoot you while you're eating your steak.'

'You're getting yourself all wound up over nothing.'

She pointed at the gun on the shelf. 'That is not nothing. It wouldn't be here unless you were in danger. What have you got yourself into? Does this have something to do with the attack on Davidson?'

'I don't know what it's about.' He hated making up

impromptu excuses. Once you start lying, the lies just continue to flow. One lie is bolstered by another and then another. She was concerned and he understood that. But running away to LA wasn't the answer. He already knew in his heart and soul what the answer was, but he didn't want to accept it. He might sit and wait for something to happen, which was giving the power to the hitman, or he might turn the tables and get the hitman first. 'Give me a couple of days to sort this out. If it doesn't resolve itself, I'll do as you say.'

'Promise?' She leaned into him and let him hug her.

'I promise.' He kissed her on the lips. His father had told him never to make a promise he couldn't keep, and he was afraid that he had just broken that rule. He'd enjoyed his sojourn in Santa Monica and he might live there someday. Right now, however, he had work to do in Belfast.

INSTEAD OF GOING OUT, they had eaten what was in the fridge and drank too much wine. It had changed the atmosphere. They'd tumbled into bed and made love several times until they both drifted away. Wilson woke about three o'clock. Reid was fast asleep beside him. He climbed out of bed and went into the living room. He called Jack Duane's number on his mobile phone. It went to voicemail. 'We need to talk.' He closed the phone and went back to bed.

CHAPTER FIVE

Rory Browne was dining alone in the Mourne Seafood Bar on Bank Street. It gave him space to think. He'd been single for a year and had no desire to get back into the scene. Since arriving in Belfast, he'd had over twenty sexual encounters. He'd enjoyed most of them at the time, but they left him feeling empty afterwards. He wanted to be monogamous for a change but needed time to sort himself out before starting a relationship. He would soon be thirty and his sexual awakening had come late. He had tried to hide his sexuality, but now it was out in the open he didn't give a damn. If people weren't ready to accept him for who he was, it was their problem. It pissed him off though that he lived in the only place in the United Kingdom that still clung to traditional views on social issues like gay marriage and abortion. It was time for Northern Ireland to join the twenty-first century. But that wasn't about to happen when, politically, the place was still mired in the seventeenth century and the word 'no' still featured prominently in most of the political rhetoric.

He enjoyed his meal and then took a table outside to finish his wine. It was a warm evening and although the outside area was the realm of the smokers, he found a quiet corner facing Kelly's Cellars. Irish music poured out of the bar and he found his humour lightening. He thought back to his conversation with the boss. He needed to grow up regarding Moira McElvaney. He didn't resent her. It was more that he envied her, sensing she was more talented in the job than he was. Everyone realised there was a close relationship between her and Wilson. He didn't think there was anything sexual in their relationship, although there might have been at one point. Wilson's reputation with women travelled before him, but he had seen nothing to suggest anything was going on with her. As he poured the remnants of his half-bottle into his glass, he saw a regular from the Belfast gay scene exiting the bar opposite alone. The man's name was Charles Heavey.

Heavey glanced around. Noticing Browne, he walked across the road and sat down, uninvited, on an empty stool. 'Didn't know this was your local.'

'It's not. I just had a meal in Mourne's and I finished up out here.' Browne nodded at the empty bottle on the table. Heavey was camp enough to make it noticeable. He was in his early fifties, had a square face that was falling to fat and a full head of well-coiffed grey hair. He was attractive in a mature way and not at all Browne's type.

'I haven't seen you around lately. Have you dropped out?' Heavey asked.

'Sort of.'

'Going steady?'

'Not really.'

'Looking for a bit of excitement?'

'Not at all. Just finishing my wine and heading home.'

'You used to be friendly with Vincent Carmody or 'Fab Vinny' as he calls himself, didn't you?'

'I used to be.'

'Have you seen him lately?'

'Thankfully no.'

'Yes, Vincent is an acquired taste. He can be quite a handful.'

Browne didn't like to be reminded of his affair with Carmody. He downed his drink and went to stand up. Heavey put his hand on Browne's arm and drew a sharp look in response. 'Can we just talk for a few more minutes, no ulterior motives?'

Browne nodded and sat.

'It's just that Vinny appears to have dropped out as well. I was wondering whether you two had dropped out together.'

'No, Vincent and I are through.'

'Vinny has been my go-to man in the past. And he's disappeared.'

'Maybe he's gone on holiday.'

'And maybe he's not. The last time I saw him he wouldn't have had the price of a bus ticket to Portrush never mind a long holiday.'

'Where are we going with this?'

'You're a police officer.'

'Yes.'

'What if something has happened to Vinny?'

'What sort of something?'

'Something bad.'

'Go to Musgrave Street and lodge a missing person's report.'

'I heard that you're a detective.'

'I am.'

'Can't you lodge a missing person's report?'

'No. Look, Vincent is hardly Mister Reliable. Don't you think you're being alarmist?'

'Maybe, but I doubt it. Vinny isn't the only one of my contacts that's gone missing.'

'Did you or someone else lodge a missing person's report for that person?'

'Yes.'

'And?'

'And nothing, there hasn't been a word from the police since.'

Browne took out his notebook and pen. 'Give me his name.'

'Roger Whyte, that's spelled W-h-y-t-e.'

Browne put the book away. 'I'll look into it.' He rose.

'And Vinny?'

'Later. I know how to find you.'

Browne walked off towards Royal Avenue. There was a downside to being a police officer. He couldn't count the number of times some friend of his parents had called round for a cup of tea only to explain that they had received a speeding fine the previous day and ask could he do anything about it. His standard answer was that the best thing to do was to pay the fine and take the points on their licence. There was no way that he would investigate a missing person. There was a whole squad of people in Musgrave Street whose job that was. Let them deal with it.

CHAPTER SIX

Wilson woke early and slipped out of bed. Reid was still fast asleep. Outside, the sun was already up and it promised to be another scorching day in a summer full of scorching days. He slipped on his jogging gear and beat the well-worn path along the Lagan to the Titanic Centre and back. He smelled coffee as soon as he returned home and after checking in with a 'Good Morning' he headed to the shower, taking care to bring his mobile phone. He checked his messages, nothing from Jack.

Reid had breakfast on the table by the time he emerged from the bedroom singing about 'what a lucky guy he was'.

'How can you be so bloody cheery?' Reid sipped her coffee. 'I've just downed a couple of painkillers. If your head isn't hurting, I'd advise seeing a doctor.'

He removed the cup from her hand and laid it on the table, then took her in his arms and kissed her. 'Okay, doctor, what do you think?'

'I think you should tell me why you're contacting Jack in the middle of the night.' The microwave pinged, she removed two croissants and handed one to Wilson. 'I'm not up to facing eggs this morning. What's with Jack?'

'He started this whole assassination business, now he's gone dark, although Davis tells me that he's in town.'

'Is their affair still going on? That must be a record for Jack.'

'I have to say, Davis looks well on it.'

'I hope you're not trying to make me jealous. Jack is always coming on to me you know.' She finished eating her croissant, drank her coffee and put the cup in the dishwasher. She picked up a packet of headache tablets. 'I have a heavy day and I might need these. What did we agree: three days, or was it two?'

'I thought it was as soon as possible.'

'I think you should spend at least part of today drafting your resignation letter.' She swept out of the room before he could answer.

He took his cup and sat on the couch, which stood in front of a picture window through which there was a vista over the city. He didn't have to wonder whether she meant to accept the offer of the job in LA. He had three days to resolve the assassination threat or she would insist that he tender his resignation. Either way, in just a few days, he would be forced to lose one of the two things he loved most. He didn't know whether he could live without either one. Why the hell hadn't Duane called him back?

CHAPTER SEVEN

Wilson smiled when he entered the squad room and saw that Moira was barring Duane from entering his office.

'Who is this character?' Moira said as Wilson approached. 'He walks into the squad room as though he owns the place and makes a beeline for your office.'

'DS Moira McElvaney meet DCI Jack Duane of the Garda Síochána,' Wilson said. 'Or some element thereof.'

Duane was beaming from ear to ear. 'I think I'm in love.'

Moira stood aside.

'Where did you find this firebrand?' Duane continued. 'Is that hair real? How can I get to know her better? Is she married?'

Moira walked away.

Wilson opened the door to his office, ushered Duane in and closed the door behind him.

'Glad to see you took the advice on the gun.' Duane sat in the visitor's chair.

'It's that obvious?' Wilson sat.

'To the practised eye.'

'You obviously got my message.'

'At a most inconvenient time, but we won't go into that. Seriously though, where did you find her?'

'She was in the squad but then went away for a while. She's one of the best detectives I've worked with.'

'I wouldn't like to get on the wrong side of her. The name of the guy who's after you is Philly Brennan, and this isn't his first dance by any manner of means. Philly has kept Dublin's undertakers in business for years.'

'Do you have any idea where he is now?'

'Of course. He's in a parked car about fifty yards down the road from the entrance to this station.'

'Don't shit me, Jack.'

'I shit you not. I've been on him for the past couple of days. Apparently, he's had a busy schedule, but now you've arrived at the top of the list.'

Wilson stood up.

Duane stood to block his exit. 'Where are you off to, hoss?'

'I'm going out there to get the bastard.'

'No you're not. He's parked legally and he's probably paid his parking tickets as well. There's no weapon in his car, but there'll be one nearby, probably in another car parked somewhere close. You have no earthly reason to go near him other than to tip him off that you know what he's about. It won't stop him trying to complete the contract. He'll just be a lot more careful about how he does it.'

Wilson retook his seat. 'Reid has given me three days to solve this problem, or she wants me to resign from the PSNI and go to America with her. I can't wait around for this guy to decide when he'd like to kill me. If he doesn't act soon, I will. I don't want to lose Reid and I don't want to give up my job.'

'Let's make a plan then. Philly is still above ground and free because he's cautious, which means he won't be easily pushed into what they call precipitate action.'

'What do you have in mind?'

'The impetus for action has to come from somewhere he

trusts. I have some ideas in that direction. The problem is that Philly is no ordinary hitman. If we can manage to force his hand, there's no guarantee that you're coming out of this alive.'

'That's the risk we'll have to take.'

'It's the risk you'll have to take. You're the target. Philly will do whatever it takes to kill you. He's the equivalent of your King Rat, Mad Dog and the Shankill Butchers. Have you forgotten what such characters are like? They don't just kill to pay the bills, they enjoy what they do. We've had eighteen murders so far in the south and there's still a list of intended victims out there.'

'So, what do we do?'

'I'll make some calls and we'll see how we can screw up Philly's agenda. In the meantime, you find somewhere that's the perfect killing ground for a man with an AK-47 and a Smith & Wesson Magnum.'

'Thanks, Jack.'

'Don't thank me yet, Ian. You realise that there won't be an arrest here. This ends with either you or Philly zipped up in a plastic bag.'

Moira watched the two men in the office. She had no idea exactly what they were discussing, but it was something serious. Like Duane, she had noticed the bulge under Wilson's left arm. She had only ever seen him wearing his gun when there was an operation underway. A detective superintendent of the PSNI and a Garda DCI with their heads together spelled trouble for someone. Wilson had briefed her on the cases under investigation when she had rejoined the squad. She saw nothing that would require a firearm intervention. Sammy Rice had disappeared, probably never to be seen again, and few people in Belfast would lament the fact. She hadn't yet crossed swords with the current crop of criminals but knew they were mainly former soldiers and so-called reformed paramilitaries. She'd reviewed the profiles of Davie Best and his pal Eddie Hills. They dressed and behaved like businessmen but had ruthlessly culled the old Rice and McGreary gangs. They appeared to have the EQ of an amoeba. She took a longer look at Duane. He had the look of a hard man. She'd seen his type before. Seeing that Duane was preparing to leave, she returned to her search for drone clubs in East Belfast. It was a shot in the dark, but sometimes they were the best shots of all. She sensed someone behind her and pivoted to see Duane looming over her.

'Nice to have met you, Moira. It was a rocky start, but I think we'll get on like a house on fire.'

Moira glanced at DC Siobhan O'Neill, who was shuffling paper nervously. 'Sorry about the inconvenience, sir, but I'm sure you understand.'

'Of course I do, you have a good day now.'

As soon as Duane left, she nodded at Graham. 'Fancy a coffee in the cafeteria, Harry?'

He recognised an order when he saw one and rose from his seat. 'I'd love one.'

O'Neill watched them leave the squad room together. She hadn't taken to Moira. Something about her was unsettling. Maybe it was the way she always seemed to watch and listen more than anyone else. She wondered whether Moira had copped her unease when Duane approached them. She trusted him to keep his mouth shut, if only to protect the boss.

HALF A DOZEN other officers were seated in the cafeteria. 'I'll get the coffees,' Moira said and nodded at a table well away from the others.

Graham sat down and Moira joined him with two steaming cups of coffee. 'What's with this Duane guy?' she asked when they were settled.

'He's a cross between a copper and a spook from down

south. He and the boss have gotten tight lately. I haven't had anything to do with him and I'm happy enough for that.' He felt Moira's eyes boring into him. He'd forgotten how intense she was. He wondered if she was ever off the job. 'I can tell you one thing, I wouldn't like to meet him in a dark alley.'

'They've worked some cases together?'

'You know the boss, he keeps his cards close to his chest. I think they've teamed up on one or two investigations; they certainly worked together on the Aughnacloy business when that gang over there shot Jock McDevitt.' He sipped his coffee.

Moira made a mental note to look up the recent cases. 'Is there any reason O'Neill should feel uneasy around him?'

'Not that I know of. You're a woman, does he give off a bad vibe?'

'I think he'd go after anything in a skirt, but he didn't creep me out.' She sipped her coffee. 'Did you notice that the boss is wearing his gun?'

'I saw him load it up yesterday.'

'Anything I should know about?'

'Not that I'm aware.'

'Anything to do with Peter Davidson?'

'I think so. The guy the boss thinks assaulted him has disappeared. We've put out a bulletin on him and launched a European arrest warrant.'

Moira sat back. She smelled trouble, but it was clearly something that Wilson wanted to keep to himself and possibly his new best buddy. She had only just met Duane, but if she were in trouble, she reckoned he'd be the man she'd want in her corner. She wanted to help Wilson but would not push herself forward. 'How are the kids getting on?'

Graham sighed with relief. Nobody liked being the subject of a Moira McElvaney probing.

CHAPTER EIGHT

Browne used his finger to remove the rheum from the corner of his eye. He'd woken at two-thirty in the morning and found it impossible to get back to sleep. That wasn't the norm. He had the reputation of being able to sleep on a bed of nails. He'd lain awake wondering what was on his mind that refused to allow him to sleep. He finally decided that it had something to do with the conversation he'd had with Charles Heavey. Maybe he'd been too offhand in dismissing him. One friend going missing was possible. Two might be too much of a coincidence. It was worth checking out. Once he decided to act, he was able to get a couple of hours' sleep. He then rose early and was at the station before any other member of the squad arrived. He looked up the file on Roger Whyte and saw it comprised only one item, the missing person's report. The name of the officer investigating was included and as he had expected he was in Musgrave Street. He left a message at the desk that he had some business to transact outside.

Browne headed into town and picked up a coffee and a Danish pastry. He made his way to Donegall Quay, where he sat on a bench and enjoyed his breakfast in the bright sunshine. It was a beautiful morning and he had to force himself to get up and walk around the corner to Musgrave Street Station.

He showed his warrant card when checking in at the desk and asked for DC Stuart Ward. The CID squad room on the second floor was more than double the size of the Murder Squad room at Tennent Street. He asked for Ward and was pointed towards an overweight, bald, middle-aged man with the kind of moustache that had gone out in the seventies and never come back. Ward's desk was in the corner of the room. He walked over and introduced himself. Ward tilted his chair back and emitted a loud fart. 'What can I do for you?'

Browne assumed the fart was a reflection of Ward's contempt for a senior officer who was twenty years his junior. He tried not to breathe. If bottled, Ward's farts would breach some UN convention or other. 'You're the officer responsible for looking into the disappearance of Roger Whyte. I was wondering how the investigation is going.'

Frown lines stood out on Ward's fleshy face. 'Where did you say you were from?'

'The Murder Squad, Tennent Street.'

'Has Whyte's body been found?'

'Not that I know of.'

'Then why are you so interested in him?'

'I have a friend who's worried about him.'

Ward stroked his double chin. 'What kind of friend?'

'I don't think that's relevant.'

'You have shirt-lifter personal friends?'

'I have lots of personal friends. Has there been any advancement on the investigation into Whyte's disappearance?'

'There's no advancement. A couple of uniforms dropped by his place, but there was no answer. They asked the neighbours. It seems Whyte led what they called an active social life. There were people dropping by and he liked to take long holidays from time to time. Those kind of people are often like that.'

'What kind of people are they?'

'Mr Whyte was a well-known homosexual. Maybe he went off to live in a gay commune in California. They do things like that.'

Browne was getting irate. He didn't see much point in continuing. 'What do you intend to do about his disappearance?'

'Most of them turn up sooner or later.' Ward turned back to his computer. 'Tell your friend that he'll probably arrive home unscathed one of these days.'

Browne stormed out before he said something unpleasant. On the way, he received some curious looks from the officers he passed.

Zero effort had been spent on finding out what had happened to Whyte. The poor man might have fallen off a bridge into the Lagan and nobody in the PSNI gave a damn. And that appeared to count double because he was gay.

As BROWNE RETURNED to Tennent Street, he saw DCI Duane climbing into the rear of a white van. There was an empty seat beside the driver, but he knew Duane was more than an ordinary copper so he accepted it as strange rather than unusual.

He was glad to see that Wilson was alone in his office and O'Neill was the only other person present in the squad room. He knocked on Wilson's door.

Wilson was removing his shoulder holster and thinking about what Duane had told him. He motioned Browne to enter and take a seat. 'What's the problem?'

Browne told him about his conversation with Heavey and his epiphany in the middle of the night, and about his visit to Musgrave Street and his encounter with Ward.

'What did you expect?' Wilson said. 'Last year, the Police Ombudsman examined the PSNI's response to missing people and declared it woeful. He examined six cases in detail and more than fifty serving officers were disciplined. Maybe your guy Ward was among them. They tend to wait until someone returns home, or a corpse is found.'

'I got the impression that Whyte's sexual orientation played a part in the decision to do nothing this time.'

'I can see the lack of competence, and that's already been established, but I think your paranoia might be showing now. Why should sexual orientation matter?'

'Because many people in Northern Ireland still dismiss homosexuals as evil sodomites. At least, that's what the clergy preach from the pulpits every Sunday.'

'That may be so, but following up on a missing person isn't any of our business and we have enough to be going on with at the moment. Keep an eye on it and if it becomes our business, we'll deal with it then.'

'Okay, boss.' Browne stood up and went to the door. 'But I have a strange feeling about this one. I've never woken up in the middle of the night like that before.'

'Welcome to the club.'

CHAPTER NINE

Wilson reflected on his discussion with Duane. The fact that a contract killer was sitting in a car fifty yards away from the station convinced him that he was in mortal danger this time. He was already unable to sleep and had found himself searching every strange face he encountered. He rubbed his hands on his trousers. It was a fine summer's morning but not yet warm enough to warrant the sweat on his palms. He'd stood up to murderers before; men who would have slit his throat as quick as look at him. And he had been scared witless. Anyone who said that they hadn't felt fear when their life was threatened was a either a liar or a fool. There was a lot of life left in him and he didn't want it taken away. He understood why Reid wanted to run, but that was just one option he was looking at right now.

He had a good idea who was behind the plot. All the dots were in place and he had already joined them. The initial meeting with the hitman was held in the south of France and that's where Helen McCann lives. Davidson had got them close to putting the cuffs on her. She would have felt the cold wind blowing around her ankles. Hiring a hitman was exactly the reaction he expected from McCann. She wasn't the type who took prisoners. She had demonstrated her ruthlessness. The question was: what to do about it? He could take Reid's advice and run with her to California. She would earn the big bucks and he would be the house-husband. He might not enjoy the lack of gainful employment, but at least he would be alive. The other option would be to stay and fight. He agreed with Duane that the fight option would end with someone in a body bag. He had a choice to make. Once the dice rolled, however, there would be no going back; the decision would create its own dynamic.

He'd never run from anything in his life. In both sport and career, he had jumped at every challenge. But that was when he was young and naive, and when he felt he was immortal. He thought about Reid. He wanted so much to spend the rest of his life with her. No one would blame him if he submitted his resignation and left Belfast. He wasn't sure that the PSNI was something that he wanted to give up his life for. But if he ran, he would have to spend the rest of his life knowing that he hadn't stood up when it counted. It was not a decision to make in haste. He saw that Moira had returned and that she was staring at him. He motioned her to come.

'What's up, boss?'

There was no point in bullshitting her. 'We have a little situation at the moment.' He saw the look on her face and knew that she was about to speak. 'No, it's nothing that you can help with. Something has come up on the investigation that Peter was handling. It nearly got him killed and I don't want to involve you until I know that it's safe.'

'Boss, you know I look up to you a lot. We all do. But if you have a fault, it's that you take on too much yourself. I saw the expressions earlier on your and Duane's faces and both of you are strong individuals. So I know that something bad is going down.'

'We'll sort it out. If I need your help, I'll ask.' He needed to move away from his predicament. 'How are things going on the review of the Helen's Bay investigation?'

'I went there yesterday evening and looked at the site. I was wondering why the killer chose that place to torch the car. Few people would have known about the turnoff onto Coastguard Avenue. Maybe he lived around there at some point in his life. There was no CCTV, but I learned that people sometimes fly drones in that area so maybe someone was out that day. It's unlikely, but I'm contacting drone clubs in the area. Most of them have websites and if they agree to put up a post asking members whether they were in the area that day, we might get a strike.'

He looked at her with admiration. She was a wet week back in the job and already she had opened two new lines of inquiry. She might nail Best and Hills, but he wouldn't count on it. 'Keep it up. You'll get him.'

Moira stood. 'You are one of the most frustrating men I've ever met. You and that Duane character still live in the world where the guys would handle it. That might be a mistake.'

She left the office and he sat back in his chair. It was typical Moira. She was right. The organisation he joined prized machismo. Maybe it was time he and it evolved.

CHAPTER TEN

Moira settled herself at a table just inside the door of McHugh's on Queen's Square. She ordered a tonic water and had just been served when Stephanie Reid entered.

'Sorry,' Reid sat down and picked up a menu. 'I'd hoped to get away a little earlier. It's a busy day. I was a little surprised when you invited me to lunch. I guessed it was urgent though. We've been getting along well since your return from the US, but lunching together is ratcheting the relationship up to another level.'

They both laughed.

'How are you settling in?' Reid asked. The waitress arrived and she ordered a sparkling water.

'Okay, I suppose. It's not the same. A lot of the old crew are gone and so I'm trying to build a bond with the new recruits. But I'll get there.'

There was a silence as they examined the lunch menu. The waitress returned with Reid's drink and they both ordered the boxty and haddock.

'Cheers,' Reid raised her glass.

Moira touched her glass to Reid's.

'What's the subject?' Reid asked.

Moira smiled. It was so like Reid to get to the point quickly. She hadn't been too keen on her at the start. Wilson had been involved with Kate McCann when Moira joined the squad. Moira was a working-class girl and she was in awe of Kate, the Queen's Council, who always wore beautiful clothes and had the bearing that the privileged wear so well. She'd seen Reid as a man-eater out to lure Wilson away from his intended partner. Maybe her response to Reid was driven by a desire to protect Wilson, or maybe there was a bit of jealousy in there. But that was back then and Kate McCann was history. Reid was a far better fit for Wilson than the aristocratic Kate. 'Something is going on that the boss wants to keep me out of. I was wondering whether you'd tell me what it is.'

'How do you know that I'm aware of what it is?'

'You care for the boss and you'd be the first to notice if there was a problem.'

'What if he wouldn't like me to tell you what I know? Wouldn't he have told you himself if he wanted you to know?'

The two dishes arrived.

'He's wearing a gun,' Moira said. 'So whatever the secret is, it's dangerous. A guy called Jack Duane stopped by the office this morning. He gives off a dodgy vibe. He and the boss discussed something that looked super-serious. They probably don't think so but maybe they need some help.'

'You're putting me in a difficult position.' Reid picked at her food. You and I didn't get off to a good start. And I'd be lying if I said that I was unhappy went you headed west with your boyfriend. But I know you care about Ian and that you're totally loyal. And I also know that he wouldn't appreciate me telling you something that he wouldn't tell you himself.'

'I was wrong about you and the boss and I'm happy to admit it. You're good together. I don't want you to break a confidence, but I think the boss is in danger and I want to help.'

'Someone has taken out a contract on Ian's life. A hitman has been employed and I feel that things are coming to a head.'

Moira's fork stopped in mid-air. 'You're joking?'

'I don't joke where Ian's life is concerned.'

Moira raised the fork to her mouth and chewed without tasting the food. 'Does he have any idea who placed the contract?'

'I think so. It has something to do with the investigation that Peter Davidson was working on.'

'And how does Duane figure in all this?'

'He was the first to get wind of the conspiracy. The hitman is someone that Dublin has an eye on because of his connection to a drugs gang. Jack passed the intelligence to PSNI Castlereagh but you know what that means.'

'Jennings?'

Reid nodded. 'I want Ian to resign. My mother died recently and left me a small house in Santa Monica. A hospital in Los Angeles has offered me a job. So we could leave tomorrow.'

Moira was still trying to assimilate the fact that Wilson's life was in danger and now there was the possibility that he would simply resign and run away. 'Maybe that won't be enough.'

'What do you mean?'

'Do you think they won't follow him to the US? Someone wants the boss dead. He knows something that's clearly a risk for someone important. Perhaps they won't rest until he's in the ground.'

'Really? I assumed that once he was out of Northern Ireland, he would be safe. I can see that assumption might have been false.' Reid closed her cutlery and abandoned her lunch. 'Now you know, what do you intend to do?'

'I don't know, but I won't sit on my hands.'

CHAPTER ELEVEN

Wilson spent the afternoon in the office trying to work out a plan that might have a chance of succeeding. Duane was sure that this Brennan guy would be into heavy weaponry. That meant something like an Uzi or an AK-47. He needed to choose a place where there were no civilians. If he had to die, he wasn't about to take a bunch of innocents with him. That meant an enclosed area that he knew and where there was no chance of bystanders. He had considered a half-dozen potential sites, but they all failed on one or other of the criteria he had set. He took out a map of Belfast. There had to be somewhere. It came to him, the warehouse in East Belfast where Sammy Rice had met his end. It would be ironic if he were to meet his own end there. He called Duane.

'I think I know a place.'

'I've been on to our guy in Philly Brennan's gang and he'll do the necessary to put pressure on for the hit to be sooner rather than later. What's your idea?'

Wilson told him about the warehouse fitting the bill, especially regarding possible civilian casualties.

'It seems ideal. I'm waiting for a call from Dublin. Hopefully, tonight will be the night. I have some guys sitting on Philly and his mate.'

'Get back when you can and thanks, Jack.'

'Anytime. Sure, it'll be craic. I've wanted to take Philly off the board for quite a while.'

Wilson didn't like the sound of the latter remark. 'I wish I had your confidence.'

Browne spent the afternoon pondering. He was a little pissed off with the way Wilson had dismissed his request to look into Roger Whyte's disappearance. Maybe if Wilson had seen the scant effort that Ward had made, he wouldn't have been so dismissive. But the boss was strangely preoccupied these days. It looked sometimes like he was on another planet. Wilson was right, of course, when he said that it was none of their business. It would only become their business if Whyte's corpse turned up. But that would be too late for Whyte. There was the added factor that he felt that Ward and his colleagues considered Whyte to be less worthy of their attention because he was gay. Indignation flared in him every time he realised that for some people the disappearance of a homosexual counted less than any other disappearance. The same could possibly be said for an indigent or a foreigner.

He spent the afternoon being angry with both Ward and the boss. He fanned the anger because it justified the decision he'd made to ignore Wilson's edict and look into Whyte's disappearance himself. There was also the nagging question of Vincent Carmody's disappearance. The absences of Whyte and Carmody might have nothing to do with one another, but then again they might. The boss had taught him not to accept coincidences. He would contact Heavey and go with him to Whyte's residence to see what they might learn. He would have to keep things quiet in case the boss found out, but he was damned if he'd allow Ward and his pals to short-change Whyte because of his sexual orientation.

MOIRA SPENT most of the afternoon on the phone speaking with the organisers of the four drone societies in the city. What she had learned had both encouraged and discouraged her. On the positive side, most of the members were fanatical about flying their drones and transferred the video they shot to their phones or computers. So, if anyone flew that afternoon there was a good possibility that they had caught something on film. On the negative side, many were doubtful that their members would have been in the Helen's Bay area because the terrain there is devoid of features.

While she worked away on her line of inquiry, she decided she would follow Wilson when he left the station. If some bastard was lying in wait to kill Wilson, he'd have to deal with her as well. She had already removed her Glock from the gun cabinet in the office and loaded a magazine. She was ready to move when he did.

CHAPTER TWELVE

Jack phoned Wilson just before five. 'It's on. Philly is under pressure. As I speak, he's sitting in a stolen Audi A8 with Dublin licence plates just down the street from the station. You lead him to the warehouse and go inside. I'll be close. I'm informed that the weapon involved is an AK-47, so if you have a Kevlar vest handy, I'd bring it along. See you there.'

Wilson's heart was racing as he put down the phone. He was about to face a hitman who had never failed a contract. He knew the kind of damage an AK-47 would do in the hands of an experienced shooter and in an enclosed space. He inhaled a deep breath and let the air out slowly, repeating the exercise several times. His first impulse was to pick up the phone and call Reid. If he was about to die, he wanted at least to hear her voice one more time. He decided against calling her. She might hear something in his voice and that might affect his resolve. He contemplated placing a call to his mother but decided instead to visit her if things worked out. They were the two most important people in his life and the thought of being without them hurt him.

He tried to envisage a scenario that might avoid confrontation but knew there was no way out. He could call in an armed response team, but the hit wouldn't go down until the last moment and he would still be in danger. The best way to protect himself was to show that anyone who came after him would be met with maximum force. He slipped on his shoulder holster and made his way downstairs to the storeroom. He signed for a Kevlar vest, put it on and went out to his car.

MOIRA SAW Wilson leave his office and head downstairs. She closed her computer and picked up her bag with her Glock inside. She watched from a corner of the courtyard as he made his way to his car. She saw him leave and then jumped into her small Ford and took off after him. She was so focused on Wilson that at first she took no notice of the Audi that was behind him or the transit van that was behind her.

WILSON DROVE to the Crumlin Road, where he joined the A12 and the took the M3 across the Lagan. It was the journey he made every day on his way home and it wouldn't raise a red flag for anyone stalking him. He recognised that this was another of those existential moments in his life. He had already survived a bomb blast that had killed a dozen others. Maybe this time his luck would run out. He took the slip road down to Middlepath Street and headed for the Ballymacarrett Road. A bout of déjà vu hit him as he pulled in through the open gate of the abandoned warehouse where Sammy Rice had lost his life.

He exited the car and made his way to the grey concrete block building. The lock had already been opened, which meant Duane was already inside. He pulled open the door and walked into the empty space. When the door closed behind him, the interior was pitch-black. He gave his eyes several minutes to get used to the darkness. There weren't many places to hide. He moved to the rear, casting a glance upwards to the first floor where the offices were located. The rooms appeared deserted. He prayed that Duane was somewhere up there.

THE AUDI A8 with the Dublin licence plates slowed down before turning into the gate on the left-hand side of the road. Moira drove past but kept an eye on the mirror. She watched the van follow the Audi. She turned right at the next junction and immediately made a U-turn to drive back the way she had come. She pulled up across from the gate and saw a man take what looked like an assault rifle from the rear of the van and hand it to a second man, who then moved towards a large building with steel double doors. She turned her car off, removed her gun and slid out of the driver's seat.

PHILLY BRENNAN CRADLED the AK-47 and appraised the situation. He didn't like it. There was something off about it. He told himself he'd find the arsehole in Dublin who had moved the hit up. This wasn't the way he operated. Slow and steady wins the race was his motto. He held the assault rifle close. Instead of going into the warehouse he circled around the building. He half-expected to find the place crawling with PSNI officers. He'd been assured that no information on the hit or the possible subject had been leaked, but he wasn't a first–timer. The organisation that didn't leak like a sieve didn't exist. Leaks didn't bother him. Half the men he'd taken out had been expecting it.

The building was rundown and looked abandoned. It was rectangular, about a hundred and fifty feet long and there were no windows so it would be dark as soon as he entered. He'd done his reconnaissance. He took a deep breath. Ah fuck, he thought, it's time to start the fireworks. He went to the door and slipped inside, crouching low and keeping close to the wall. The interior was as dark as the pit of hell. He stayed low, waiting for his eyes to acclimatise to the darkness.

Wilson saw the figure slip through the door and move to the side. It was one of those occasions where the rules of engagement were fuzzy. His adversary was carrying an assault weapon and a cry of 'Stop police' might allow him to fire. But it would also expose him and a burst from an AK-47 might catch him before he got a shot off.

Moira sneaked through the gate and made her way along a bushy perimeter fence until she came up behind the van. The driver was smoking a cigarette and drumming his fingers on the steering wheel. The engine was running, ready to make a quick exit. The man with the assault rifle had done a swift recce of the area and was now inside the building. Not for the first time she thought that men shouldn't be born with the ability to create testosterone. They seem to be bent on reliving Old West clichés. This one was a recreation of the gunfight at the OK Corral in a deserted building in East Belfast. She crouched and moved along the side of the van until she came level with the driver's door. She jerked the door open and put the Glock into the man's face. 'Move one fucking muscle and I'll blow your head off.'

The cigarette dropped from the man's lips and he stared ahead without moving.

'Okay, now that we've established who's boss, get out of the van and lie flat on the ground.' She backed away and the man did as he was told. When he was on the ground, she handcuffed him. 'You move and you're dead,' she whispered in his ear. She listened, but there was no sound from the warehouse.

. . .

Wilson knew Brennan was waiting for his eyes to become accustomed to the dark. As soon as they were, he would spot Wilson at the rear of the building and all hell would break loose. Wilson lay flat and pointed his gun where he saw Brennan crouching. 'PSNI. Drop your weapon.'

Brennan heard the shout from the rear and decided this was his chance. He fired off a quick burst in the direction he was sure he'd heard his target. He'd asked for a forty-round magazine and his burst used thirty shots.

The empty warehouse resonated with the grating sound of gunfire and the wall behind Wilson exploded, showering him with shards of shattered brickwork. He fired six shots in the direction of the flash from the muzzle of the AK-47.

Duane had been watching Brennan through night-vision glasses and had had a bead on him from the moment he entered the warehouse. As soon as the first burst was fired, he'd turned on his gun's laser sight and shot three times. Brennan was lying prone on the ground. 'It's okay, Ian, he's hit.'

Wilson stood up and walked forward. He looked at the wall behind him, which was peppered with bullet holes. The vertical pattern showed that he would certainly have been hit if he hadn't been lying flat. Duane joined him and they walked over to the still body of Philly Brennan. He had pitched forward, so Duane turned him over with his foot. Brennan had taken shots to the shoulder, the legs and the side. But it was the shot to the head that had killed him.

'Not like it is in the movies, eh Ian?'

The door moved and both men pointed their guns in that direction.

Moira sighed with relief when she saw Wilson and Duane towering over the motionless body. They weren't exactly Butch Cassidy and the Sundance Kid, but standing there, guns in hand, they were a decent Irish approximation.

'What the hell are you doing here?' Wilson asked.

'I followed you from the station. I thought you might need some help.'

'You didn't think we were up to the task?' Duane asked.

'Something like that,' Moira said. 'I've disabled the guy outside who supplied the weapon.'

Duane started for the door. Wilson and Moira followed him. The van driver was where Moira had left him. Duane picked him up and manhandled him into the rear of the van. 'Shite. He's a loose end, but I'll take care of it.'

Wilson didn't like the sound of that.

'Who'll make the call?' Duane asked.

'I'll do it,' Wilson said. 'I'm in this up to my neck, but Moira was never here.'

'I suppose so,' Duane said. 'She's the only one who doesn't deserve to have a pile of shit thrown at them.'

'Where's your car?' Wilson asked Moira.

'Outside.'

'Get the hell out of here, now.' He pushed her shoulder. 'Go on.'

'No way,' Moira said. 'It's not time to send the girlie on her way.'

Wilson took out his mobile as he walked back into the building. He didn't care about the shit he'd have to take. He had survived and as he looked at the body slumped by the wall, he felt no guilt. The dead man was a murderer who had accepted money to kill him. The guilt would kick in later.

CHAPTER THIRTEEN

Browne left work at five and went straight to meet Heavey at Ryan's Bar on the Lisburn Road. The resolve that he had been building up all afternoon to go against the wishes of his superior was melting as he got closer to actually doing it. He hoped that Heavey wouldn't show and he could go home and forget about the whole business. His hopes were dashed when he arrived at the bar and saw Heavey sitting in the rear, sipping a glass of white wine. He ordered a pint of lager, waited for the drink to be poured and then joined Heavey. 'Did you do as I asked?'

'Good evening to you too,' Heavey said.

Ryan's was popular with students, but since it was the summer holidays, there was only a scattering of patrons.

'I've checked with all our mutual acquaintances. Nobody has seen hide nor hair of Roger in more than three weeks. They're all as concerned for him as I am. What did you learn at Musgrave Street?'

'It appears they're not anxious about homosexuals disappearing.' He didn't bother to add a comment on the PSNI's obvious failures on the subject of disappeared individuals.

'So, what's the next step?'

'Why do you think we're meeting here?' Browne sipped his pint. Even at six o'clock in the evening, it was hot outside. The news said it was hotter in Belfast than it was in Lisbon. That was one for the books. 'The next step is a visit to Whyte's flat. Any luck with a key?'

Heavey shook his head.

'That means breaking and entering, which I suppose you're aware is a crime, even for a police officer.' What sort of idiocy had he got himself into, he thought. 'Let's finish up here and get on with it.' He slammed his glass on the table, drawing looks from the other patrons.

It took them less than five minutes to arrive at Whyte's address in Elmwood Mews. A small metal plaque fixed to the wall beside a letter-box bore the legend 'Mr Roger Whyte Esq.' Browne looked around before producing a pack of lock-picks from his pocket. He selected two and put them in the lock. After a bit of fiddling, the lock sprung open. He pushed Heavey inside and followed behind him. They entered a dark corridor with a set of stairs on the left. Browne closed the door and followed Heavey upstairs. At the top, they entered a large living room reminiscent of the studies of Browne's university professors. The chairs were large and comfortable and from another era. Original works of art covered the walls and books filled every nook and cranny. The only concessions to modernity were a modem, a state-of-the-art music system and a forty-inch flat-screen television. The rest of the flat was stuck in the early twentieth century.

'How old is Whyte?' Browne asked.

'Mid-fifties.' Heavey was moving around the room, letting his hand slide over the furniture.

'Figures.' Browne found a small kitchen at the rear of the room. It was meticulously clean. It mirrored the situation in the living room. There was no sign of a *Marie Celeste* situation. If Whyte had left, he hadn't done so in a hurry. He moved on to the single bedroom and bathroom. The bed was made and the bathroom was spotless. The whole flat spoke of someone obsessive about cleanliness. Browne was no forensic expert, but there was nothing to suggest that anything of a violent nature had occurred in the flat. He returned to the living room and found Heavey flicking through a folio. 'Everything looks normal. You've been here before, what do you think? Is there anything out of place?'

Concentration lines furrowed Heavey's brow as he held out the folio. 'He's writing the great Irish novel and has been at it for the past ten years. It's all in here, handwritten. He would never have left it here if he were going away somewhere. It's his most valuable possession.'

'Maybe he left it here by accident.'

'Not Roger. Look at this place. He's the most organised man you'll meet in your life. He wasn't the type to have accidents with things important to him.'

'What does Roger do for a living?'

'He worked for an investment firm in London. He quit and started investing for himself. As you can see, he was comfortably off.'

'Did he have a partner?' Browne noticed some photographs of two men taken in various European cities.

'As I understand it, he had one about twenty years ago in London. The poor fellow died of AIDS, apparently.'

Browne was getting angry with himself again. He shouldn't be doing this. He was a professional police officer behaving like some amateur sleuth. If Whyte was genuinely missing, someone in the PSNI should be making the necessary inquiries. But the point is they weren't. There was a desk at the end of the room. He wanted to examine it but, if he did, his fingerprints would be all over it and the contents. He was in a bind. Whyte could walk in his front door at any moment and find two men wandering around his flat. And one of those men was a serving police officer. But if Whyte had come to some harm, he was obliged to investigate or to at least push the system to investigate it.

'What do you intend to do?' Heavey asked.

'I don't know. There are procedures and protocols for this kind of situation and I'm breaking most of them. We've already committed one crime and I'd like that to be the last one.'

'I have a terrible feeling that Roger has been the victim of foul play.'

'Okay, I'll have one of my colleagues check the hospitals tomorrow. My boss has told me to keep away from the investigation and leave it up to Missing Persons. So, I must keep him in the dark about this and that might lead to trouble down the line.'

'I understand that I'm putting you in a difficult position, but I'm really concerned for Roger.'

'We'll check the hospitals then we'll see.'

'What about Vincent? I'm concerned for him as well.'

'Vincent can wait. Let's see if we can find Whyte first.'

CHAPTER FOURTEEN

Contrary to popular belief, police forces are not thrilled when one of their officers kills a successful hitman in a shoot-out. That was why Wilson, Duane and Moira were occupying adjoining interview rooms in Strandtown Police Station. The van driver had been taken to Musgrave Street and a forensic team was examining the warehouse. The PSNI's *Manual of Policy, Procedure and Guidance on Conflict Management* sets out in Chapter 9 the rules with respect to police use of firearms. Wilson knew well that officers were not permitted to roam around with an issued weapon like the Glock, shooting it off at will. As a senior and long-serving officer, he knew the regulations by heart. He realised there would now be an investigation into the shooting, and the Police Ombudsman's Office would carry it out. He was relieved that it wouldn't be an internal investigation because that might involve DCC Jennings and the outcome might not be as impartial as he would wish. The major issue in his favour was that he hadn't dealt the cards but was instead reacting to a threat to his person. That issue was covered in the manual and the fact he was an intended murder victim would help his case. What might not be so favourable was that someone might easily deduce that he had lured the potential murderer to the warehouse intending to have a shoot-out. The presence of Duane on the upper floor would lend credence to that theory. However, he knew they would send Duane on his way to Dublin post-haste, and his whole involvement in what happened in the warehouse would be erased. You couldn't have a Garda detective involved in a shoot-out in Belfast. What about Moira? She was carrying a gun but hadn't fired it. If she explained that she was following her boss and came upon the murderer and his quartermaster by accident, she might skate with a reprimand for having the weapon on her person. That left him. He would be the man at the investigation's centre and he would have to get his story straight and stick to it.

The door to the room opened and Chief Superintendent Stuart Upton entered, carrying two plastic cups.

'Where do they get the water from?' Upton put the two cups down quickly on the table. 'You'd need special gloves to carry those cups, they have my hands burned off.'

Wilson had met Upton on a management course and liked him. He was a big, bluff, no-nonsense copper. He looked into the cup and saw milky tea. 'I hope it's better than the slop in Tennent Street.'

Upton sat down across from him. 'Fat chance of that. Give it time to cool though.' He stared into Wilson's eyes. 'You'll be keeping the lights burning late at HQ this evening. I've had a call from your chief super. I've never heard that level of concern from a superior for a subordinate. What the hell sort of effect do you have on these women? Whatever it is, bottle it and sell it. Davis has the reputation of being a ballbreaker, except with you.'

Wilson tested the tea. It was hot and slop. He'd already called Reid and given her a potted version of the event. He hadn't been able to work out whether she was relieved or not, given the tirade she'd launched at him, but he knew she'd be worrying about him. 'How long will I be here?'

'Until they tell me that you can go.' Upton sipped his tea. 'They have to work out whether you created a shit-storm, or whether it's something they can spin positively. I can just imagine the lads over in the media centre trying to write the press release.'

'It was a good shoot-out. They'll find out he shot first and he had a bloody AK-47.'

'Not my business. I'm not supposed to question you. That comes later. In fact, nobody is supposed to talk to you about what happened until someone at HQ works out what did happen first, if you know what I mean.'

Wilson nodded. A story was being constructed.

'I'm here as a colleague to have a cup of tea with you, but if you'd care to tell me a story while we enjoy our tea then I'm up for listening.'

Wilson started his story at the point where he heard that someone had concluded a contract for his assassination and continued to the shoot-out in the warehouse.

Upton listened attentively. 'Hell of a story. You're bloody lucky to have come out of that one alive. I won't ask how you got yourself into the situation where someone wants you dead. You must have pissed them off rightly. Maybe they'll have another go?'

'I don't think so. What's happening with Duane and my sergeant?'

'We're going to pack your sergeant off home as soon as she's made and signed a statement. She's had a bit of help from her federation representative.'

'What about Duane?'

Upton shook his head. 'Don't know any Duane. Apparently, there was a guy in the warehouse though when the shoot-out started.' He looked at his watch. 'But he was released five minutes ago.'

'So, I'm here alone.'

'Until Media Affairs comes up with a statement. I understand the chief constable will be wanting a word when he's free. I don't know whether that will be here or at HQ. You're a lucky man, Ian, in lots of ways. You've a few enemies but a lot of friends.'

'Thanks, Stuart. Could you try to pressure them at HQ? My partner is waiting at home and eager to give me hell.'

Upton went to the door and opened it. 'She has that reputation.'

CHAPTER FIFTEEN

The door didn't open again for more than an hour. When it did, the man who entered was Chief Constable Norman Baird, dressed in full uniform. He took off his cap and put it on the table before sitting down. Wilson stood and Baird waved him back to his seat.

'No formalities,' Baird said. 'Are you a student of history?'

'Not particularly.'

'There was a famous Irish general in the French Army called Marshal McMahon. Louis the fourteenth was reviewing his Irish troops and he turned to McMahon and said, "My Irish troops give me more trouble than the rest of the French Army." McMahon is supposed to have replied, "The enemy has the same complaint." You no doubt understand the link. You give me more trouble than all my senior officers, but I reckon the criminals might have the same complaint. Having said that, I'm getting a little tired of having to save your bacon.'

'Sorry, sir.'

'I don't believe a word of it. And don't put on an innocent face, it doesn't become you. The DCC is having an orgasm at HQ because he believes you've really done it this time. All the same, I bet you have a way of slipping the noose. And it'll have something to do with that pal of yours from Dublin. I have half an hour, so no bullshit, just tell me the real story.'

Wilson began. 'DCI Jack Duane of the Garda Special Branch received information that someone had put out a contract on the life of a PSNI officer and, following your own logic, he reckoned it might be me.' Wilson continued for the next twenty-five minutes describing exactly what had happened and leaving nothing out.

'What did you do to justify such attention? Anything to do with your run-in with Pratley and the Drugs Squad?'

'It isn't Best's style. He wouldn't shit on his own doorstep. I have my suspicions, sir, but I'd like to keep them to myself for the moment.'

'What if they try again?'

'I can't say for certain, but I think they'll reflect on what happened today and decide that it's better to avoid a replay, for the moment at least.'

'But you can't guarantee it.'

'No, I can't guarantee it.'

'And it's something I shouldn't know about.'

Wilson nodded.

Baird took out a folded sheet of A4 paper from his pocket and handed it to Wilson. 'That's the statement we intend to put out. Too many people know about the shooting to deny that it ever happened.'

Wilson read the statement. It was a typical Media Affairs production. A senior police officer had been the subject of an assassination attempt in Belfast. Shots were exchanged and the assassin fled. The theory was that a dissident republican group was responsible for the attack. Wilson handed the paper back. 'That should do it. What about my sergeant?'

'She was never there. By the way, she's waiting outside the station. I've also had several calls from Chief Superintendent Davis. There are many people who envy the loyalty you engender in your colleagues. As for Duane, he should be back in Dublin by now, where his bosses are waiting to give him a rocket up the arse. The deceased has been packed up and will be found dead somewhere outside Dublin tomorrow. It's handy they're having a drugs war down there at the moment. He'll be just another casualty. So the whole mess is being cleaned up and that only leaves your date with the Police Ombudsman's Office. You can't avoid it and I'm sure you can handle it.' He stood up and picked up his hat. 'I'm late for a dinner engagement, but I wouldn't have missed this for the world. You're free to leave.'

'What about the DCC?'

'Pity, he'll have to get over it. For some people, orgasms are all too short. I'm sure we'll run into each other again.'

They went to the door together. 'Is that son of yours bulking up?' Wilson said.

'He's in the gym every day.'

WILSON SAW Moira's jalopy sitting by the kerb. He walked over, opened the passenger door and sat in 'Take me back to my car. It should be still parked outside the warehouse.'

The starting motor ground, the gears squealed and the car jolted forward.

'What am I to do with you?' he said as soon as they were in motion.

'I was having your back.'

'Duane had my back.'

'I didn't know that.'

'But you knew something was going down. Who told you?'

There was silence in the car.

'I need to know,' he said. 'No repercussions.'

'I had lunch with Reid. My fault, I invited her. She was beside herself with worry.' She came to a stop behind his car.

He opened the door and turned to face her. 'Thanks for the lift. See you tomorrow.'

CHAPTER SIXTEEN

Reid was waiting for him at the door of the apartment. He assumed Moira had called ahead to let her know he was on his way. She tried to punch him, but he caught her arms and held her. They had had passionate kisses before, but the kiss that Reid planted on his lips contained more than passion. He sensed the relief and he wasn't about to tell her that it might be short-lived. The adrenaline rush was quite a few hours ago and he was now suffering the down after the high.

She broke the kiss and held his head in her hands. 'You look tired.'

'I wouldn't say no to a drink.'

Reid walked to the drinks cabinet and poured a large whiskey and a gin and tonic.

Wilson collapsed onto the couch. 'It's been a long and trying day.'

She left their drinks on the coffee table and sat down beside him. 'What will they do now?'

They sat holding each other and he told her about his meeting with Baird.

'So you're not suspended?'

'No, but there's an element at HQ who'd like to see that.'

'But the threat is over?'

For now, he thought as he nodded his head.

'The next time something like this happens, you're resigning. You might have been killed.' She hugged him.

That was their plan, he thought. Peter Davidson had got too close. So now they knew he was coming for them, Brennan's attempt on his life might not be the last. They had far too much to lose. It wasn't only the war chest they had built up using Carson Nominees and God only knew what other financial vehicles, it was also the corruption they had fostered and the murders they had organised. While bringing down Helen McCann would remove one block from the edifice, it might not bring down the whole rotten cabal. Most citizens lived their lives without ever seeing or feeling the cancer that was taking place around them. Davidson was ninety per cent of the way to proving that Helen McCann had ordered Jackie Carlisle's death. That had made Davidson a target. But McCann also knew it was him who was behind Davidson's investigation. He tried to put the whole mess out of his mind and enjoy the moment with the woman he loved. He picked up his drink and noticed that his hands were shaking.

Reid was watching. 'It's the adrenaline. It's left your body and your mind is confronted with the enormity of what happened in the warehouse.'

'I think I might have killed a man.'

'Or maybe Jack did.'

'I need to know. They'll dig the slugs out during the autopsy.'

She stroked his cheek. 'He was trying to kill you. What you did was self-defence.'

Had he lured Brennan to the warehouse to kill him or just to stop him from killing? He couldn't answer that question yet. For now, he was either a cold-blooded killer or a copper defending his life.

. . .

It wasn't Jack Duane's first time being hauled over the coals. Chief Superintendent Nolan was red-faced and spitting expletives faster than his lips could move. He was in such a rage that once or twice he nearly lost his dentures. Duane sat rigid before him. He knew that Nolan had had a dressing down from the Justice Minister and was passing the kick to the rightful miscreant. The problem was that Duane didn't give a damn about the kick. He'd enjoyed the shoot-out so much he would take half a dozen kicks. He lived for the adrenaline. He wasn't the kind of copper who hid in the office filling out forms. He'd taken a killer off the board today and in doing so he had sent a message. Some unfortunate rambler would find Brennan's body in a lane in north County Dublin tomorrow morning. The media would report the death as part of the ongoing tit-for-tat drug murders that plagued the city. But the players would know that Jack Duane had taken out Philly Brennan, and that was what mattered.

Nolan was running out of puff like a fire that flames and then dies. He slumped back in his chair. 'Fuck you, Jack, you're going to be the death of me. Either that or you're going to get me fired. Some days I wonder if you're worth the trouble.'

'Think positively. Another scumbag is out of the picture. We haven't made Ireland great again, but we have made the place a bit safer.'

'You're getting too close to that northern copper.'

'Probably.' Wilson wasn't the only northern copper he was getting close to. Yvonne Davis had called him twice on his way back to Dublin. The first call to make sure he was okay, and the second to tell him that everything in Belfast was arranged. Life had taught him to be unemotional, and while her concern touched him, he wasn't sure how to deal with the fact that she cared for him. For him, it was all about the sex. He was an adrenaline junkie, excitement was his drug. He looked at the pale-faced man across the desk, who probably couldn't even spell the word 'excitement'. The highlight of Nolan's life was when his village team scored a goal against their local rivals. He stood. 'I'm tired. It's been a bruising day. I think I'll have two pints and then go to bed. You should do the same. It will prepare you for whatever fuck-up I get involved in tomorrow.'

MOIRA FORKED a mouthful of microwaved chicken madras into her mouth. She tried not to look at her new surroundings, which would send the most cheerful person into a fit of depression. Her old flat had been cosy, whereas this dump would need a make-over just to make it habitable. She didn't need to stay here. She had a cheque in her possession for the sum of ten thousand dollars. Frank Shea had sent it to her as a thank you for keeping him out of jail. Maybe she would never cash it. She didn't help Frank for the money. She finished her meal and deposited its plastic container in the trash. She wasn't sorry that she'd followed Wilson to the warehouse, but she didn't like having to shop Reid. Her mind was full of questions. Had she been right to come back to Belfast? Why does the grass always seem greener on the other side of the hill for some people? And why did she have to be one of those people?

CHAPTER SEVENTEEN

Browne was at the station early. He wanted to be there when O'Neill arrived so he could get her working on a background profile for Roger Whyte. He hadn't slept well again. It bothered him that he'd ignored Wilson's instruction and was running his own private investigation. He wished Heavey hadn't involved him. So what if Vincent Carmody and Roger Whyte were missing? Knowing Vinny, they had probably gone off together, especially if Roger had money. Browne never wanted to see Vinny again, and yet he'd gone with Heavey to Whyte's flat. That had been a huge mistake. Why had he allowed himself to be drawn into Heavey's paranoia? Breaking and entering Whyte's flat had produced nothing. There wasn't any blood lying around and apparently nothing was missing. People vanish every day for many different reasons.

He let O'Neill sit down before he approached her desk. 'I need a favour.'

'Fire away.' O'Neill switched on her computer.

'I need you to do a background profile on a Roger Whyte with an address in Elmwood Mews.'

'Anything in particular?'

'Everything you can find. Is financial information out of the question?'

'Bank stuff, yes, but I can check things like credit rating.'

'Just get me everything you can.'

'No problem.'

'Also, can you check with the hospitals across the province to see if either Whyte or a Vincent Carmody have been admitted recently?'

O'Neill wrote the names in her notebook.

He went back to his desk and tried to concentrate on putting the papers together for the DPP on the murder of Colin Payne, the police whistle-blower who'd been drowned in a slurry tank. There was no way to follow up Whyte's disappearance on his own. There was too much legwork involved and he would need experienced detectives like Graham and Moira if he were to investigate. Somehow he'd have to get the boss onside.

WILSON SLEPT LATE. It crossed his mind that Reid may have slipped something into his drink the previous evening because he had no memory of falling asleep or getting himself to bed. She had already left when he rose and his head was feeling fuzzy. He downed a couple of painkillers and followed them with two cups of strong coffee. He was relieved to see there were no messages on his phone. He showered, dressed and turned on the television in time to catch the news from BBC Northern Ireland.

A modified version of the statement Baird had shown him was read out. It was terse and contained the minimum amount of information. If Media Affairs intended to create a 'one-day wonder', he believed they had succeeded. There was no mention of who the officer was or of possible fatalities. There was no follow-up expected. The people who needed to know what happened were informed and that was the end of the matter. There would be handshakes all round on an incident well covered up.

Except somebody had tried to kill him. Maybe the next time they would be better prepared or Duane wouldn't be on hand. It was a sobering thought that he couldn't allow to dominate his thinking. After one more cup of coffee, he headed to the station.

THE DESK SERGEANT's greeting was a little cheerier than usual. It might have been Wilson's imagination, or perhaps, despite the lid on the affair, word had got out as to the identity of the officer whose life had been threatened. If so, he'd soon be receiving a call from Jock McDevitt, the crime correspondent for the *Belfast Chronicle*. That wasn't an eventuality he looked forward to. The sergeant pointed up, which was the signal that Wilson had an immediate audience with the chief super. His steps seemed more laden as he made his way up the three floors to his boss's office.

CHIEF SUPERINTENDENT DAVIS closed the meeting she was holding as soon as she was told of Wilson's arrival. She waited until they were alone in the office before inviting him to sit. 'How are you?'

'Still here.'

'It was a close-run thing. The warehouse has been closed off, but word has it that thirty shots struck the wall where you were hiding.'

'He must have been a lousy shot.'

'There's no point in being blasé. Someone wants you dead. I want to know who.'

'I hear it's a dissident republican group.'

'Cut the crap, Ian. I'm trying to have an adult conversation here. First Peter Davidson and now you. I think someone's cage must be well and truly rattled. There's nothing much on at the moment, maybe you should take a week off.'

He shook his head. 'It's over for a while. Well, I hope it is, since they took my weapon away yesterday.'

'You and Jack seem to think you're immortal. The bad news is, you aren't. You know who's behind it, or at least you have a good idea.'

He didn't speak.

'Something else I'm not supposed to know?' she said.

He didn't answer.

'I think I'll suggest trauma counselling,' she said. 'It's the first time I've seen you speechless.'

'It appears that I'll be doing a lot of talking in the next few days to the Police Ombudsman's team. They might not be so adept at accepting the dissident republican theory as the general population. But you can count on me being discreet. Especially where Duane's involvement is concerned.'

'These people mean business. If you know who they are, get them behind bars as quickly as possible.'

'I'm working on it.'

'Okay, get to it and no more gunplay.'

He stood. 'It wasn't my call.'

'Why don't I believe it?'

Wilson entered the squad room but didn't go to his office. He stood at the top of the room and called the team together. He explained to them what had happened at the warehouse, excluding the information that Moira had been on hand. He knew there were rumours around, but he expected the squad to keep quiet about what he'd told them.

'This situation is serious, boss,' Graham said when he'd finished. 'It's got to be the Carlisle investigation.'

'It might have been Best,' Wilson said.

'Davie's not that stupid,' Graham said. 'And he's got guys

on his team who blew up half of Afghanistan and wouldn't have worried about taking out you and a dozen innocent bystanders. It's Carlisle and it's money.'

'I will handle Carlisle.'

'What about Helen's Bay?' Moira said.

'That's your priority.' He moved towards his office. Once inside, he flopped into his chair. Davis and Graham were right. Davidson had lifted the wrong rock and the snake hiding underneath was proving venomous. He needed to get busy. Moira and he had already proved to be an effective team. If they couldn't finish what Peter started, it would be a surprise to him.

He noticed Browne lurking around outside his office. His sergeant was not the easiest to get along with, but he was an honest, clever young copper who would probably go places. Anyone taking Moira's place had a lot to live up to and Rory was getting there. If only he would try to be a little more personable. He motioned him to come into the office.

'What's all the shuffling about?' Wilson asked as soon as Rory entered.

'You'll be angry when you hear what I've done.'

'Sit down.' Wilson prepared himself for the confession.

'I ignored your instruction to stay away from the Whyte disappearance.'

'And?'

'Last evening I met with the guy Heavey who told me about the disappearance and we went to Whyte's flat.'

The hesitation was there again. 'I can't keep waiting for this story. Get on with it.'

'We rang, but there was no one there. So I picked the lock and we went inside. There was no sign of Whyte, and Heavey reckoned that nothing was missing.'

'Any sign of a struggle?'

Browne shook his head. 'The place was scrupulously clean. There was no upturned furniture, no blood visible to the naked eye. The flat looked as though the occupant had just gone down the road for a pint.'

'What made you follow up on this when I told you to let it go?'

'It was just the way Ward dismissed the disappearance.'

'People will get pissed if we tramp over their territory.'

'Whyte was an obsessive-compulsive. Everything had to be just so. You can see it in the flat. He lived a regulated life. There were certain things that had to be done at certain times and on certain days. Guys like that don't just drop off the radar. His friend Heavey isn't the only one who's concerned. Everybody who knows him is worried.'

Wilson hadn't looked on Browne as an intuitive copper, but maybe he'd got that wrong. 'Get your jacket. We're going to Musgrave Street.'

CHAPTER EIGHTEEN

After checking in with the desk sergeant, Wilson and Browne made their way to the office of DCI Noel Jones, head of the Missing Persons unit of the PSNI. Wilson shook hands with Jones and introduced Browne.

'Can I get you guys a tea?' Jones asked and pointed to two chairs.

'I think we'll pass.' Wilson sat.

'Good call. Did you hear about a republican group targeting an unnamed officer?' Jones said. 'Rumours abound.'

'You wouldn't want to believe everything you hear,' Wilson said. Jones had been one of his colleagues in the old days when he had worked in Musgrave Street and Donald Spence ran CID. In those days, Jones had a full head of reddish hair and the start of a beer-belly. Over the years, the hair had thinned to a few strategically placed strands and the belly had taken over the body. While several months of plentiful sunshine had left even the most sun-shy of Irish people with a light tan, Jones's round countenance was still alabaster white.

'Aye, I'm aware of that. What can I do for you?'

'DS Browne was here yesterday looking into the disappearance of a Roger Whyte,' Wilson said. 'Whyte's friends are concerned for his safety. As in they fear something has happened to him.'

Jones tapped keys on his computer and then turned the screen around to face the two men. It showed a vertical listing of missing persons and their photos. Roger Whyte was at the top. Jones gave them an opportunity to look at the screen before turning it back. He tapped some more keys and the printer beside him spat out five A4 pages. 'This is what we've collected. We have a description, where he was last seen, the clothes he was wearing when last seen, his vehicle, his telephone number. We've checked social media. You know the drill.'

'And that's led nowhere?' Wilson asked.

Jones shook his head. 'We've put out requests for information on the Internet but so far nothing. There are people on our list who have been missing since 1962. Many people are just unhappy with their lives and opt out. Check out the homeless shelters, they're full of runners.'

'I wouldn't class Whyte with them,' Browne said. 'He lives in a nice flat, he worked in financial services and had made enough money to afford to live off his investments. On the surface, he had no reason to disappear.'

'What do you think, Ian?' Jones asked.

'There has to be a judgement call that Whyte has been the victim of foul play if we're to take the case on. I need to hear that from you.'

'I think we've taken it as far as we can,' Jones said. 'I don't know that I can conclude that Whyte has been the victim of some evil deed. But if you have the resources to take the case on, you can have it.'

Wilson looked at Browne, who nodded. 'Apparently, we have the resources.'

'We'll need everything you've got,' Browne said.

'I'll have the file sent over before close of play. But don't be surprised if it's no more than the machine spat out. If he turns up, you'll let us know?'

Wilson nodded and stood. He extended his hand. 'Good to see you again, Noel.'

Jones shook. 'Good to see you too, Ian. There's no truth in the rumour that you were the police officer in question, is there?'

'Not a word of truth.'

Jones winked. 'Aye, well, take care of yourself.'

'WHAT DO WE DO NOW, BOSS?' Browne asked, once they had left the building.

'Go through Whyte's life with a fine-tooth comb.'

'I've already started that process. I asked O'Neill to dig up what she could on Whyte.'

Wilson valued initiative but not insubordination. 'You and I need to have a talk about how hierarchy works in the PSNI.'

'I'm sorry, boss.'

'You're taking this too personally for my liking. Is there something that you want to tell me? If there is, now is the time.'

Browne shook his head.

CHAPTER NINETEEN

Wilson gathered the team around the whiteboard. 'Roger Whyte has been missing for almost a month. He is a man of regular habits and his friends are worried that he's come to harm. Our colleagues in Missing Persons have gone as far as they can and they're happy to let us run with it. They're sending over the file as we speak. I understand Siobhan is already looking into Whyte's life. I want to go deep: bank statements, credit cards, ATM withdrawals. By this evening I want this whiteboard covered in information on Whyte's life.' He turned to Graham. 'Harry, you're working with Rory on this one. Get to it.'

WILSON WAS JUST ABOUT to shut his office door when Moira put her hand out to stop him. She walked in after him and closed the door. 'What's with the statement issued by the media people?'

'Case closed.' Wilson sat and motioned for Moira to do the same. 'HQ arranged everything. Brennan's body has probably been found by now, and he will be treated as another victim of the drugs war in Dublin. Forensics will clean up the warehouse. The Gardaí arrested the van driver. All is well in our little world up here. Didn't they fill you in at Strandtown?'

'The chief super checked my gun and confirmed that it hadn't been fired. Then he told me to piss off home and forget that I was ever at the warehouse.'

'Sound advice.'

'You and Duane only got the hitman; whoever was behind it is still out there and might try again.'

'They might.'

'And you're okay about that?'

'Have you ever had an AK-47 loosed off in your direction?'

She shook her head. 'I take it you're not okay.'

'Somebody will have to pay. How are things going on Helen's Bay?'

'I've put the word out to the drone clubs and I'm looking into Best's and Hills' backgrounds to see if either of them has an association with Helen's Bay.'

That was sound police work. She'd made more progress in a week than they had in the previous three months. The case was alive again. He knew she was the best person to replace Davidson on the Carlisle investigation and he knew she would jump at the chance. The downside was that he would be putting her in danger. He opened his desk drawer and took out the file that Peter had made on his investigation. It was all there, from the interviews at the hospice to the finding of the mobile phone at the airport. It also contained the name of the person at the end of the phone call from the murderer. He put it on the desk between them and made a snap decision. 'I want you to have a look at this file. I want you to read it with an open mind because I haven't given it to you yet.'

She picked up the file and ran through the pages. It was organised like a murder book, with sections on the victim, details of the interviews and statements taken. She noticed the name of Jackie Carlisle as the victim.

'This was Peter's investigation,' he said. 'And a damn fine job he did too.'

Moira closed the file. 'This is what both he and you almost got killed for.'

'That's why I haven't decided yet who to give the continuation of the investigation to.'

'I'll read it and I'll probably want it.'

'It won't be your decision. It'll be mine. How can I be sure that you'll manage it after what you did yesterday? Duane and I knew what we were heading into, but you tagged along with no idea of the danger or the consequences for you. How do you think I would have felt if you'd been killed or injured on my account?'

'I'm sorry, boss.'

'No you're not. You'd do it again in a heartbeat. But that file is dangerous. You'll see why when you've read it. And going off half-cocked will get people hurt. Read the file and then we'll talk.'

He watched her leave the room. She was the kind of person he liked having in his corner, but he really wasn't happy about giving her such a dangerous assignment. He switched on his computer and tried to deal with administrative tasks. It was all so much bullshit. Today wasn't the day to be thinking about budgets or overtime allocations. Whoever cleaned up after Duane had dumped Brennan's body in a lane like it was a sack of potatoes. He was having difficulty coming to grips with the fact that he might have taken a life. It was the opposite of what he had dedicated himself to. It all depended on whether he had lured Brennan to the warehouse to kill him. He had followed the correct protocol and he remembered giving the shouted warning. But would they believe him?

His computer pinged indicating an email. The Police Ombudsman's Office would like to know when Detective Superintendent Ian Wilson would be available for an interview.

CHAPTER TWENTY

Wilson emerged from his office at five-thirty and went to the whiteboard. Browne and O'Neill had worked hard since he returned from Musgrave Street. A new board had been set up with an eleven-by-fourteen-inch black-and-white photo of Roger Whyte at the top. According to his date of birth, which was below the photo, Whyte was fifty-five years old. He looked older. His hair was snow-white, thin on top but plentiful at the sides. The face was oval and soft, the cheeks depressed and fleshy, the lips thin and the mouth small. His eyes looked sharp and Wilson thought he saw a curiosity there. 'Gather round children, while Rory fills us in on what he's found so far about our missing person.'

Browne stepped forward and tapped the board beside the photo. 'This is Roger Whyte from a photo supplied by Musgrave Street. He was born in Ballymena on March 25th, 1963, which makes him fifty-five years of age. He attended St Louis Grammar School before obtaining a first-class honours degree in classics from Oxford. After university, he became a successful investment banker in the City of London with a small private bank. When a larger rival purchased the bank, Whyte had a financial windfall and retired. He returned to

Belfast five years ago and bought his flat in Elmwood Mews. He was last seen on July 11th. He is a practising homosexual and well-known within the gay community. He is not active on social media. His bank account is at the Ulster Bank and we've requested a court order to examine his statements. Harry and I will check his flat tomorrow morning.'

'Good work,' Wilson said. 'I received a request from the Police Ombudsman's Office for an interview concerning the shooting in Ballymacarrett. I have no idea how the investigation will impact on my work, but Moira and Rory are more than capable of keeping the ship on course. Although Whyte is considered a missing person, we will treat him as a victim of violence and this as a murder inquiry. We don't have a body and there's a possibility that we might never have one. We start by interviewing everyone who's been in contact with him over the past few months.'

'On it, boss,' Browne said.

'Moira will continue with the Helen's Bay case for the moment. You can give us a quick rundown.'

Moira explained the two new lines of inquiry she had opened. 'I might need Siobhan depending on how the inquiries proceed.'

'Okay, let's head home and get at it early tomorrow,' Wilson said, bringing the briefing to a close.

WILSON HAD TOLD Reid that he would meet her at the Crown as soon as she finished work. When he pushed in the door he encountered a sea of tourists taking selfies while downing pints of Guinness in front of the ornate décor of the pub. He hated the summer crowds, but it was the price he paid for having the most famous pub in Belfast as his local. Since the signing of the peace accord, Northern Ireland had entered a kind of golden age, embracing values that were continental as much as British. Tourists flocked to the Titanic Centre and jumped on buses promising a tour of the *Game of Thrones* sites. Restaurants and pubs served dishes other than boxty and Wilson's favourite haunt wasn't only a pub but a tourist attraction. The barman caught his eye and directed him towards a snug at the far end of the bar. Wilson nodded and signalled for a pint of Guinness. He pushed through the throng of smartphone-wielding tourists and entered the calm of the snug.

'Who's been a bad boy then?' Jock McDevitt looked up from the book he was reading. 'I knew you'd come in here sooner or later.'

Wilson sighed and settled himself into a seat across from McDevitt. 'You've been quiet. What are you drinking?'

'I'm off the booze.' McDevitt put the book into his messenger bag. 'I'm on antibiotics for a throat infection. Why didn't you tell me someone was out to kill you?'

'I've listened to this bullshit all day. I have no idea who started this bloody rumour, but I'm not involved.' Wilson's pint arrived and he paid.

'Pull the other one. I have it on the best authority so you might as well let me into the secret. Off the record.'

Wilson sighed. 'How's the Hollywood business going?'

'We're in development. They're looking for an actor who can lie while keeping a straight face. I'm not new to this game and I smell something very juicy in this story. I haven't seen this level of cover-up in a long time. That "dissident republican" bullshit gets dragged out every time something spooky happens. You might as well tell me now because I'll ferret out the truth.'

Wilson felt a sense of relief when Reid appeared. She kissed McDevitt on the check and Wilson on the lips before sitting beside him. 'What are you fellows up to?'

'There's a rumour around that I'm the police officer who was shot at yesterday,' Wilson said. 'Jock has bought into this fantasy, so will you please disabuse him.'

'Gin and tonic,' Reid said.

'Sorry.' Wilson did the necessary.

Reid looked at McDevitt. 'Ian is not the police officer involved.'

'My God,' McDevitt said. 'He's trained her to lie as convincingly as himself. Have you no shame, woman?'

Reid's gin and tonic arrived. She glanced at the glass of water in front of McDevitt.

'He's on the dry,' Wilson said.

'You guys are a better double act than Hope and Crosby,' McDevitt said. 'But I'll get the truth out of you yet.' He picked up his messenger bag. 'I must leave you, folks. I have an assignation with a confidential informant. But I'll be seeing you soon.'

Reid waited until McDevitt left. 'He'll find out, you know that. Maybe you should confide in him.'

Wilson shook his head. 'He'll want to go further and I can't have that.'

'Why do I feel that we're at the beginning of the end rather than the end of the beginning? You haven't even told me the whole story.'

'Someone tried to kill me because of what I know, but I also don't know the whole story. The last thing I'll do is put you in danger.'

'I asked the hospital in LA to put the job on hold.'

'And?'

'They can't, but jobs are coming up all the time and they want me.'

Every time she spoke about the job in LA he felt her longing. 'Want to go and eat somewhere?'

'No, let's pick up some takeaway and a good bottle of wine. We'll have a nice bath together and enjoy each other's company.'

He finished his drink. 'I think I love you.'

'I think you do too.'

CHAPTER TWENTY-ONE

He lay back on the couch. It was such a futile exercise, but he had to appease his parents. The irony of it was that they were the ones he held responsible for the way he was. He looked across at Dr Rose Aronowitz and wondered was it Freud who started the tradition of the Jewish psychiatrist. It was so like his parents to choose an Aronowitz over a Maguire. She was ten years older than him, lived with her husband in a four-bed detached house in Finaghy and had three children attending the local primary school. As soon as his parents insisted that he seek professional help and suggested Dr Aronowitz, he'd researched her on the Internet. When he agreed to be her patient, he stalked her, her husband and her children. He had a large gallery of photos of them and he knew more about their lives than they knew about each other. He had already decided that if she found out too much about him, he would kill her and her husband, maybe even her children. He often thought about killing people. In fact, he always thought about it. He'd heard that most men think about sex every ten seconds, but for him it was killing. Since he was a teenager, he had fantasised about killing just about everyone in his life. That included his parents, teachers and classmates.

Most of all he would have liked to kill his classmates. There were parts of him that nobody should ever find out about. Parts he didn't understand himself.

He watched Dr Rose as she made her notes. To carry out this charade, he had been forced to create another character, an alternate or an avatar. He'd always been good at drama. Maybe he should have followed up on it? Anyway, the character he created was gentle and didn't want to kill anyone. However, he couldn't be perfect. There were too many strange instances in his past. He had to have problems. Otherwise why would he be attending a psychiatrist? He'd discovered that Dr Rose's brief was to find out why everyone who came into contact with him was left with the feeling that there was something odd about him. He suspected that his parents' disquiet perhaps centred on their fear about what he might do to them. He couldn't deny that he'd had fantasies about killing them, but there were elements of the perfect fantasy missing from that scenario. He had no desire to have sex with either parent. He had been in and out of therapy since his teen years and Dr Rose was the end of the road. What she didn't know was that he had found the cure for what was bothering him all by himself. How could he tell her that the answer to his problem was his desire to drug homosexuals, rape them and murder them?

'Tell me about yourself.' Aronowitz's tone was soft and professional.

Her eyes looked interested behind her large dark-framed glasses. Or perhaps it was her professional manner, and he'd find at the end of their session that she had covered her notebook with doodles. Telling her about himself was the last thing he wanted to do. He'd read dozens of books on psychology and had already made what he considered to be a credible diagnosis of his situation. He wondered whether he should present the symptoms of narcissistic personality disorder where he would display a grandiose sense of self-importance and entitlement, be preoccupied with fantasies of unlimited power, lack empathy and require excessive admiration. But that wasn't even a character he could play. He opted instead for antisocial personality disorder, whose sufferers are deceitful and manipulative for personal profit or gain. That was something his parents would recognise straight away.

His research into psychology had made him realise the collage of mental disorders his whole life had been. If Dr Rose had his real story, she might even come to the same conclusion as him. He was one of those rare psychopaths willing to take his feelings of dissociation from the human race to the limit of torturing a human being before taking his life.

He lay back and reeled off the life of the character he had created, beginning at memories from when he was three. He didn't know how many sessions his parents had paid for and he didn't care. He had a whole other life story ready to disgorge. It was a game he was good at and enjoyed playing. While his mouth was fleshing out the character he wanted Dr Rose to get to know, his mind was watching the films he'd made of the deaths of Whyte and Carmody. Whoever said that a human couldn't think and operate on two levels hadn't met him.

CHAPTER TWENTY-TWO

As soon as Wilson had arrived at the station, the desk sergeant had pointed upstairs. When he entered Davis's office, she was at the coffee table with a visitor. They both stood.

'Ian, this is Senior Investigating Officer Colm Matthews from the Police Ombudsman's Office.'

Matthews extended his hand.

Wilson shook. 'Detective Superintendent Ian Wilson.'

Matthews had a firm handshake. He looked to be in his mid-forties and carried himself like a copper. His face was round and his eyes peered out from behind a pair of not very strong lenses.

'I saw you play,' Matthews let go his hand. 'I used to play myself, at a much more modest level.'

Wilson fancied he could tell what rugby position someone played from their body shape. That would not be so easy today when some backs have the build of forwards, but it would have been possible in Matthews' time. He was maybe five-feet-nine tall and had probably put on weight since he played. 'Winger?' Wilson guessed.

Matthews smiled. 'How could you tell?'

'It's a gift.'

They sat and Wilson was pleased to see that it was a tea and biscuits meeting. He poured himself a cup of tea.

'You're over your ordeal?' Matthews said.

'I've been in an explosion,' Wilson said. 'Being shot at and missed doesn't rate.'

'The damage caused by the explosion finished your career,' Matthews said.

'Such as it was, yes.' Wilson sipped his tea.

'You're far too modest,' Matthews said.

'Senior Investigating Officer Matthews wishes to launch the investigation into the shooting,' Davis said.

'Please call me Colm, my full moniker is unwieldy.'

'All our full monikers are unwieldy,' Davis said. 'How long do you think the investigation will take?'

'We'd like to move as quickly as possible,' Matthews said. 'There are always complaints from the press that we're slow in getting the reports out, but we need to be as thorough as possible. That no one was injured eases the situation somewhat.'

'We're here to assist you in every way possible,' Davis said.

'Perhaps we could start with a visit to the scene of the shooting,' Matthews said. 'Perhaps DS Wilson might accompany me.'

Wilson nodded. 'When would you like to go?'

'Forensics have finished their work,' Matthews said. 'Would you be free later this morning?'

'Is eleven o'clock all right?' Wilson said.

Matthews nodded, stood and extended his hand to Davis. 'Thanks for the tea.'

Davis shook.

Matthews turned to Wilson. 'See you at eleven at Ballymacarrett.'

'It's a date.'

Wilson and Davis watched Matthews leave. 'Be careful of

that one,' Davis said when the door closed. 'You're sure that you're solid on the shooting?'

Wilson didn't answer. 'He's not one of ours?'

'No, before you came in we had a short meet and greet. He was an inspector in the Royal Bahamas Police Force for over ten years before he joined the Police Ombudsman's Office here six years ago.'

'So he didn't come to Belfast for the sunshine. No connection to our friend at HQ?'

'Jennings? Not on the surface. But one never knows.'

'The octopus's tentacles have a long reach.'

'Why didn't you and Jack arrest the shooter?'

'On what grounds? Until he walked into the warehouse cradling an AK-47 he'd done nothing wrong.'

'You could have arrested the quartermaster?'

'They would have replaced him within hours. The only possibility of no casualties was when Brennan ignored my warning and started shooting. I suppose Jack and I should count our lucky stars that we prevailed.'

'Just be careful with Matthews. You need to get this off your plate.'

'Speaking of which, we've just launched a new investigation.'

'Thank you for informing me. It must be insignificant if you're telling me at the start.'

'A man named Roger Whyte disappeared almost a month ago. His friends are very concerned for his safety.'

'What about Missing Persons?'

'They've passed the case to us.'

'At your request, what's the interest for you?'

'I don't know. Maybe I want to scratch an itch.'

'Be my guest, as long as you don't scratch it on overtime.'

DAVIS RETURNED to her desk and watched the door close. He

was a handsome devil and the perfect Shakespearean character, suffering as he did the slings and arrows of outrageous fortune. A flawed man who engendered love and hate in equal measure. Some day he would come undone and she would be very sad. She sighed and went back to work.

CHAPTER TWENTY-THREE

Harry Graham missed Davidson more than he would admit. They had formed an attachment based on their shared background as Shankill boys and had developed a good social and work bond. He envied Peter his new life in the sun. He loved his wife, and the girls were a joy, but life was a struggle and would continue to be for the foreseeable future. Sometimes he hankered back to the old days when George Whitehouse was the sergeant and he, Peter, Eric and Ronald had laboured in the squad room. Happy days, he thought, but deep down he knew he was looking at the past through rose-coloured glasses. The new crew were more serious and drank less and that was for the best. They were a lot sharper than the old boys, probably because they were better educated. It was strange how the new coppers had evolved from the old timers much as Best and Hills had emerged from the old gangsters. He wasn't sure which set was better. He wasn't one of those who credited criminals like Sammy Rice with having some kind of honour code. Rice killed as easily as Best and Hills would.

'Ready to go?'

Graham came out of his daydream and saw DS Browne standing at his desk. 'Absolutely, sergeant.'

'What's with you, Harry? You looked like you were away with the fairies.'

They headed downstairs. 'Family, kids, school, mortgage, it never seems to stop.'

Browne slapped him on the shoulder. 'You're never in bad humour, but I suppose the pressures of family life and the job must be hard.'

'Wait until you have three small ones to clothe and feed and keep a roof over their heads.' He realised what a stupid remark that was. Browne would probably never have the pleasure of rolling up a nappy full of shit, cleaning a bottom and slapping on a new Pampers. Things were changing though. Gay couples could adopt in other places, although that wasn't likely to happen in Northern Ireland any time soon. Graham had learned to live and let live. He'd been raised in the Protestant heartland, but he'd long ago rejected the politics of division. He'd seen too much of the blood and gore it produced.

They took one of the station cars and drove to Elmwood Mews, parking in the yard in front of Whyte's flat.

'Let's take a look.' Browne climbed out of the car and knocked on the door several times. When he received no answer, he worked his magic with the lock-picks.

They put on latex gloves before entering the hallway. Browne climbed the stairs.

'You've been here before?'

'Yes, once with one of Whyte's friends. I thought I said.'

'No, you didn't.'

'The boss knows.'

They entered the living room together. 'You take the bedroom and the bathroom.' Browne indicated the area at the rear of the flat. 'I'll do the living room and the kitchen.'

Graham went towards the bedroom.

Browne went straight for the desk he had seen on his previous visit. A filing cabinet supported one side of the desk. He pulled out the large drawer revealing a series of files. Each had a small label at the top and the subjects were the ones found in any home. Seeing the neatness of the filing he felt that Whyte's OCD would come in useful. There was a thick file of bank statements that would have to be examined in detail. He had requested a forensic team to examine the flat with a concentration on whether it was a crime scene. He removed the bank file and closed the cabinet; Forensics could deal with the rest. He picked up a diary from the desk. Whyte's obsession with detail was opportune. His movements were annotated for every day of the week. Browne flicked through the pages and saw why Whyte was described as a creature of habit.

Graham did a quick search of the bathroom. There were more smelly bottles and antiperspirants than in his wife's cabinet at home. There were six bottles with tablets in them, but he would leave those to the forensic boys as well. He moved on to the main bedroom. There was nothing of note. The room was as neat as a pin and the bed had been made with military precision. There were three books on the bedside table: two novels and a guide on investments to make in the next crash. Not another one, he'd survived the last recession, but he didn't like to think what another cut in his salary would mean for his family's future. They were scraping by as it was. He did a quick inspection of the floor but saw no signs of blood. The closets were fully stocked with clothes that looked expensive and the drawers were filled with ironed shirts, socks and underwear. The laundry basket in the corner of the room was empty. To Graham's experienced eye, there was no reason to think that Whyte had come to harm in his flat. He went into the living room.

Browne handed him the diary. 'You could set your clock by this guy.'

Graham flicked through the pages of the small book.

'There are probably a hell of a lot of leads to follow up here. There's no obvious sign of blood or a struggle that I can see.' He dropped the book into an evidence bag and sealed it.

'I'm inclined to agree,' Browne said. 'If Whyte has come to harm, it didn't happen in his home. But I suppose we must wait for Forensics to confirm that. We need to establish a timeline for July 11th and 12th.'

'Maybe he went out on a march,' Graham said tongue-in-cheek. The twelfth of July holiday in Northern Ireland was the main day of the marching season when many of the Protestant population celebrated the victory of William of Orange over King James at the Battle of the Boyne.

'I wish he'd picked a better day to disappear than one with all that mayhem going on.'

'Where to next?' Graham asked.

'We need to draw up a list of his friends and organise some interviews. Someone might know something useful.' Browne handed the file of bank statements to Graham. 'He didn't disappear because of financial difficulties anyway.'

Graham looked at the last document in the file and whistled. 'Four hundred and twenty grand in the bank.' His own account was fifteen hundred overdrawn, as it was every month. 'We need to check it's still there. Some boys in this town would gut you for a small percentage of that.' He removed an evidence bag from his pocket, dropped the bank file in and sealed it.

'Might it be the motive for the disappearance?'

'It might indeed.'

CHAPTER TWENTY-FOUR

Wilson drove into the yard in front of the warehouse on the Ballymacarrett Road and parked next to a Skoda Octavia. He cut the engine and exited the car. As he approached the door, he saw that the lock the forensic team had put on had already been opened. He found Matthews inside, inspecting the wall at the rear. The investigator turned as soon as he heard Wilson approach.

Wilson looked at his watch. 'Am I late?' He knew that he wasn't.

'No,' Matthews said. 'I arrived early.'

Matthews wasn't a good liar and this wasn't a good start to their relationship. 'You wouldn't have been trying to steal a march on me?' Wilson asked.

'Perish the thought, I just don't want to waste your time.' Matthews took out a sheaf of paper and shone a torch on it. 'This is the statement you signed at Strandtown station after the shooting. What were you doing here?'

Wilson walked to the centre of the warehouse and pointed down. 'Shine your torch on the ground.'

Matthews did as he was requested. He saw the dark stain on the concrete floor.

'That stain is Sammy Rice's blood. I think this is the spot where he was murdered. The case is still open and we're still searching for Rice's body and his killer. I come here occasionally hoping I'll get inspiration that'll help me move the case forward.'

Matthews nodded his head as though the answer seemed feasible enough. 'Where were you when the assassin entered the warehouse?'

Wilson moved to the area that Matthews was examining when he entered. 'Here.'

'And what were you doing there?'

'Praying for inspiration, as far as I remember.'

'And you heard the door open?'

'Yes, and I saw a man silhouetted against the light carrying an assault weapon. I dropped to the ground, shouted a warning and kept my head down while he sprayed the wall behind me. Then I returned fire in his direction and he must have decamped. It all happened so quickly.'

'And you hit no one.'

'I don't know. I kept my head down until I heard the noise of an engine starting up outside. Then I knew he was gone. I called it in, but I had no idea of the type of vehicle he escaped in.'

'It must have been traumatic.'

'I would have preferred a bun fight. I've been a copper for a good while, but I've never been subjected to a burst of fire from an automatic weapon. It's not the most pleasant sensation to have bullets flying around your head. Adrenaline kicks in, you remember your training and you react.'

'Have you any idea how many shots you fired?'

'No. It seemed like six, but my gun was taken from me when the squad car arrived. I didn't check the magazine.'

Matthews walked towards the front of the warehouse where Brennan had been shot. He shone his torch on a patch of what looked like blood. 'Could you have hit the assailant?'

'I might have. My shots weren't well directed. I'm sure Strandtown would have checked with the hospitals.'

Matthews shone his torch on the wall above the patch. 'It looks like six bullets hit this wall. How many bullets were in the magazine?'

'There should have been seventeen, but I'm not sure.'

'Forensic found six shells.'

'Then I must have fired six.'

'Thank you, detective superintendent, that'll be all for now.'

'Let me know when you need me again.'

'I'll do that.'

Wilson left the warehouse confident that he had answered all Matthews' questions. He noted that there had been no small talk about rugby this time. He'd need to look up Matthews' background. There couldn't have been many shooting incidents investigated by the Royal Bahamas Police.

CHAPTER TWENTY-FIVE

Charles Heavey stood up from the wooden bench in the reception area when Browne and Graham returned from Elmwood Mews. 'DS Browne,' he said before they disappeared.

Browne turned to Graham. 'This is Charles Heavey, Whyte's friend.'

Graham and Heavey shook hands.

'I'll deal with this,' Browne said. 'Log the evidence and then let Siobhan take a look at the financial statements.'

'Yes, sergeant.' Graham started up the stairs.

'What's happening?' Heavey said.

'My boss has agreed to investigate Whyte's disappearance. We've been to Elmwood Mews and there'll be a forensic examination of the flat. I doubt if anything happened there. You should stay out of this. We'll interview you in due course, but please don't come to the station again.'

'What about Vincent? I'm worried about him and so are a lot of others.'

'One thing at a time. Investigating the disappearance of Whyte will use up a lot of our resources.'

'What if the disappearances are connected?'

'They're most likely not. Vinny is a butterfly. He could have hooked up with someone and gone off to Paris on an adventure. Sooner or later he'll turn up.'

'What if he doesn't?'

'Then we'll look for him when we find Whyte. Now leave us to do our job.'

'There's a lot of disquiet in the LGBT community about the way cases involving gender-diverse individuals are being handled by the PSNI. There's talk about sending a delegation to the chief constable.'

'They can do whatever they want. Don't come to the station again. If you need any news, phone me.'

Browne turned and climbed the stairs. He was worrying that he would become the 'LGBT man' in the Murder Squad. He glanced at the boss's office and saw it was empty. He walked ahead to the whiteboard.

Moira was keeping her head down. There'd been no mention of the warehouse or of her being there. She knew that the Police Ombudsman's Office was investigating the shooting and since they hadn't contacted her, she assumed that her involvement had been erased. It wouldn't have mattered because there was nothing she could have added since she hadn't taken part in the events inside the warehouse. But it might have contributed to the idea that there had been some level of premeditation on Wilson's part. She was plodding through the details of the lives of Davie Best and Eddie Hills. One or both had to have some prior connection with Coastguard Avenue in Helen's Bay. So far she had come up with nothing. Neither man had been born or raised locally or appeared to have relations living in the area. But if they were the culprits, there had to be some reason they knew of a small turnoff that ended at the edge of the sea. She had checked with the drone clubs and they had put the word out by email to their members. It was doubtful, but something might come of it. Her search for another line of inquiry had so far come up dry. She needed action. She would prefer to be working on the Whyte disappearance. There was more flesh on the bones to pick in that case. She appreciated the boss's strategy of easing her back into the job, but right now she didn't need to spend her days behind a desk. She needed to be out there and she believed that her salvation lay in the Carlisle investigation. Davidson had done a fine piece of detecting and the conclusion was there for all to see: Helen McCann had been instrumental in the murder of Jackie Carlisle. She saw the danger in the case. That was part of its attraction.

WILSON TOOK his time in returning to the office. There was nothing urgent and he fancied a stroll along the Lagan. The Titanic Centre was close-by, and he parked there. He considered a coffee at the Galley Café but tourists were jammed into the small space and the reception area was thronged. He strolled back towards the SSE Arena and bought a coffee from a shop that had picnic tables in front.

It was a beautiful summer's day, so he sat for a while and watched the tourists trailing from town along his jogging path. Then he took out his phone and brought up the front page of *The Irish Times*. The lead article described the finding of the body of Philly Brennan on a back road in a place called Ballyboghill in north County Dublin. The Garda statement said that Brennan appeared to be the victim of the current feud between rival drug gangs. He had been shot several times and the fatal shot had been to the head. Wilson closed his phone. Whoever shot Brennan had been accurate in his shooting. His shots had been wild so maybe he got lucky, or maybe he wasn't the killer. There was no point in asking Duane because he would just receive the answer that Duane assumed he'd want to hear. The whole Brennan affair brought him no nearer to pinning Jackie Carlisle's murder on Helen McCann. He was certain that she had been the instigator and that Simon Jackson had carried out the murder. Was Jackson a contractor, or was Special Branch behind the operation? It had all the hall-marks of a Black Bob operation. But he needed more proof and there was only one way to get it. He needed to lay his hands on Jackson.

CHAPTER TWENTY-SIX

'What have we got?' Wilson looked at Browne and Graham as they sat before him.

Browne ran through the search at the flat.

'Four hundred and twenty thousand in the bank,' Wilson said. 'Let's assume he owns the flat, that's another two hundred thousand. Our friend Whyte was not short of a few pounds.'

'Siobhan has been looking into his background,' Browne said. 'He may have received as much as two million when the bank he worked for was taken over.'

Wilson whistled. 'Two million. I suppose all this was common knowledge.'

'Anyone with a computer and an Internet connection could have discovered it,' Browne said.

'We have a very strong motive for murder then,' Wilson said. 'But first, we must check whether any of the money has disappeared along with Whyte. We also need to check on the inheritors. Get Siobhan busy on tracing Whyte's family. How close was this guy Heavey to him?'

'According to the diary,' Browne said. 'They had lunch every second Wednesday.'

'The eleventh of July was a Wednesday,' Graham noted.

'Maybe that was the second Wednesday,' Wilson said. 'We need to get working on a timeline. It's time to use some shoe leather. We need to dig up a lot of information over the next few days.' Considering the level of Whyte's bank account it's probable that his friends are right to be concerned for him. Someone might have abducted him or maybe something worse. They would only find out when they examined all the information. 'When will Forensics look at the flat?'

'I'll get on to them,' Browne said.

'The urgency level has moved up. It's one thing for a man with problems to go missing. Guys like that are found working as porters in some out of the way hotel in the Scottish Highlands. But a single man without a worry in the world and a huge bank balance doesn't disappear himself.'

'Maybe he was hit on the head and he's wandering around with amnesia,' Graham said.

'It's a possibility,' Wilson said. 'Even if it is remote, it's worth checking out.'

'Siobhan has checked with the hospitals,' Browne said. 'There's no sign of him there under his own name. I'll get her to check for amnesia cases. There can't be many.'

'This man has been missing for a month,' Wilson said. 'We're way behind on this case so we have to get moving. I want to speak to Heavey.'

'I've already done that, boss,' Browne said. It worried him that Heavey might run off at the mouth and drag Vincent Carmody into the picture.

'Doesn't matter,' Wilson said. 'Write up your interviews. I need to get a feel for Whyte from the horse's mouth. I'll go to him. Where does he work?'

'He's a librarian at the McClay Library in Queen's University,' Browne said. 'But I don't think he has any further information.'

'I'll be the judge of that.' Wilson didn't know why his

sergeant was resistant. Maybe it was time he took over the investigation himself. There was a very good possibility that Whyte had come to harm. But with no corpse, they were at a disadvantage. Their only hope was to generate the maximum amount of information and to try to identify the last person who saw Whyte alive. 'Harry, you'll keep the murder book up to date.'

'You're sure he's been murdered, boss?' Graham said.

'We'll keep an open mind,' Wilson said. 'But I can see why his friends are worried.'

Browne had been writing in his notebook. 'There are a lot of issues we have to cover.'

'Call Heavey and tell him I'm on my way. We're playing catch-up here and that's not a position I like to find myself in.'

'We're on it, boss,' Browne said.

Wilson picked up his jacket and left.

Browne watched him go. He dialled the number of the McClay Library and said a silent prayer that Heavey wouldn't mention Carmody's disappearance.

CHAPTER TWENTY-SEVEN

Parking within Queen's University is restricted and the security guard who stopped Wilson at the entrance was not thrilled when he was shown a PSNI warrant card. Wilson told him his destination and the guard gave him a map and indicated an area where he might park. The McClay Library was at the rear of the campus beside the Botanic Gardens. Wilson parked his car where the guard had indicated and put his 'Police on Duty' plastic card where it was visible. He didn't want to find a wheel booted when he exited. The library building was an ultra-modern edifice of glass and red brick and out of character with the old university buildings he passed on the way to his destination. The lobby seemed to have been designed by an architect more accustomed to working on hotels. As soon as Wilson entered, a man approached with his right hand extended.

'Detective Superintendent Wilson.'

He didn't add 'I suppose' as some people might have. Wilson nodded and shook. 'Mr Heavey.'

'Dr Heavey. Would you prefer to speak in my office? I'm afraid it's a little cramped though. Perhaps the cafeteria would be more comfortable?'

Wilson looked around. There were a series of white tables and modern-looking orange armchairs in the reception area, none of which were occupied. 'What about here?'

'Perfect.' Heavey led the way to the table furthest from the entrance and sat.

Wilson thought that Heavey couldn't look more like a librarian if he had gone into a costumier and ordered a librarian costume. He wore a tweed herringbone jacket with leather patches on the elbows and brown corduroy trousers. He sported a red bow tie with his light blue shirt. When he crossed his legs, he displayed Pringle multicoloured socks sticking out of his English brogues.

'I'm so glad you followed up on Roger's disappearance.'

'It's our job to pursue an investigation where we believe someone has disappeared in unusual circumstances. What can you tell me about your friend? Try to think of something that you haven't already discussed with DS Browne.'

'Roger is smart, he got a double first at Oxford. He's well-read, articulate, generous, an excellent conversationalist and an all-round decent fellow.'

'Does he have a particular friend?'

'Roger doesn't have a partner, superintendent. He had a long-term partner in London who died. I've never known him to have a partner since he returned to Belfast.'

'Does he have any family?'

'Not that I'm aware of.'

'You said he is generous.'

'He's always the first to pay for meals, drinks and the like. We never talked about money, but I think he is rather well-to-do. I get the impression that he is clever with money.'

'Did people ever borrow from him?'

'Knowing Roger, I wouldn't be at all surprised. Some would say he has a cavalier approach to money.'

'What you're saying is that he throws it around?'

'Not exactly, but he is generous with his friends.'

'Would you be so good as to draw up a list of these friends?'

'I'd be happy to. Do you think his disappearance has something to do with money?'

'At the start of an investigation, we look into every possibility. I don't wish to pry, Dr Heavey, but did you have a sexual relationship with Mr Whyte?'

'A dalliance, once. We weren't suited. Roger's tastes are for younger men.'

'He is promiscuous?'

'It's such a judgemental word, I'm afraid I can't say.'

'Did he have many lovers?'

'He said so. But he never brought a lover home. As I told your sergeant, he is an obsessive-compulsive and wouldn't be able to support anyone messing up his flat.'

Wilson stood. 'Thanks for your time, Dr Heavey. You won't forget that list for me. You can drop it into the station or pop it in the post.' He took a business card from his pocket and placed it on the table.

'I hope you find Roger safe and well. He's a very dear friend.' Heavey fought back a theatrical tear.

'We'll do our best.' He didn't know whether it was natural intuition or the experience of almost twenty years on the job, but he doubted he would bring Roger Whyte safely home.

CHAPTER TWENTY-EIGHT

Wilson went to the whiteboard as soon as he arrived back at the station. He'd zeroed in on Whyte's apparent wealth as the motive for his disappearance. 'Anyone used Whyte's credit card since July 12th?' he asked O'Neill.

'No, boss. As far as anyone can tell there's been no sign of Whyte since July 12th.'

'You dig up any relatives yet?'

'His father died when he was young, I've asked for the death certificate. His mother raised him, and she's in a care home in Bangor. I think she might be the best source of information on other family members.'

'She must be the next of kin. So she'd inherit if anything happened to her son.'

'Unless he left a will.'

'Where are Rory and Harry?'

'They're out checking the timeline. Heavey and Whyte had lunch in Deanes on the eleventh. That looks like the last sighting of Whyte before he disappeared.'

That made Heavey a more important witness than Wilson had realised. He took out his phone and called Browne. 'Any news on the forensic inspection?'

'Tomorrow, at the soonest.'

'You didn't find a will during your search of the flat did you?'

'No, but I can pass the message on to Forensics to look for one.'

'Do that, and see if they can find any correspondence from a lawyer as well. We need to know who the beneficiaries are.'

'Okay, boss.'

Wilson put his phone away. He was on his way back to his office when the duty sergeant stuck his head around the door. 'Bloke downstairs, something-or-other Matthews, wants to come up to see you.'

'Send him up,' Wilson said. Senior Investigating Officer Matthews was turning out to be more trouble than the brains at HQ had expected. He continued into his office and was seated by the time Matthews knocked on the door.

Wilson motioned him in and pointed at the visitor's chair. 'Can I offer you a tea? It's from a machine, so the quality will be inferior to that available in the chief super's office.'

Matthews gave a wan smile. 'No thanks.'

'What can I do for you?'

Matthews took out a notebook and placed it on the desk. He flicked through a couple of pages. 'I've never seen an event so easy to understand. The would-be assassin is fled and vanished and all we're left with is your recollection, some bullet holes and some shell casings. There are no witnesses. How fortunate that the whole event took place outside the public's gaze.'

'Some people might look on that as a positive. None of us want innocent bystanders caught up in an exchange of gunfire.'

'Perhaps that was why the assassin attacked while you were in the warehouse.'

Wilson recognised a cynical remark when he heard one. 'Those kinds of people don't tend to be model citizens, but I'll remember to ask him why he chose the warehouse when we catch up with him.'

'If you catch up with him.'

'I suppose I have a more positive view of the PSNI's abilities.'

'This whole affair is hardly worth the expense of an investigation.'

'I understand it's obligatory in the case of an officer firing his weapon.'

'It is. But why do I think that I'm being snowed?'

'What gives you the impression you're being snowed?'

'I know there was a shoot-out in the warehouse and you've been upfront about using your weapon. I've checked with all the local hospitals and nobody has shown up with a bullet wound. And you are also unscathed. You are one lucky man.'

'That's what the doctor said when I woke up in hospital after being caught in the bomb blast. I wasn't so sure considering that half my right thigh was torn up and my rugby career was over. But both there and in the warehouse, I suppose I was lucky to survive. It beats the hell out of the alternative.'

'And so was your assailant.'

'We were both lucky.'

'The fact that it is all so clear-cut smells wrong to me. Why didn't he keep firing? An assault weapon trumps a Glock 17 any day of the week.'

'Maybe he wasn't expecting me to shoot back.' He told himself to keep the answers short and concise.

Matthews stood. 'People say that I worry too much about trifles. They say that I'm pedantic, but I think the job we do is important.'

'I tend to agree with you.' And them, Wilson thought.

'Would you agree to a polygraph?'

'I'd consider it an insult to be asked to take one.'

'There are a few more things I have to look into, so I might be back.'

'I'll still be here.'

Maybe there was more to the Royal Bahamas Police Force than Wilson had imagined. There were several good reasons why HQ had buried the real events at the warehouse, not the least of which would be the Garda DCI on the scene, and the dead body, and the need to explain why someone wanted Wilson dead. It wasn't in his nature to lie. But he was so far committed that it would be difficult to pull out. His reason for playing along was personal. If all the facts of the shoot-out came out, HQ would be obliged to put him on administrative leave, which would open the door for Reid to insist on a move to California. He wasn't dismissing the idea, but there was something he had to do before he would be ready to leave Belfast.

CHAPTER TWENTY-NINE

The team stood at the whiteboard, to which details had been added hourly. Browne gave a rundown of his and Graham's activities. They had spent the afternoon checking Whyte's movements on the eleventh of July. Whyte was a gentleman of leisure and spent a good deal of his time in the old-fashioned pursuits of reading, writing and dining with friends. All that was missing was the butler. It was apparent from his diary that Whyte didn't cook. He took breakfast every morning at Clements Café and a black-clad waitress confirmed that he had breakfasted there regularly until recently. She wasn't sure when she had seen him last but the twelfth was a good estimate. He was a creature of habit and his breakfast of choice was a pot of Earl Grey tea and a bagel with scrambled egg.

Browne and Graham had moved on to Deanes restaurant where, after a quick check with the reservations book, it was confirmed that Whyte had lunched with a guest there on the eleventh. None of the wait staff remembered what time he had left, but the credit card receipt for the bill showed that Whyte had settled it at 14:31. The guest's name written in the diary was Charles Heavey. They then went to Whyte's flat at

Elmwood Mews to take another look at the neighbourhood. It was a residential area where there were always people milling around. But would anyone remember a middle-aged man and tie it to a specific day, especially if it was the day before the biggest holiday in the province? It was something that might amuse the uniforms.

'We must do a proper canvas of the area,' Wilson said.

'Uniforms and a flyer,' Moira said.

Wilson nodded. 'Siobhan make up a flyer and we'll have one in every house. Use the missing person template, the black-and-white photo and specify the eleventh and twelfth of July.'

'What else do we have?' Wilson asked.

'The credit card payment at Deanes was the last use of the card,' O'Neill said. 'I've gone through most of the financials and it appears he's made two large payments to his friend Charles Heavey, ten thousand pounds each time.'

'Heavey told me Whyte was generous,' Wilson said. 'Now I know what he meant.' He turned and looked at Browne. 'What do we know about Heavey?'

'Not much,' Browne said. 'I've only met him casually. Can't say I like him.'

'As far as we know,' Wilson said. 'He's the last person who saw Whyte alive. Siobhan, run a check on him and see why he needed to borrow twenty thousand pounds. I still favour the money motive here. We also need to speak to Whyte's mother. I need to be out of Belfast tomorrow and I fancy a trip to Bangor so I will visit the nursing home. Did anyone check if Whyte had a mobile phone?'

Nobody answered.

'Then find out.' He looked at Browne. 'You didn't see one at the flat?'

'No, boss. When I was there with Heavey he didn't mention a mobile phone.'

'Any idea what the significance of that is?' Wilson asked.

'We should get on to technical and take a look at his calls and messages,' Moira said. 'Also we could ask them where the phone is now.'

'If it's still charged,' O'Neill said.

'Keep working on the timeline,' Wilson said. 'Whyte might have met someone after he left Deanes, either that or Heavey is in the frame.'

Browne didn't much like the sound of that.

'Keep at it,' Wilson continued. 'The investigator from the Police Ombudsman's Office might be around tomorrow looking for me. Tell him I'm busy.' He started towards his office.

Moira touched his arm. 'A word, boss.'

He motioned her to follow him.

'What's up?' he asked when they were inside the office.

'I'm doing nothing while waiting for something to happen on this Helen's Bay case. I've been running through what we have on Best and Hills, but neither has an obvious link to Helen's Bay. I suppose it's out of the question to go down to Best's club and ask them.'

'I don't think you'd get very far.' He sensed Moira's frustration. Working a case where there is little or no evidence is no pleasure. There has to be movement and Helen's Bay was at a full-stop for too long.

'I need action, boss.'

'I can't pull Rory off the Whyte case. He's the one that initiated it. And I haven't decided whether to involve you with Carlisle yet.'

'I've been through Peter's file. There's enough to bring Helen McCann in for an interview.'

'Her seat wouldn't be warmed when the highest priced lawyer in town would knock on the door demanding her release, and we'd be left with egg on our faces. When I bring her in, I'll have enough evidence to put her away.'

'And if you bring her in, boss, it'll look personal.'

'I know.'

'Peter did a hell of a job. A lot of the dots are already connected. It's a pity the Jackson guy has disappeared. Peter could have him for the assault and that might squeeze him on the Carlisle murder.'

'You haven't met Simon Jackson. When you do, you'll understand why that scenario will never happen.' Wilson's phone beeped. He looked at the message. It was from McDevitt: 'It's been confirmed. Meet at the usual place?' Wilson sighed.

'What's up?'

'Senior Investigating Officer Matthews is smelling a rat in the official version of what went down at the warehouse. He's one of those guys who will poke around in a dead fire to find the only ember still lighting and then fan it until the fire is raging again. I might appreciate his dedication if he were focused on someone else.'

'You have to make sure he doesn't find that ember.'

'You're a university graduate. Was it Shakespeare who coined the phrase "Oh, what a tangled web we weave when first we practice to deceive"?'

'No, it was Walter Scott.'

'Well he was right. Matthews is irritating me and that's not an easy thing to do. The text was from McDevitt. He claims that he has proof that I'm the officer involved in the shooting. That means there's a leak at HQ and the whole story is within an inch of coming out.'

'Then HQ will have to deal with it.'

Wilson was glad she was back. They worked well together and he liked her. He had ambivalent feelings about the failure of her relationship with Brendan. He was sad for her that things hadn't worked out in the US. She deserved something more than being a detective sergeant in the PSNI. But Moira was looking happy for the first time since she returned.

'I want to take over Peter's file.'

'This assassination shit is because of that investigation. You don't bring down people like Helen McCann without collateral damage. I don't want that to be your future.' He stood up. 'Get off home. McDevitt is waiting for me in the Crown. Maybe I can convince him not to publish the story, but with McDevitt there'll have to be a quid pro quo.'

CHAPTER THIRTY

Browne was standing outside the dump on Broadway that Vincent Carmody called home. The rundown building must be one step away from being condemned. He had visited Vinny's place several times while they had been together. Every time he recalled their brief fling bile came into his throat. They had met within weeks of his arrival in Belfast and a wiser head would have observed the scene before jumping in feet first. Their time together had been a salutary experience for him and it would not be repeated. He fingered the lock-picks in his pocket. He knew he was on a fool's errand. Unless Vinny returned, Heavey would continue to link the Whyte and Carmody disappearances and his relationship with Vincent Carmody would be exposed. He would be compromised and Wilson would take him off the case in a heartbeat. He approached the front door and bent to open the lock. The piece of crap opened almost immediately, and he pushed inside. The two-up-two-down house had been split into upper and lower flats with a staircase on the left-hand wall. Carmody occupied the ground floor. The door to the upper flat was hanging off its hinges. He used the picks to open the white panel door on the right of the stairs.

The living room looked like a bomb had hit it. Carmody could have used some of Whyte's OCD. Browne didn't like to think that he had been so obsessively in love with Vinny that he had ignored the filth the man lived in. He imagined the fun the forensic team would have lifting fingerprints. The place looked like it hadn't been cleaned in months so no doubt his prints would be found here too. It wasn't the fingerprints that bothered him though, it was someone viewing the text messages that had passed between Vinny and him. He could feel his face reddening as he moved through the litter towards the rear of the building. It was already bad enough being pointed out as the gay copper. What would his colleagues think when they read the lovelorn messages he'd sent?

The kitchen was a mess of dirty plates, burned pots and oil marks on the ceiling and walls. Trash was overflowing from a black bag in the corner. A stack of empty pizza boxes sat inside the back door. If the rats hadn't already taken up residence, they soon would. He opened the fridge and got the sour rancid smell of stale milk. Without touching the bottle, he bent and read the label. The milk was out of date by two weeks. The fridge was empty save for a single plastic bag on the middle shelf containing Carmody's stash of pot and a couple of pills. He remembered Carmody's body. There wasn't an ounce of excess fat on it.

He moved on to the bedroom and had a sudden memory of him and Vinny lying naked on a foul mattress. Tears came to his eyes. How could he have been so fucking stupid?

It was clear that Carmody hadn't been home for some time. How much time was anyone's guess. The whole scenario was a screw-up. A part of Browne knew he should tell the team about this second disappearance. Another part said, if Whyte appears tomorrow, you'll look like a fool, and if you add Carmody to the list and they both turn up, you'll be the village idiot. The smart strategy was to see where the Whyte investigation went before bringing Carmody into it. If the boss's theory was correct and Whyte's disappearance was money-related, there would be no link to Carmody, who didn't have a penny.

He made his way back through the living room and closed the door of the flat behind him. He opened the front door and found himself face to face with a young woman. She was small and frail with arms as thin as pipe cleaners. Her face was lived-in and her hair had streaks of green and red in it. She could be anything from fifteen to thirty.

'I saw you goin' in, so I did,' she said.

'My friend lives here.'

She looked him up and down, and her brow furrowed. 'You're a friend o' that wee rat Vinny?'

Browne nodded. There was a look of disbelief on her face.

'You smell like a peeler.'

'I'm just a friend.'

'Where the fuck is he then?'

'I thought you might know.'

'I gave the wee bastard twenty quid three weeks ago for to buy me some pot and I haven't seen the thievin' fucker since. My boyfriend is gonna kill him if he doesn't give me me money back.'

'Do you remember what day you gave him the money?'

'Do I look like I walk about with a fuckin' calendar in me pocket?'

Browne produced his wallet. 'If you remember, I might help you out.'

She stared at the leather wallet. 'It was the week after the twelfth. I remember it was a Friday so that would be what, the eighteenth?' Her eyes never wavered from the wallet.

He removed a twenty-pound note and handed it to her. 'I'll get it from Vinny when I see him.'

She snatched the note from his hand. 'Aye, good luck wi' that. You can't trust the sodomites, that's what me da always says.' She gave him a sly smile, pocketed the money and walked up the street.

Browne rushed off in the opposite direction. He'd been a fool to come here. Vinny was off God only knew where. And that young woman would remember that Browne had been to his flat.

CHAPTER THIRTY-ONE

'I've been here since four o'clock and I've only just got a snug,' McDevitt said. 'These bloody tourists are a plague.'

Wilson dropped on the seat. 'God be with the old days when the tourists wouldn't come to Belfast because they were afraid of being bombed or shot.'

'Don't be so bloody sarcastic. You know what I mean. I was reading an article the other day about how the Venetians are more than a little annoyed about the influx of tourists in the summer.'

'Then we should be thankful that the summer here only lasts a few weeks.'

'The tourists don't come here for the sun, unless they can't read weather reports. They come here for the craic and for characters like you and me.'

Wilson had signalled for a pint of Guinness on the way through the bar and it arrived. 'Still on the antibiotics?'

McDevitt nodded. 'Three more days. I can feel the throat getting better already.'

'But you must finish the course to get the full benefit.'

McDevitt scowled. 'I didn't think a week could last so long.'

A week was nothing, Wilson thought, thinking about his lessons in patience in the hospital and rehabilitation.

'Hard day?' McDevitt asked.

Wilson drained half his pint as an answer.

'No sign of the good lady?'

'Away to Coleraine to give a lecture.'

'She still pining for the shores of the Pacific?'

'Aye, like yourself.'

'My agent is asking about a follow-up book. Have you got anything for me?'

Wilson shook his head. 'Not at the moment.'

'I was thinking of a plot myself. It's about a police officer who someone is trying to kill. I haven't worked out who or why yet, maybe you could help with that?'

'I'm not a creative like yourself. I'm just a poor copper trying to do his job.' He finished the other half of his pint and called for a refill.

'I'll never forget that you saved my life and I'll never do you a bad turn, but word has slipped out from on high that you're the copper they tried to kill in East Belfast.' McDevitt held up his hand. 'Don't waste your breath denying it. I have it on the best authority. I won't write about it, but I'm concerned. I take deep objection to someone wanting to kill my best friend.' McDevitt's voice was shaking.

'Ah, Jock, I didn't know you cared.'

McDevitt took out a handkerchief and blew his nose. 'It's no fucking joke.'

Wilson wasn't joking. He was touched. He put his hand on Jock's shoulder.

'I might be able to help,' McDevitt said.

'I don't need help. It wasn't such a big deal. A guy cornered me in the warehouse where Sammy Rice was killed and fired a blast from an AK-47. I was lucky I had my weapon on me and I fired back. He ran and I stayed down. I heard a car leaving and I got up. That was it.'

'So he's still out there?'

'I presume so.'

'And you've still got your weapon handy?'

'They took it off me. It's standard practice when you fire your gun. The shooting is being investigated by the Police Ombudsman's Office, that's standard as well.'

'Do you know who's behind it?'

Wilson didn't answer.

'You have an idea.'

Wilson nodded.

'And you won't tell me.'

'No.' Wilson sipped his drink. 'Changing the subject, we're looking into the disappearance of a man called Roger Whyte, ever run across him?'

McDevitt thought for a moment before shaking his head. 'The name means nothing to me.'

'He lives in Elmwood Mews. We'll do a door-to-door in the area and put a flyer in every letter-box. But it wouldn't hurt to have a piece in the *Chronicle*.'

'Lots of people go missing. What's the wrinkle with this guy?'

'He has a very healthy bank balance and maybe more assets we haven't discovered yet.'

'Now that is interesting.'

'I don't know if his disappearance is linked to his wealth, but it's as good a place as any to start.'

'What do they say, there are three reasons to kill someone: sex, money or revenge. Have you ruled out the other two?'

'I'll move on to them when I've checked the money angle out. What about a piece in the paper? Whyte disappeared around the twelfth of July. We're looking for anyone who had contact with him around that date.'

'You know that Belfast goes crazy on the days leading up to the twelfth and for several days after. Half the Protestant population probably don't even know what planet they were on over that period.'

'We know the problem. Still, someone might remember meeting him.'

McDevitt stroked his chin. 'Things are quiet at the moment. I suppose I might be able to work up an angle.'

'Good man. I hear they have a great green tea here, I don't suppose you'd fancy a cup?'

CHAPTER THIRTY-TWO

What the hell had she been thinking of when she had returned to Belfast? Moira had studied psychology as part of her degree course so she understood the concept of 'buyer's remorse'. Summer would soon draw to a close. The days would get shorter and it would be dark when she got up in the morning and dark when she returned to her garret in the evening. In the meantime, she would spend her time praying for some drone-nerd to offer a piece of film showing what had happened at Helen's Bay the day someone used a brand-new BMW as a funeral pyre. Maybe she had been a little rash in turning down Frank Shea's offer. Life in the US was getting complicated and Belfast had represented an uncomplicated alternative, or at least it seemed that way. But uncomplicated also meant boring and Moira didn't do boring so well.

She had finished what passed for her dinner and was contemplating an evening in front of the box when her eyes fell on the file on the investigation into Jackie Carlisle's death. Putting Helen McCann in jail wouldn't be easy, but it would be fun, and dangerous, maybe even very dangerous. She pulled out her laptop and surfed. There were over two thousand pages with mentions of Helen McCann and almost as many with mentions of her daughter Kate. Moira didn't yet have a printer and made a mental note to get one. She went to the Wikipedia site and looked at Helen's profile. There were details of her early life, her scholastic achievements, her marriage to a famous older man, her resumé as a business-woman and a list of her board appointments. It was anodyne. The focus was on Helen McCann the public person and there was nothing about who Helen McCann actually was. She must have had some drive and energy to go from humble beginnings to being the top of her class at Queen's University.

If they were going to bring the investigation to a conclusion, they'd have to adopt a different approach. Peter Davidson had followed the trail of evidence regarding Carlisle's death. She would centre her research on Helen McCann. She would start by reading each of the two thousand online entries mentioning McCann. That should give her some insight into McCann's psychology. McCann couldn't be brought down by a frontal attack. Wilson was right about that. Bringing her in to help with inquiries, would only put her on high alert. The best way to bring her down would be to get inside the protective ring she's built around her. And that would mean getting to know her as well as she knew herself. Moira opened the website of a computer supply company and ordered a cheap laser printer and two boxes of copy paper. It was time to get to work.

He had connected his phone to the television and was playing the videos he'd made. His parents' living room filled the screen and the camera moved to the still figure of Roger Whyte lying on his mother's treasured Persian carpet. Whyte was catatonic, his eyes bulged and his face was in a rictus of fear. The older man was his first and he had made a mistake on the quantity of the drug he had used. He paused the picture and moved closer to the screen, reliving the excitement he had felt. Whyte looked scared to death. He restarted the video and his own face leaped onto the screen. He looked exultant. He had discovered his reason for living.

He felt no emotion for Whyte. It was always like that. He'd wondered why people had cried at the deaths of his grandparents. It was on occasions of either great sadness or great joy that he realised how different he was. He stared again at Whyte's startled face. The worms will have been feasting on that face. Whyte had promised him untold wealth if he would only let him live. But it wasn't about money. It was about satisfying his need. Once he had revealed himself, there was no way he could let Whyte go.

The video continued. He entered the picture frame again, pulled down Whyte's trousers and his Y-fronts, revealing his white, flabby posterior. Then he opened his own fly and displayed his erect penis. He climbed on Whyte and raped him. He could feel his penis growing now as he watched himself invading the older man. He smiled as he watched the performance. He could easily have had sex with Whyte. That had been Whyte's intention when they had had gone off together. But that hadn't been his intention. He watched until the recording finished and then stopped the picture at the point where he stood on the screen standing over Whyte's body.

There was a part of him that would like to show Dr Rose his home movies. He wondered what she would think of them. The recording would say so much more about him than an hour of listening to his ramblings. He was sure that she had already worked out he was homosexual, especially since he didn't hide it from her. He had attempted to come out at sixteen, but his parents' Christian faith wouldn't allow them to accept that their son was cursed and destined for hell. Then they made the gross mistake of sending him to a gay conversion facility in the US to be 'cured'. The stupid fools thought he had some kind of disease. They believed that hours of indoctrination accompanied by a bit of scourging and some ice-cold water baths would give them back their blue-eyed boy. The effect had been the opposite. His counsellor had been 'cured' but still managed to rape him. The experience allowed him to channel the anger and hate he felt, not for himself but for others with the same sexual orientation. It was the first step on the path to the man he has become. He realised that the sooner he was 'cured', the sooner he would be released from the grip of the pseudo-psychologists and their crazy theories.

Back in Belfast, he often saw his mother staring at him. He responded with a smile, but he knew she didn't totally believe in his conversion. His parents didn't realise that what made them uneasy about him had nothing to do with his sexual orientation and everything to do with the anger and hate he felt for everyone around him. He sat staring at the final still image of his first foray into murder and a thrill ran through him.

CHAPTER THIRTY-THREE

Wilson pounded the concrete on the Laganside path that was the habitual route for his morning run. He had remained a little too long in McDevitt's company the previous evening and had eaten only a snack before going to bed. Reid hadn't shown up by the time he'd got home and he assumed that the after-lecture festivities were the reason for her delay. This morning's run had the dual purpose of clearing his head and allowing him to reflect on the happenings of the past few days. His willingness to play his part in the story the brains at HQ had cobbled together meant he was still potentially in danger. They also hadn't bargained on the dogged Senior Investigating Officer Matthews. Within the force, an admonishment by the Police Ombudsman's Office was unpleasant, but it wasn't the end of the world. Serving officers were more worried when an investigation into their activities was being undertaken by Professional Services. He was learning the hard way that the Ombudsman's Office was not to be dismissed lightly and that he had been naive in thinking that the officers of the Royal Bahamas Police Force might not be as serious as those of the PSNI. Matthews was teaching him a lesson about underestimating the opposition that he should have learned years ago on the rugby field. He was also loath to admit that the attempt on his life had shaken him. It is a truism that police officers do a dangerous job. Putting one's life at risk is very easy in theory but quite a different story when facing a hail of bullets from an AK-47. He had been offered counselling and had turned it down. Perhaps he'd been a little hasty. He decided to try to put the issue from his mind.

Wilson's proposed incursion into an investigation that up to now had been led by Sergeant Browne, had nothing to do with competence and a lot to do with his desire to have a morning free of Matthews. He had no idea why Whyte had disappeared, but he believed that he had come to no good. He was also sure that the motive for the disappearance was money. How the disappearance and the money were connected would be the major line of inquiry. He passed the Titanic Centre on his left and continued running. He was on autopilot as far as the run was concerned and his mind was clearing.

It was also time to decide on the future of the Carlisle investigation. He knew Moira was eager to take it over, and she would be the perfect choice to further the investigation. However, the attempt on his life had shown how dangerous it is to poke a bear and he knew he wouldn't be able to live with himself if a decision of his led to her death. He turned and headed for home. The murder cases of Grant and Malone were still open, Sammy Rice's death was also a mystery and Jackie Carlisle had also been murdered. A lightbulb went off in his head. What if all these deaths are connected? He'd tell Moira that he was giving her the Carlisle investigation when he arrived back from Bangor.

He found the Sunny Days Care Home quite easily. It was located on a rise just off Seacliff Road, in a prime position with a view over Belfast Lough. He parked in front of the large two-storey red-bricked building, guessing that in former times it might have been a small hotel catering to the summer holiday crowd from Belfast. That would have been in the days when the price of a two-week holiday in Spain was beyond the pocket of most working-class families. Times had changed and so had the demographic. Seaside towns like Bangor now mostly catered for geriatrics. A businessperson would justify the change of use by citing the laws of supply and demand.

The reception area had maintained an old-world atmosphere reminiscent of a 1950s hotel, which probably suited most of the residents. A middle-aged woman stood behind a polished oak mid-level desk.

'Good morning,' Wilson said. He looked for a name-tag on the woman's ample chest; there was none. Sunny Days had bought into the full 1950s vibe.

The woman looked him up and down before responding. 'Good morning, how can I help you? If you're looking for a place for an aged relative, I'm afraid we have no vacancies.'

Wilson took out his warrant card. 'Detective Superintendent Ian Wilson, I called yesterday. I want to have a word with a resident, Mrs Norma Whyte.'

'And the director approved?'

'Apparently.'

The receptionist called over a young woman dressed in a white orderly jacket. 'Miriam take this police officer to see Mrs Whyte.'

Miriam smiled at Wilson. 'Follow me, please.'

Wilson fell into step and they walked to a door at the left of reception. Miriam punched in a code on a keypad and a buzzing noise indicated the door was ready for opening. Wilson pushed it and held it back to permit her to enter. They walked along a corridor with doors on either side, most of them ajar.

'We have a few wanderers so the door to reception is always locked,' Miriam said.

As if to prove a point, an old lady approached them. She stood in front of Wilson. 'Have you come to take me home?'

Wilson was about to answer in the negative when Miriam interrupted. 'Yes, Mrs Cassidy, this is the driver of the car your son sent. But he has to have a cup of tea first. When he's finished, we'll come and find you.'

'Thank you.' The old lady continued along the corridor.

'Alzheimer's,' Miriam said. 'You see what I mean about the front door. Mrs Whyte is on the ground floor. She's not one of our wanderers.' They continued along to the end of the corridor and she knocked on the final door on the left.

'Come in,' the voice was faint but distinct.

Miriam opened the door. 'A visitor for you, Norma.' She held the door open to permit Wilson to enter.

Norma Whyte sat in a wheelchair staring through a large window. She turned the wheelchair around when Wilson entered. The room was large and more like a suite, with a sitting area and a coffee table as well as a bedroom.

This is the way it ends, he thought. The frail woman was dressed in a woollen cardigan and plaid skirt. Her hair was totally white and well-coiffed, but the face beneath was thin and pallid. The dark circles under her eyes indicated that all was not well with Norma Whyte. He took out his warrant card and introduced himself.

'Take a seat, superintendent.' Her tone was soft and sibilant. 'I've been expecting someone from the constabulary to visit me. Has something happened to Roger?'

Wilson hadn't expected the direct approach. 'I'm afraid your son hasn't been seen since the twelfth of July and his disappearance is now the subject of a PSNI inquiry. Why were you expecting someone from the police?'

'Because my son visits me every Sunday at precisely midday. Not at five minutes to twelve, nor five minutes past twelve. He lives by a regular schedule. When he didn't visit a few weeks ago, I knew something was wrong.'

'So, you have no idea where your son is?'

'No idea in the wide world.'

'You don't appear unduly worried.'

'How old are you, superintendent?'

'Forty-one.'

'I'm seventy-eight and I'm sitting in this wheelchair because of a stroke five years ago that left me paralysed on the left side. If Roger is missing, I can do nothing about it. That's your job.'

'I hope you don't mind if I get personal.'

'I expect it.'

'This must be one of the best rooms here. Who pays for it?'

'My son pays for it.'

'And if we can't locate him?'

'Roger has always been rather clever, even as a child. He told me that he has made provision to have my stay here paid until I leave.'

'It must cost a lot.'

'Roger is not short of money.'

Wilson was thinking of the four hundred and twenty thousand in Whyte's bank account. A long-term stay in Sunny Days would put quite a dent in that sum. 'We've seen his bank account, he has something over four hundred thousand pounds in it.'

'He has considerably more than that. He collected over two million pounds when he sold his shares in that bank. He's also a shareholder in Sunny Days.'

'Did he ever tell you he was in danger?'

'No. On his visits we discussed books, TV, plays and films he'd seen lately, that kind of thing.'

'He's an only child?'

'My husband died two years after he was born. I never remarried.'

'Have you nephews and nieces?'

'I'm the youngest of three, my brother and sister are dead.

They had no children. My husband was born in Canada. We've totally lost touch with that side of the family.'

That would be a job for O'Neill. 'Is there anything you think might be relevant to our investigation?'

'I'm sure you know that Roger is gay. He never hid the fact. He came out at a very early age.'

Wilson nodded. 'Do you know if your son has made a will?'

'I have no idea. If he has, I wouldn't expect to inherit. Roger is informed on my life expectancy.'

'Thank you, Mrs Whyte, you've been most helpful.'

'You'll come back, won't you?'

'Yes, of course.' He stood. Her hand felt like tissue paper when he took it. There was no shake just a touch.

On the way back to the reception he passed Mrs Cassidy, who was asking another visitor whether he was there to take her home. There was no Miriam to intervene and when the man said 'No', the old woman cried.

CHAPTER THIRTY-FOUR

There were four Post-its on Wilson's computer screen when he returned to the office. Each had the same message, 'Matthews called', and a time. He tore the notes from the screen, bundled them up and tossed them in his wastebasket. The man from the Police Ombudsman's Office would have to wait. He called O'Neill to his office and told her about Whyte's Canadian connection and the lack of heirs on the maternal side of his family.

'It appears possible that Roger Whyte had other banks accounts and other investments,' Wilson continued. 'The four hundred and twenty thousand pounds might just be the tip of the iceberg. We need to find a figure for his exact wealth. His mother said he received over two million pounds for his share in the bank's takeover. We need to find out where it is. He's also a shareholder in Sunny Days, so follow that up.'

'I'll do my best. It would be quicker if we could find his accountant or have a look at his latest tax declaration.'

'Get working. If money is the motive, we need every piece of information we can dig up. Where are Rory and Harry?'

She shrugged her shoulders.

'Okay, concentrate on the financial information.'

The news on the inheritors was good and bad. Good in that there was no one on the maternal side and bad because there could be many inheritors on the paternal side, all hidden in the Canadian woods. He was becoming more and more convinced that Whyte's jackpot was the reason for his disappearance. He turned on his computer and brought up his emails. There were two from Matthews complaining that his phone messages were being ignored. Wilson deleted them and was about to get down to work when his mobile phone rang. There was no caller ID and he sighed as he pressed the green button.

'Colm Matthews here.'

'Good afternoon, Colm.'

'I've been trying to get in touch with you all morning.'

'I've been out on an investigation, meeting a witness in Bangor. I've only just returned to the office and I was in conference with one of my team until now.'

'If I hadn't read your excellent record as a police officer, I might think you were trying to avoid me.'

'I wish I had the time to just avoid someone. I'm available whenever you want me.'

'Excellent. I'm downstairs, so I'll be straight up.'

Wilson opened his drawer and threw his mobile into it before slamming it shut. He looked up to see Matthews standing at his door.

'I know you're busy,' Matthews said as he entered. 'I'll try to be as quick as possible.'

Wilson pointed at his visitor's chair. 'Take the weight off your legs.'

Matthews smiled and sat. 'It's been a while since I heard that phrase.'

'Let's get to it.'

Matthews' smile faded. 'I went out to the Ballymacarrett Road and talked to the local residents. There's a lot of confusion about the sequence of events.'

Wilson didn't respond.

'The police presence was noted by most of the people living in the warehouse's vicinity. They saw some police activity, including an ambulance, and then after a lull there was a second phase of police activity. That scenario doesn't seem to gel with the official PSNI account. Why two phases of activity?'

'How many witness statements have you taken in your career?'

'Hundreds.'

'Then I don't have to tell you that memory doesn't work like a videotape or a computer, it's constructed, so memories can change over time, particularly when we're questioned about them. How many times have you taken statements from two witnesses to the same event?'

'I know what you're getting at. I think every detective in the world has seen *Rashomon*. I asked PSNI HQ about the body cams, but apparently, the responders weren't wearing them. That alone is unusual.'

'Why don't you tell me what's on your mind?'

'I'm certain there was a shooting event at the warehouse. I doubt it went down in the manner you and your colleagues in the PSNI say it did.'

'You've examined the scene and spoken to the residents, the first responding officers and me. How do you think it went down?'

'I've also spoken to the ambulance crew. And even though all the accounts tally, I think there's something wrong. Maybe you could call it "the reverse *Rashomon* effect". The accounts differ ever so slightly, but they all confirm each other.'

'And that's a sin?'

Matthews stopped and left a pregnant pause. It was a tactic that all police officers knew of and which Wilson regularly used. Normally, he would wait his questioner out.

Matthews was aggravating him and he assumed that it was intentional.

'You haven't answered my question,' Wilson said. 'How do you think it went down?'

'I think that maybe you shot your attacker and killed him.'

'And what did I do with the body?'

'An ambulance took it away and it has been disposed of somehow.'

'Let's assume that somebody in the criminal fraternity attempted to assassinate me and I killed my attacker. What reason on God's earth would the PSNI, or I, have to suppress that fact?'

'That's a question that's been troubling me. I've checked with the hospitals and they have no record of a gunshot victim in the days after the event.'

Wilson saw that Matthews' brow was furrowed with frown lines. 'It's our job to be a doubting Thomas. But sometimes the simplest explanation is the truth. You're not looking at Dirty Harry here. I'm not some gun-happy idiot. Someone tried to shoot me and I shot back.'

Matthews stood. 'I've taken up enough of your time. I'll be discussing the case with the chief investigating officer.'

And I haven't seen the last of you, Wilson thought.

'I suppose you've pondered why some "dissident republican" might want to kill you.'

'I've made a lot of enemies in my time on the force. I've put many people in jail and I'm sure some of them hold a grudge. And no, I am not happy that someone tried to kill me. And it bothers the hell out of me that they might try again. This time no one got hurt. The next time we might not be so lucky.'

Matthews hesitated before offering Wilson his hand. 'We'll be in touch.'

CHAPTER THIRTY-FIVE

The Helen's Bay case was not advancing, so Moira spent the morning researching Helen McCann. It was a formidable task that involved downloading hundreds of pages from the Internet. McCann had been a personality in Ulster for over thirty years. Moira remembered a famous graphic from *Rolling Stone* magazine showing the world in the grasp of the Goldman Sachs vampire squid; she saw a parallel to Helen McCann and Ulster – the woman's tentacles seemed to stretch everywhere. The mass of paper on her desk was about a quarter of the information publicly available on McCann. Even when she had accumulated all of it, she knew it would only be the information that McCann wanted to show the world. The part that wasn't in the public domain would contain all the juicy stuff. And that was where she would find the reason for Jackie Carlisle's death and the assassination attempt on Wilson.

Before she had worked in the Murder Squad and got to know Helen's daughter Kate, Moira had had no idea that a creature like Helen McCann existed. Like many of her fellow citizens, she would have described Northern Ireland as a patriarchal society. It was all about Edward Carson and a succession of male voices. Not many women had infiltrated that world. So she was intrigued to discover that a woman was actually at the centre of the province's business and political life.

Moira ploughed through the paper mountain in anticipation of the day she would get to dig into the unseen treasure that had to exist. She picked up the latest mention of the McCann family in *Hello* magazine. Kate McCann QC and her investment banker fiancé Daniel Lattimer had announced their nuptials, which would take place on the Lattimer estate outside Ballymoney. She contemplated showing the announcement to Wilson, but he had enough on his plate. He'd learn about it sooner or later, and she doubted it would have much impact on him. Kate McCann had been consigned to history. She wondered what was happening with her own ex. She hadn't heard a word from Brendan since leaving Boston and she didn't expect to hear from him until she found an invitation to his wedding in her letter-box. That was the way of the world and she had no regrets.

Wilson entered the squad room and went straight to his office. She was just going to approach him about taking over the Carlisle investigation when the investigator from the Police Ombudsman's Office arrived and went straight to Wilson's door. She settled down to read more about the life and times of Helen McCann.

Browne and Graham had used up a good proportion of shoe leather traipsing around Belfast visiting Whyte's haunts and inquiring into his movements on July 11th and 12th. However, they had little to show for it. Everyone knew Whyte but the dates were a blur to those people who had been celebrating Protestant Ulster's sacred day. If Whyte could have chosen a day to disappear, he couldn't have chosen a better one. A secondary problem was that, aside from the lunch engagement with Heavey, there were no other agenda items for those two days. Given that Whyte was a creature of habit, the two police officers used the entries of the previous week as a guide, but the reality was Whyte could have been anywhere or nowhere. He might well have spent the day at his flat and disappeared from there.

O'Neill had mocked up a poster and the local uniforms had distributed two hundred copies around the University area. Graham would have the dubious pleasure of sifting through the responses. It was approaching one o'clock and they ended their quest with a pub lunch. Graham was about to recommend a local hostelry in the Shankill area when he saw that his superior had other ideas.

'We'll try Kelly's Cellars,' Browne said.

'Suits me,' Graham said without enthusiasm. His wife had made him a sandwich for lunch and it was sitting in the top drawer of his desk. His financial situation didn't extend to buying lunch. The kids needed new shoes more than he needed to eat out.

'I picked the venue, so lunch is on me.'

Graham noticed that it was a beautiful day and the sun was shining on Belfast.

'Ever work on a disappearance before?' Browne asked when they were seated in the corner examining their menus.

'One or two.' Graham was busy selecting his lunch.

'What happened?'

'What usually happens when people drop off the radar. They wander home when their money runs out or they get bored. Of course, some of them are never heard of again or turn up dead. Your friend Whyte could be in that last category.'

'He's not my friend. I didn't even know the guy. And he hasn't turned up dead yet.'

'I think he will.'

The waitress appeared and they both chose the beef boxty.

Graham added a pint of Guinness while Browne stuck with water.

'What makes you so sure he's dead?' Browne asked.

'If he wasn't dead, the boss wouldn't have taken the case. He has a nose for death. There are two people we need to talk to: his doctor and his accountant. If the doctor gives him a clean bill of health, it's unlikely that he's developed amnesia and wandered off or thrown himself off a tall building.'

'And the accountant?'

The drinks arrived and Graham took a large slug from his glass. 'If we're wrong and he lost four hundred and twenty thousand, we have to look at the bottom of tall buildings or in the Lagan.'

'I didn't know you were a comedian.'

The food arrived and cut their conversation short. The lack of progress disappointed Browne. He had hoped that someone would remember seeing Whyte on the evening of the eleventh. There was a possibility that a connection would be found between the disappearances of Whyte and Carmody, and he was apprehensive about what would happen when the boss discovered that he was holding back information. If the girl outside Carmody's flat was reliable, the two men had disappeared at different times. But that didn't mean that the cases weren't connected. He wished to God that Carmody would turn up, dead or alive. His thoughts were interrupted by his ringing mobile phone.

Wilson spoke as soon as Browne answered. 'The forensic boys have finished at Whyte's flat. The team leader, Finlay, will meet us there at two o'clock.' The background noise of clinking glasses and raucous laughter indicated that Browne and Graham were enjoying a pub lunch. He envied them.

'See you there, boss,' Browne said, ending the call.

CHAPTER THIRTY-SIX

Wilson was standing at the door of the flat in Elmwood Mews when Browne, Graham and Finlay arrived together. Finlay produced a key that opened the door. The three detectives looked at each other and laughed.

'It was in a small fissure in the brickwork,' Finlay said. 'It was cleverly hidden and impossible to see with the naked eye.' He led the way up the stairs and into the living room.

Wilson looked around. One wall was floor-to-ceiling bookshelves, loaded with volumes. The furniture was antique, expensive and comfortable. The carpets were Persian and there was a hint of cigar smoke in the air. The picture he had been building up in his mind of Roger Whyte as an erudite, cultured man was accurate.

'At least six different sets of fingerprints. One of them belongs to Sergeant Browne and one is female,' Finlay said.

Wilson looked at Browne.

'Sorry, boss.'

'So, five unidentified sets of prints,' Finlay continued.

'Heavey?' Wilson asked.

'I'll get him into the station for elimination,' Browne said. 'And there may well be a cleaning lady.'

'If he left, he didn't leave in a hurry,' Finlay said. 'The dishes have been put away. He doesn't appear to have packed any clothes. There are no signs of a struggle or of the furniture being rearranged.' He moved to the desk. 'The filing cabinet contained all his private papers, which we've bagged.' He nodded at a large plastic bag. 'We've dusted the papers for prints. Only one set matches with those we found in the room and we're assuming they belong to Whyte. Not a speck of blood in the flat. The medicine cabinet has a cornucopia of drugs, most of which are on prescription except for some small blue pills I understand assist with erections. He apparently has problems with his bowel movements. There are medicines to help him go and others to help him stop going.' He looked at Wilson. 'I think we can safely say that if something bad happened to Mr Whyte, it didn't happen here.'

Wilson walked around the room. He didn't bother to don the latex gloves. There was a crystal whiskey decanter on a side table. He removed the stopper and smelled the contents. It was top-drawer. He opened a polished oak humidor and took out a cigar, the label read *Romeo y Julieta*. Another premium brand.

He moved to the rear of the flat. The bedroom furniture was expensive, the sheets crisp white Egyptian cotton. They would have to get their finger out on this one. Roger Whyte was dead. Since the body hadn't turned up, it must be concealed somewhere, which made life difficult but not impossible. They wouldn't know the cause of death, or the time of death other than the last day he was seen. There was probably forensic evidence on the body that would point to the killer, but unless they found the body that evidence didn't exist. He returned to the living room and nodded at the plastic bag Finlay had indicated. 'Harry, get that bag back to the station.' He shook hands with Finlay. 'Good job.'

'Sorry we couldn't be more help,' Finlay said.

'You can't manufacture evidence,' Wilson said.

They all smiled. If they had done, it wouldn't be the first time.

'Take the key, Sergeant Browne,' Wilson said as he headed out the door. 'And I want to see you and Graham as soon as we get back to the station.'

CHAPTER THIRTY-SEVEN

The team assembled at the whiteboard. Wilson began by outlining the results of the forensic examination of the flat, or rather the lack of results. O'Neill had already emptied the contents of the plastic bag and stacked them on her desk. 'We have to assume that Roger Whyte is dead and that we are conducting a murder inquiry. At first I wasn't sure that he was deceased, but now I'm convinced. I'll be speaking to the chief super this evening so she can inform HQ and we'll get the machine wound up to assist us. We're starting late in this game, and it hurts that we have no corpse and no forensic evidence to go on. We are going to have to rely on old-fashioned police work. We've already delved into Whyte's life. This morning I interviewed his mother. It appears he is, or rather was, a very wealthy man. We're all aware that money is probably the most powerful motive for murder. According to his mother, the Whytes are not a large family in Northern Ireland. So there may not be many beneficiaries here. We need to locate a will if it exists.' He looked at the stacked documents on O'Neill's table. 'Okay, Siobhan, you've scanned the material, run us through it,' he said.

'There are documents for several banks, letters from his

stockbroker and correspondence with his legal adviser. We're well set up to formulate a clear picture of his wealth. There's no sign of a will in the papers, but it's possible he has one lodged with his lawyer. I should have a better picture by tomorrow.'

'The last sighting of him was leaving Deanes after his lunch with Heavey,' Wilson said. 'We need to look at the CCTV for central Belfast on July 11th and 12th. If he wasn't killed at his flat, and it seems certain he wasn't, we need to follow his movements. I don't just mean CCTV from PSNI cameras. I want every piece of footage that shows Whyte on those dates. That's down to Rory and Harry.'

There was a collective sigh from the team. Nobody liked to spend hours looking through grainy images.

'I know, I know,' Wilson said. 'But we have to work with what we've got until we get something better.'

'What if it's not about the money?' Browne asked.

'It's the most obvious motive,' Moira said.

Wilson stared at Browne. 'What are you thinking?'

'Nothing, other than that we're putting all our eggs in one basket.'

'It's a working hypothesis until we get something better,' Wilson said. 'There's no evidence that Whyte had any enemies. He appears to have led a quiet life. It's a puzzle.'

'What about Whyte's phone records?' Moira said.

'I'm on it,' O'Neill said. 'Along with half a million other things.'

'Lines of inquiry, people,' Wilson said. 'We need as many lines of inquiry as we can think of. Get to it.'

The team was dispersing when O'Neill touched Wilson's arm. He turned and she thrust a book into his hand. 'It's his photo album. I already looked at it and I think you should too.'

Wilson took it to his office. He put the book on the desk and opened the cover. There was a title page and written in meticulous calligraphy was the legend 'Roger and Niran,

London 1995–2005'. He opened the first page to a full-sized professionally produced photo of Whyte with his arm around the shoulders of a slight Asian man. He continued flipping the pages and examining the contents. Every photo showed a happy couple or individual. The smiles were always in place. That was the motif until halfway through the book when the smiles faded and the slight Asian man looked even slighter and the skin hung on his narrow face. The remainder of the album depicted the wastage that AIDS can wreak on the human body. The final photo was of a grave. Wilson closed the album and sat back. He wondered whether the person who had taken Whyte's life had looked at the photo album. Anyone who had would have recognised the pain he had already suffered. But in the killer's case, it probably wouldn't have made any difference.

CHAPTER THIRTY-EIGHT

His feet felt like two lead weights as he climbed the stairs to Davis's office. He wasn't sure whether she had been busy all afternoon or whether she preferred to deal with him at the end of her day. He knocked on her door and walked in. She was sitting at her desk poring over a large report. It was Wilson's vision of hell.

'I hope you don't feel as glum as you look.' She marked her page and put the report aside.

'I'm feeling my age.' Wilson fell into the visitor's chair.

'Get away with you.' She opened her desk drawer, removed two glasses and a whiskey bottle, and poured two large shots.

'Looks like you had a hard day.' Wilson took the glass that she had slid across the desk.

They touched glasses and drank.

'Now the world feels better,' she said.

'They don't manufacture enough of this stuff to make the world feel better. If you want to feel better about the world, get out of policing.'

'Too late. I assume the investigation by Senior Investigating Officer Matthews isn't going according to plan.'

'He's like an aggravating fly that keeps coming back the more you bat it away.'

'Does he remind you of anyone in particular?'

He smiled for the first time that afternoon. 'I suppose if he wasn't investigating me, I'd appreciate him.'

'Somehow or other I don't see you two becoming friends.'

'I don't like lying.'

'This is about making sure that it never comes out that a Garda officer was in the warehouse with you and that the assassin was a hitman with a Dublin drug connection. It's white-lying.'

'Matthews is discussing the case with the chief investigating officer.' He sipped his drink. 'Any word from Jack?'

'He's gone dark.' She laughed. 'I'm joking. He has a visitor from Quantico and he's showing him the west of Ireland.'

'Can I have his life? He gets to swan around with some Yank and I have Matthews climbing all over me. Anyway, that's not why I came to see you.'

'And there was I hoping it was just a friendly visit.'

Wilson recited the story of how he had become enmeshed in the disappearance of Roger Whyte.

'Who approved the use of the forensic team?'

'I think it was you.'

She opened a file on her desk. 'This is the latest budget plan for the station.' She put the report under his nose. 'Show me where there's a budget for forensic examinations.'

'The guy is dead. As soon as you inform HQ we're leading a murder investigation, there'll be a budget for forensic.'

'When will you learn that it's a new world, the bean counters have taken over. They're trumpeting in London that austerity is over, but that's just talk for the press.' She closed the file and put it away. 'How do you know that Whyte is dead? If he arrives home tomorrow, HQ will demand an explanation for the expenditure on the forensic examination of his flat.'

'He won't arrive home tomorrow.' He offered his glass for a refill. 'Make it a small one. I was sceptical myself, and I suppose I mainly took an interest to distract myself from Matthews, but now I'm a true believer. I don't know where he is, and I don't know who killed him, but he's dead and someone murdered him. I intend to find out the how and the who.'

She poured them both a small measure. 'I have to work late tonight.'

'No overtime?'

'I worked sixty hours last week and no overtime payment. It's our duty.'

'McDevitt will have a small piece on Whyte's disappearance in the *Chronicle* tomorrow so we need to crank up the PSNI machine. I have the team looking at the CCTV footage, but the uniforms will have to do the house-to-house and we need to do a press briefing. We have to put this out to the public.'

'I'll pass the word along. I don't want you in the DCC's office for the foreseeable future. He's already hauled me over the coals for the warehouse caper. I'm sure he'd love to shop you, but leaking what happened in Ballymacarrett could end his career.'

Wilson emptied his glass and stood. 'Whyte was a decent man who by and large kept himself to himself. I want to get the bastard who took his life.'

CHAPTER THIRTY-NINE

Reid tossed her surgical gown into the wicker basket in the corner of the autopsy room. It had been a long day. Sometimes she tired of her daily life of blood-spattered corpses, formalin-soaked dissections, anguished relatives and scornful barristers. As she plopped into her chair to write up her notes, she wondered how many dead bodies she had cut up. She remembered the Congo, dozens of bloodied and bruised bodies, heaps of cadavers. She hadn't been sleeping well. It had something to do with the threat to Ian's life, but it was also about her life. She'd spoken to older colleagues at conferences. They were all living on the edge of PTSD occasioned by years of confronting violence and the grave, and the steady emotional damage from dissecting thousands of bodies. The medical profession inevitably involves blood and gore, but she could have avoided much of that by joining a general medical practice. Except that one day she picked up a copy of *Simpson's Forensic Medicine* and her life changed forever. She found herself fascinated by the gallery of stranglings, knifings, shootings and electrocutions that the book contained. That small act of picking up a book had influenced the direction of her life. Her chosen profession made her a dispassionate observer of other people's deaths. Each post-mortem was like another piece being chipped off the rock of her life. Having been so dispassionate about other deaths, she had been completely unprepared for the grief she felt at her mother's death. She'd hardly known the woman and had hated her for most of her life, but a part of her disappeared along with her mother.

She finished her notes and went across to the mirror. There were dark circles under her eyes that hadn't been there when she returned from California. She knew it would be difficult to get Ian to leave Belfast. She would have to edge him towards the door marked 'Exit'. But it would have to happen, for both their sakes

WILSON LOOKED up from the bench in the snug as the door opened and Reid entered. Her smile hit him like a bolt of sunshine and warmed his body. She looked beautiful but tired. He didn't know how she could do her job. He could only imagine the amount of scrubbing she had to do just to remove the smell of death.

'Double gin and tonic,' she said bending to kiss him.

'Tough day?' He ordered the drinks.

'Ever hear of Bora Bora?' She sat beside him.

'Somewhere in the Pacific.'

'Can we go there?'

'We've just had a holiday.'

'I'm not talking about a holiday.'

He saw through her smile that there was a tinge of seriousness. He knew the various stages of grief and assumed that Reid was going through them. She appeared to be in stage four: depression. They would have to work their way out. The drinks arrived and he handed hers across. 'What do you say about dinner in Holohan's followed up with some jazz at Bert's?'

She looked at him. 'Sometimes I love you to pieces.'

He leaned forward and kissed her. 'A good blast will do the both of us good.'

'How's your case?'

'I'm certain Roger Whyte is dead. There's no corpse so we won't have the benefit of your skill with the scalpel. We have no forensic and aside from the fact that Whyte was a wealthy man we have no motive. The guy's life is without a blemish. I don't think he even had a parking violation.'

'Maybe he died of natural causes. He might be in a ditch somewhere. Or maybe he was drunk and fell off a bridge into the Lagan.' She saw the scepticism in his face. 'It has happened. But you're like a gun dog, someone disappears and right away it's murder.'

'I hope Whyte turns up. He has an eighty-odd-year-old mother in a home in Bangor who's worried sick about him. I promised that I'd go back to see her when the investigation is over. I'd like to be standing beside her son when I do it.'

'Finish up that drink and let's go dancing. We're becoming too sedate.' She smiled. They had a history of clubbing and there was still a lot of the rugby player in Ian. Thankfully her schedule for tomorrow was light.

Browne woke up with a start. In his dream, a bruised and bloodied Vincent Carmody was reaching out to him, and he was trying to run away. He switched on the light beside his bed and looked at his watch. It was three-fifteen and he had never felt so awake. He slipped from the bed and put on his dressing gown. He had moved to a two-bed apartment on Malone Avenue. The second bedroom should accommodate his parents, but they never visited and they probably never would. He padded into the open-plan living room and made a cup of camomile tea. He contemplated watching some late-night TV but instead sat staring out the window at the deserted street below. It was dark outside and he felt the blackness surrounding him. He turned on all the lights in the room, but it didn't dispel the gloom.

His Presbyterian parents would stand up in chapel on Sunday and beat their breasts about being their brother's keeper. Well, I am not my brother's keeper, he thought. I have no responsibility for Vincent Carmody. In fact, he couldn't count the number of times he had wished Vinny out of his life. Despite that, he knew that he could never sleep well again until he did right by him. However, the minute he told the boss about his connection to Carmody, he would be off the case. Keeping that connection secret was a fanciful delusion. Forensics would dust Carmody's hovel and his prints would turn up all over the place. Someone would find the young woman he had given the twenty pounds to and she would describe him. O'Neill would find Carmody's phone number and read his texts including the ones they had exchanged. He put his head in his hands. They would drag him into the investigation. At twenty-nine years old, he was alone, friendless and in a job he sometimes felt unsuited for. He needed to make changes. But first, he would have to work up the courage to mention Carmody to Wilson. Or maybe there was another way out.

CHAPTER FORTY

Moira wasn't easy to impress, but she was more than impressed with DC Siobhan O'Neill. She didn't know what time her colleague had arrived that morning, but considering the amount of work she had gotten through, it must have been in the early hours. Moira stood before the whiteboard and read through the additions made since the previous evening.

'I thought my computer skills were good, but you're in a class of your own,' Moira said.

'The result of a misspent youth,' O'Neill shot back. 'I should have been out playing hockey in a little skirt and having the local lads running after me. Instead, I was in my room learning code, wolfing down chocolate biscuits and turning myself into a blimp.'

All Moira could see was an attractive curvy blond that would set many a heart racing. 'So what the hell are you doing in the PSNI? You could use your skills to go into business for yourself.'

'Why does everybody ask me that? I'll tell you why, because none of the questioners have ever worked in a start-up. And few of them would have survived the experience. It's no fun waking up in the morning afraid that you won't have the price of a coffee at the end of the week. We sold our little company and pocketed the money, but two of my partners have already lost that money and more on new ventures. They're broke, they've lost their houses, one of them has ruined his marriage and they now have no jobs. I'm not broke and I have a job. Does that answer your question?'

Moira hastily changed the subject. 'How's your mother?'

'Not good. Dementia is like another planet where the woman who was my mother now lives. And there's no way back from planet dementia. I still believe that she's in there somewhere, but another part of me knows that she's gone forever' She handed Moira a sheaf of papers. 'These are Whyte's financial records. Can you go through them? I'm not an accountant.'

Moira took the papers. 'Neither am I. But I'll look.' She went back to her desk and pulled out her chair. O'Neill might be a computer whiz but she's also a strange wee girl. Moira picked up a yellow highlighter and started on the first sheet.

WILSON'S MOUTH felt like the bottom of a parrot's cage and that's what it resembled when he looked at it in the mirror. He climbed into the shower and gave himself alternating blasts of scalding hot and freezing cold water. He couldn't remember who had recommended the hot/cold treatment, but it didn't work on his headache. From what he could remember, they had had a great time last night and he was prepared to take the pain.

The smell coming from the kitchen seemed to write the phrase 'Ulster Fry' in the air above his head as he dressed and went to the kitchen. Reid looked sensational in a cream ensemble that was more in keeping with a night out than the autopsy room. Wilson took one look at the plate containing eggs, bacon and sausage and his stomach heaved.

'Drink this before you eat.' Reid handed him a glass of a clear bubbling liquid.

'I hope it's poison.' He gulped it down in one swallow.

'You'll be a new man in five minutes.'

'Don't make empty promises.'

'Trust me, I'm a doctor.'

They both laughed. 'You're in better humour today.'

She gave him a hug and kissed him. 'That was a great night. I haven't had so much fun in a long time.'

It was good to see her so happy. She was right. They had been preoccupied since returning from the US. Then again, it was only natural to be preoccupied by the possibility that someone might kill you at any moment.

It was a beautiful summer's day outside and Wilson wished they could play truant. 'We'll head off to Rathlin this weekend, if this weather lasts.'

She looked at the kitchen clock. 'The five minutes are up. How do you feel?'

He grabbed her and held her tight. 'Like a new man.'

She felt his erection pressing against her. 'Feels like the old man to me.'

CHAPTER FORTY-ONE

Wilson stood at the whiteboard. 'The chief super has done us proud. HQ will give us uniforms for the door-to-door. Siobhan, we need to run off photos of Whyte for them. Get them done on a proper machine. There'll be a press conference at midday so it'll be on the evening news that we're concerned for his safety and all that guff. They won't say outright that we think he's dead because he might walk into a police station this afternoon with a case of amnesia. By the way, that's not about to happen.'

Browne stared at the board in shock. One name jumped out: Vincent Carmody. Heavey was playing silly buggers. He realised that his mouth was open and he closed it. The longer he kept his secret, the more it would fester within him. Wilson was looking at the money as a motive. He might be right, but Browne knew that two gay men were missing and one of them was penniless.

'I see you've been feeding McDevitt.' Moira handed Wilson a copy of the *Chronicle* with the second page exposed. 'He'd didn't do the "have you seen this man" line, but it's plain that Roger Whyte has been missing and the police are worried about his safety. I suppose the media people at HQ will have something more substantial to plant in tomorrow's edition.'

'They will, and the line will be "have you seen this man",' Wilson said. 'I want a photo of Whyte over to HQ pronto. It will have to accompany the request for information. The chief super will handle the press conference and I'll be on hand in case there are questions.' He turned and looked at the board. 'I see Heavey has come through with a list of friends. We need to speak to all of them. I want formal statements. When they last saw Whyte, was he worried about anything, had he been threatened? Rory and Harry are on that.'

'I'd like to help out there, boss,' Moira said. 'I'm still waiting for a response from the drone clubs on Helen's Bay. It might speed things up if there are three of us interviewing.'

Wilson looked from Browne to Graham and saw no objection. 'Okay, you can split up the names between you.'

'I've given DS McElvaney the financial records I've obtained,' O'Neill said.

Neither Wilson nor Moira missed the formality.

'I've started on them,' Moira said. 'One thing is clear: as Whyte's mother said, he's far wealthier than we realised. It'll probably need a court order to get the full information from his stockbroker, but the guy is a millionaire.'

Wilson looked at O'Neill. 'Have you contacted his lawyer?'

'I rang at nine o'clock. He's due in court this morning and he'll call as soon as he's free.'

'Okay,' Wilson said. 'I'll take the lawyer. He might not be forthcoming since we haven't found his client's body. If he is resistant, we'll go the court order route. Until we know any better, we follow the money. Let's get to it.'

'Why don't we take the names to the cafeteria and distribute them over coffee?' Moira said.

'Your treat?' Graham said.

Moira nodded. She was about to invite O'Neill but saw

that she was already on her way to the ladies room. She would have to find out what makes her tick.

THEY SAT at a table in the cafeteria looking at the list of ten names and addresses. 'We should do this by area,' Moira said. 'Otherwise, we'll spend a lot of time running around town.' She looked at Browne. 'Is that all right with you, Rory?'

He nodded, but there was a slight hesitation. 'There are three over by the Royal Victoria and the Falls Road, I'll take those if you like.'

Graham looked at the addresses. He was the only Belfast man of the three. 'That part of Broadway is ropey. Maybe I should handle it.'

'I hope you don't think I'm not up to an area that's ropey,' Browne said.

'No offence,' Graham said. 'But you and Moira aren't from this neck of the woods and you may not know the local geography. There are a lot of junkies down there.' He looked down at the list. 'It might be better if we did Carmody together.'

'That will cost us time.'

'There are a couple of handy addresses in the University area,' Graham said. 'They would suit you right fine.'

'What if I said I preferred the Broadway/Falls area?' Browne said.

'Boys,' Moira said. 'The purpose is to get the job done. I can see Harry's point. But we need to get the interviews over as soon as possible. Rory, you want Broadway, you've got it. I'll take University and Harry will take the rest.' She looked at the other two, neither of whom spoke. 'I'll take that as a yes.' She picked up her coffee, drank, then grimaced. Some things never change, she thought.

CHAPTER FORTY-TWO

Wilson and Davis reviewed a press statement whose content had been carefully worded to exclude anything associated with the word 'murder'. They were simply searching for a missing man. The usual suspects were gathered in the media centre at Castlereagh, where a female constable led Davis and Wilson to their places on the dais. Wilson nodded at McDevitt as he passed. There was a twinkle in the journalist's eye that he didn't like. That twinkle said that McDevitt was up for diversion. At midday, the constable picked up a hand-held microphone and professionally did her welcome patter to the assembled journalists. She introduced Wilson and Davis and handed the proceedings over to them.

Davis read her statement with the aplomb of a seasoned professional. She held up a poster-sized photo of Whyte. 'We need to find this man. Anyone who has any information as to his whereabouts can call the confidential police line. The number is on the screen. If you saw or spoke to him at any time on or since the eleventh of July, your help could prove crucial. Thank you.'

McDevitt's hand shot up. 'Is this a murder inquiry?'

'Roger Whyte is a missing person,' Davis said. 'We have no

reason to believe that he is the victim of foul play, and in the interest of not wasting police time, we'd like anyone with information to come forward.'

McDevitt continued. 'I notice you're sitting beside Detective Superintendent Wilson. Does that mean that the Murder Squad is leading the investigation?'

'DS Wilson is the SIO on this case of a missing person. It is unusual; however, his team have the skills for this investigation. Our overall concern is for the safe return of Mr Whyte, whose relatives are concerned at his disappearance. That's all, thank you.' Davis and Wilson stood.

Most of the journalists were on their feet and preparing to leave when McDevitt continued. 'Anything to report on the shooting in Ballymacarrett? Has the shooter been located?'

The exodus paused and the journalists looked to the dais. Davis gathered her papers. 'For an answer to that question, I have to refer you to the Police Ombudsman's Office.'

Wilson led the way and Davis followed him. 'That man is a pest,' she said as they exited the building.

'He sells newspapers, and sometimes we find him useful.' Wilson opened the car door for her. 'After that performance, they'll be polishing the leather on that chair they're preparing for you at HQ.'

'I know he's your friend, but he's still a pest.'

'Being a pest is part of his job description.'

HE'D MADE IT. He'd been on a high since he'd seen the piece in the *Chronicle*. Although he wasn't mentioned, it was about him. The cutting was already pasted into his album, along with still photos of his victims. Inevitably, there would be more press articles, now that Whyte's disappearance is out in the open. He would make a point of watching the news reports on all the channels. He'd make recordings. He would be famous, but in the meantime, a lot more people would die. He imagined the police running around like little ants looking for Whyte. It amused him to think they'll never find him. He wondered why they hadn't rumbled that Carmody is also missing. He deduced that nobody gave a shit about him.

Moira learned nothing new from her three interviews. She had a couple more names to pursue, but she didn't hold out much hope. Whyte kept himself to himself. Like most individuals he had a few friends, a wider circle of acquaintances and an even wider circle of casual acquaintances. The uniforms would concentrate on the third category and she didn't envy them. Every now and then a neighbour or the local shopkeeper might provide a lead, but door-to-door inquiries rarely produced the goods.

She found herself close to Bedford Street and one of her favourite haunts, the Harlem Café. She wasn't enamoured by the décor, which she found overwhelming, but she liked the coffee, the food and the eclectic mix of people. She sat at a corner table and examined her notebook while she ate. None of her interviewees could be classified as friends of Whyte. They saw him occasionally and she felt that the reason they were on the list was they had once been the missing man's sexual partners. She leafed through the pages searching for some nugget of information. Whyte wasn't a complex person. He was someone who enjoyed his own company and who found pleasure in cultural pursuits. As far as her interviewees knew, he had no interest in politics, never took drugs and liked to drink fine whiskey. It looked like Wilson was right. It had to be about the money. Otherwise, Whyte had no ostensible reason for being missing. But was it about the entirety of his wealth or the money in his pocket? People could be killed for a handful of change.

She dug into her veggie breakfast. Her liking for vegetarian food was a carryover from the States. She was treating herself because she had finally deposited Frank Shea's cheque and in a few days her bank balance would be back in the black. Cashing the cheque had been a 'will I, won't I' moment. It came down to the fact that she needed it and Frank wouldn't even miss it. A guy at a table across from her was staring. She shot him a quick 'fuck off' look. She needed a break from romance, although she doubted her admirer had romance in mind. She closed her notebook and returned it to her jacket pocket. Ever since the business with Ronald McIver, she was acutely aware of signals from those around her, especially colleagues. She had picked up vibes from both O'Neill and Browne that she wasn't keen to ignore. Reintegration into the squad would never be easy, and she understood Rory's nose being out of joint, but instinct told her that something else was the matter with him. She finished the last of her veggie sausage and pushed her plate away. She wasn't looking forward to returning to the station empty-handed, but as the boss often said, it was what it was. She paid her bill. As she passed her admirer's table, he gave her a look of disgust. She was smiling as she exited into the sunshine. She took in a deep breath. She loved Belfast.

Browne had completed his interviews. Like Moira, he had learned little titbits from Whyte's life but nothing extraordinary. Both of his interviewees were surprised when he had announced that he was gay. He had hoped it would help loosen their tongues and it had succeeded to a limited extent. Whyte had been obsessed about his former partner and had no desire to enter another long-term relationship. He was well-known in the gay community for being promiscuous and not monogamous. That might be the connection between Whyte and Carmody. Vincent was always in need of money and had worked as a male prostitute. Browne's stomach flipped at the thought of it. He hadn't even bothered to pass by

Vinny's place on Broadway. There was no point, he wasn't there. He thought about inventing an interview with Carmody but that would only dig a deeper hole than the one he was already in. He knew he was impeding the investigation and he knew it couldn't go on.

CHAPTER FORTY-THREE

The entrance to Nicholas Norwood Solicitors, one of the most preeminent legal firms in Northern Ireland, was in the middle of a row of shops on Castle Street. Wilson entered and climbed the stairs to the first floor, where a stout wooden door blocked his path to the offices proper. He pushed the button on the electronic pad and announced himself. The door buzzed and he entered. Inside, the office's stained oak panelling spoke of a long tradition of legal representation. His appointment was for two o'clock and he had been advised to be on time. The receptionist confirmed that Mr Norwood was busy and could only be available for a fifteen-minute conference. Time was money at Nicholas Norwood and Wilson didn't represent billable hours. The receptionist directed him to the rear, where a formidable-looking woman sat at a desk guarding the entrance to Norwood's office, the inner sanctum. She was middle-aged, wore the obligatory legal business suit of white blouse, black jacket and skirt, her grey hair tied back in a bun and one of the sternest countenances Wilson had seen. She was perfect for the post she occupied.

'Superintendent Wilson,' she looked at him with a level of disdain. 'Warrant card.'

He removed it from his pocket and flipped it open.

'Mr Norwood will see you now.' She pressed a hidden button beneath her desk and the door buzzed.

Wilson entered an office larger than the squad room. At one end was an enormous oak partner's desk, behind which sat a small man wearing a pair of pince-nez spectacles. The desk was piled with stalagmites formed from brown files tied together by blue or red ribbons.

Norwood stood, displaying his perfectly cut pinstriped suit. Although it was a warm day, he was wearing his jacket and his blue tie was pulled tight against his neck. His eyes blinked as he took in Wilson at a glance and then pointed at a chair in front of his desk. 'Please sit down, superintendent. I'm rather busy today.' He shuffled papers on his desk. 'However, I'm told that your visit concerns a valued client and is urgent.'

'I won't take up any more of your time than necessary. I understand that you handle legal work for Roger Whyte with an address in Elmwood Mews.'

'The firm has that pleasure.'

'You may not be aware but Mr Whyte has been missing for nearly a month.'

'I read the *Chronicle* from cover to cover each morning. How can I help you?'

'We've established that Mr Whyte was wealthy and our current line of inquiry centres on the possibility that harm may have come to him because of his wealth.'

'That would seem logical.'

'We would be interested to know if Mr Whyte had made a will.'

Norwood's head moved from side to side not in a negation but more out of habit. 'I must consider lawyer–client confidentiality.'

'We have no desire to meddle in Mr Whyte's legal affairs, but as his lawyer you are no doubt as interested as the PSNI in establishing what happened to him.'

'I have heard of you, superintendent. And most of what I have heard is positive. I can therefore trust that what I discuss will not be divulged outside this office.'

'You have my word.'

'There is a will.'

'We are spending considerable resources on searching for heirs to Mr Whyte. We understand there are few in Northern Ireland and there is a family connection to Canada. It would be a major saving in time to know if the will names an heir.'

Norwood rocked in his chair. 'I see your predicament. There is no heir. If Roger Whyte proves to be deceased, the bulk of his estate will go to charity. Now, you have the information you require and I have to prepare for a meeting.' He stood and extended his hand. 'I hope you find Mr Whyte safe and well.'

The strength of the shake surprised Wilson. 'So do I.'

He passed the secretary, half-expecting her to snarl at him, but she was concentrating on some papers.

Wilson made his way down the stairs and through the door to the street. Perhaps plots involving an heir in an overseas dominion only exist in Agatha Christie novels. If this disappearance wasn't about money, it was most likely about sex or revenge, or both. And that would mean a lot more digging into Roger Whyte's life.

CHAPTER FORTY-FOUR

Wilson had already altered 'Motive = Money' on the whiteboard by the time the team assembled for the evening briefing. He had replaced 'money' with a question mark. 'It looks like I might have got the motive wrong.' He briefed the team on the visit to Norwood's office.

'I wouldn't dismiss money as the motive just yet,' Moira said. 'I've been going over Whyte's financials and he has been very generous to some of his friends. There are lots of transfers of two or three hundred pounds into accounts that we've identified as belonging to some of the men on our list. Perhaps those sums were repaid in cash, we have no way of knowing, but there's one person who received a lot more, and that's our friend Charles Heavey. He received two transfers of ten thousand pounds. Maybe we should find out whether he's repaid Whyte because there is no evidence of bank transfers in the reverse direction.'

'Get him in,' Wilson said. 'Let's see if he has an answer.'

'On it, boss,' Moira said.

'Any news from the house-to-house?' Wilson asked.

'Too early, boss,' Graham said. 'The uniforms only started this afternoon. I'll give them a bell in the morning.'

'Anything from the interviews with Heavey's list of friends?'

Graham shook his head. 'Nothing, boss, I don't think the man really made friends. Seems to have been more of a loner. The three guys I interviewed knew him from what they called "the circuit".' He tried not to look at Browne. 'The general gay hangouts around town.'

'More of the same story with me, boss,' Moira said. 'I'm writing up my notes, but there's nothing that would raise an eyebrow.'

'What about you, Rory?' Wilson asked.

'He was pining after his partner who died in London,' Browne said. 'He's had lovers. Maybe some of the guys who got money from him were former sexual partners. But he didn't seem to have any enemies.'

'He wouldn't have topped himself?' Graham said.

'Yes, Harry,' Wilson said. 'He might have topped himself and then hidden his own body.'

'What about the Lagan?' Graham said. 'If he'd gone in there, we'd still be looking for him.'

'A body would have turned up by now,' Wilson said. He gave himself a mental slap for demeaning Harry's contribution. A leader should listen not belittle. 'Thanks for thinking outside the box, Harry. We should all follow that example. What about the CCTV?'

'The first lot of disks arrives tomorrow,' O'Neill said.

'We need to come up with another motive for Whyte's disappearance and we need to do it soon. Before we break, does anyone have anything constructive to offer?' Lack of sleep was catching up with Wilson, the investigation was stalled and he had a pile of administrative tasks waiting for him.

This is the moment to speak up, Browne thought. But something was holding him back. He glanced around the team and found Moira staring at him. Perhaps she knows. Just say it, he thought. Say it. But the words wouldn't come.

. . .

Wilson had put a limit of seven o'clock on work. Reid was already at the apartment and the steaks were in the fridge. Browne and O'Neill had left, but surprisingly Graham was still beavering away at his desk – what was rare was wonderful. Moira knocked on his door and he motioned her in.

'Hard day, boss?'

'Hard night followed by a hard day.'

'Out dancing, were we?'

'Something like that, dinner followed by multiple whiskeys, soft music and good company.' He caught the look in her eye. 'Missing Brendan?'

'We had our moments but overall no. It had to go to the next step for him and that's what burst the bubble. I wasn't the person he wanted me to be.'

He opened his filing cabinet and took out two glasses and a bottle of Jameson.

'No Crown tonight?' Moira asked.

'A quiet night at home, dinner, television.' He poured two shots and passed one to her.

'Stop, you're making me jealous.'

They touched glasses and drank. 'You didn't come here for a nightcap?'

The door opened and Graham popped his head in. 'Is this a private party or can anyone join in?'

Wilson smiled. 'The more the merrier, pull up a seat.' He fetched a third glass, gave Graham a shot and added a small measure into his and Moira's glasses.

'The old crew,' Graham toasted.

'The old crew,' Wilson and Moira said together, they touched glasses and drank.

There was a moment of silent nostalgia.

Wilson looked at Moira. 'There's something on your mind.'

'I think there's something going on with Rory.' She looked at Graham.

'I knew things would be difficult at first,' Wilson said. 'He probably views you as a threat.'

'It not that, boss,' Graham said. 'There's something on Rory's mind and I don't think it has anything to do with Moira.'

'Maybe it is my fault,' Moira said. 'This job does strange things to people, we all know that. I might just be over-reacting, but this evening when you asked whether anyone had anything to add, I was sure he was about to speak. I saw the words on his lips, but he never said them.'

'And the way he behaved when we divided up the list of names wasn't normal either,' Graham said. 'Something is up, boss.'

'I'll talk to him tomorrow.' Wilson finished his whiskey. 'Off home with the both of you, I promised to leave by seven and I am a man of my word, especially when I give it to Steph.'

Moira and Graham finished their drinks. 'Night, boss,' they said in unison as they left the office.

Wilson tried to read the report on the disposition of office furniture, which was compulsory reading for the next senior officers' meeting. Something in his bones told him that he had better get hold of the reins of this investigation. Moira was one of the most intuitive coppers he had ever worked with. If she was sure that something was up with Browne, then he was ready to believe it.

Reid had recorded the news report on the press conference and they sat on the couch watching while the steaks sizzled on the grill pan. 'Davis looks good,' she said. 'She's more confident these days.'

'Probably the result of Jack's confidence-building techniques.'

She punched him on the shoulder. 'You're terrible. You look good too, considering the shape you were in when you got up this morning.'

'I know this doctor who has a special stock of hangover cures.'

'You and Davis make a good team.'

'I was apprehensive when Donald left. We'd worked together for a hell of a long time. But Davis is turning out to be all right'

'Donald was your replacement father, and you were the son he never had.'

'Moira thinks there's something up with Rory.'

'I'd listen to her if I were you.'

'It's got to be something to do with Whyte.'

She stood and went to the stove. 'Whatever it is will have to wait until tomorrow. Get the plates out and let's enjoy dinner.'

Browne sat in the darkened living room of his flat. He had reached the point of no return. There would be a price to pay now when Wilson found out about Carmody. At the very least he was responsible for wasting the team's time. He could also be accused of perverting the course of justice. That could end his career. He hadn't wanted to expose his links with a male prostitute. And by trying to prevent that, he had undermined his professionalism. He had tried to convince himself that Carmody's disappearance wasn't linked to Whyte's. They had nothing in common: they were different ages, they had different backgrounds and levels of education, they lived different lives at opposite ends of the social scale. But deep down he knew there was a connection. Deciding to conceal Carmody's disappearance had been a misguided act of self-preservation. He would tell Wilson tomorrow and accept whatever sanction his boss deemed appropriate.

CHAPTER FORTY-FIVE

Wilson left his apartment building energised by his run, a shower and a breakfast of poached eggs on avocado toast. The sun had been beating down since early morning and the sky was clear blue. It was turning out to be the best summer in decades. Citizens of the province who worked outdoors were sporting tans, some continental holidays were being cancelled, a hosepipe ban had been introduced to conserve water, and guesthouses in coastal towns were booked out. It would be a summer that people would never forget. Wilson was just thinking that nothing bad could happen on such a beautiful day when he saw Colm Matthews climbing out of a car parked across the road from his building. He cursed.

'Good morning, detective superintendent.' Matthews crossed the road to join Wilson. 'Fabulous morning.'

'Good morning, Colm. I was just thinking the same thing.'

'I saw you and Chief Superintendent Davis on the news last night. She's a very polished performer. You two are a formidable team.'

'Rumour has it she's destined for great things.'

'A rising tide lifts all boats.'

Wilson smiled. 'Not in this case, I'm happy where I am.'

'Have you got time for a walk and maybe a coffee?'

'Why not?' They walked towards the Titanic Centre.

'I suppose you're wondering why I accosted you at your home,' Matthews said.

'I was wondering about that.'

'I wanted to talk to you outside the office.'

'Unofficially you mean.'

'I suppose so.' They passed the SSE Arena and Matthews led Wilson towards the group of shops facing the river. 'The coffees are on me.'

Wilson waited on a concrete bench outside and looked out over the Lagan. The water was a deep shade of blue and there was a steady stream of walkers making their way along the path leading to the Titanic Centre.

Matthews returned carrying two cardboard cups. He passed one to Wilson. 'I've discussed your case with my boss. He's decided that there's nothing to investigate.'

Wilson covered his sigh of relief by blowing on his coffee to cool it.

'I don't suppose you'd like to tell me what really happened?'

'Unofficially?'

'Unofficially.'

'I'm investigating the murder of a high-level political individual. It's shaking the tree and those responsible are getting nervous. The theory is that they wanted me off the case. I went to the warehouse because Sammy Rice was murdered there and Sammy was linked to these people. The hitman took his chance. He didn't get me and I didn't get him. The case is so sensitive that it can't become public knowledge.'

'The people in the PSNI look on us like we're Keystone Cops, not proper police officers.'

'I wouldn't say that.'

'We always do a professional job.'

Wilson sipped his coffee. 'I'm impressed with your work, and I'd be proud to serve alongside you.'

A small boat was heading down Belfast Lough and out to sea.

'I appreciate that. It's not pleasant investigating police officers who have excellent records and just once get involved in something illegal.'

'I've been the Professional Services route more than once.'

'I've seen the records.'

'I'm all about results. I deal with evil people who do evil things and should be brought to book for their deeds. The manual sometimes ties our hands with protocols and procedures that have been developed for ideal situations. Sometimes we're forced to step outside the boundaries. But that doesn't mean acting illegally.'

'That makes us the guardians of the guardians and it's a role we take seriously.' Matthews stood and dumped his coffee in a trash bin. He held out his hand to Wilson. 'Good luck.'

Wilson shook. 'And you.'

Matthews walked a few yards and turned. 'You tell a good story and it's important that you stick to it.'

Wilson didn't consider himself a habitual liar, but he worked in a job where the truth was sometimes blurred. As Matthews disappeared around the corner of the concert hall, he dumped his coffee and stood up. They'd both done what they had to do.

WILSON HAD JUST SETTLED in his office chair when Browne knocked on the door and entered, the frown lines on his forehead told their own story. He marked one up for Moira. 'Spit it out, Rory.'

'I'm sorry, boss, but I've been holding information back.'

'There had better be a good reason.'

'That's the point, boss, there isn't.

'What's the information?'

'Another gay man is missing.'

Wilson straightened. 'Say that again.'

'A younger gay man, Vincent Carmody, has been missing for the past couple of weeks.'

'And you've known this for how long?'

'Since Heavey first spoke with me about Whyte.'

'What class of an eejit are you? Why the hell would you withhold this information? Do you have any idea of the repercussions?'

'Carmody and I were lovers a while back. I was already involved when I discovered that he was obsessive and sometimes worked as a male prostitute. I broke it off with him.'

Wilson remembered seeing Browne with a young man in Victoria Street. They looked happy. 'There's no harm in that.'

'I didn't want my connection with him to come out. He lives in a hovel in Broadway and when Forensics dust it, my fingerprints will be all over the place. They 'll drag me into the investigation and you'll have to take me off the case.'

'You are one stupid bastard.' He was struggling to see where this bombshell was leading. One thing was certain: Rory would be off the investigation immediately. 'Is there a link between the disappearances of Whyte and Carmody?'

'I don't know, boss.'

'Perhaps they've gone missing together?'

'That thought crossed my mind. But people who know them both don't think so.'

Wilson motioned to Moira, who he knew was watching them.

She entered the office and closed the door. 'Boss?'

'We have a second missing gay man,' Wilson said. 'A Vincent Carmody with an address in Broadway.'

Moira wrote in her notebook.

'Rory was personally involved with Mr Carmody and won't be able to help us with the investigation. So you'll be deputising for me from now on. Rory will take over the Helen's Bay case.'

Moira didn't look at Browne.

'This puts a different complexion on the Whyte investigation. We need to find out whether the two disappearances are linked,' Wilson continued.

'And if they are?' Moira said.

'Let's not go there until we have more proof. We need to have a profile on Mr Carmody. There are two new lines of inquiry: Whyte and Carmody might have disappeared together, or one might be responsible for the disappearance of the other. Get Siobhan to pull everything she can get on Carmody.' He turned to Browne. 'You can help with the profile of Carmody, after that you're out. I'll give Finlay a call. I want Carmody's place given a thorough examination. And I want to look at it myself before they start. I'll meet you downstairs after I give the chief super the news.'

Browne knew that Wilson wasn't referring to him.

'What the hell was he thinking?' Wilson said as they parked outside Carmody's address. 'We've lost a lot of time because of Rory.'

'Put yourself in his shoes, boss,' Moira said. 'No one wants their sex life paraded for public consumption. I know he can't be part of the investigation, but I'm not happy about replacing him. Rory looked devastated. Losing the case is a bitter blow and I don't like profiting at someone else's expense.'

Wilson had seen the shattered look on Rory's face. Some repair work would have to be done down the line. If there was something down the line. The kind of mistake that Rory had made left the whole question of his career hanging in the balance.

On the positive side, perhaps Carmody's involvement might clear up Whyte's disappearance. It wouldn't be the first time that a date had ended in an argument. Wilson had already handled cases where a prostitute and john had done each other harm. However, there was another possibility. Perhaps the same person had disappeared Whyte and Carmody. He prayed that they were looking at the former scenario and not the latter.

Wilson did the honours with the lock-picks even though he knew the door would not have withstood a good kick from a twelve-year-old. Browne had told them that Carmody inhabited the ground-floor flat. Wilson opened the door and they slipped on their latex gloves as they entered. People often exaggerate when they describe the residences of others, but Browne was right when he called Carmody's abode a hovel. A visit by the Council would lead to the house being condemned. The first thing that hit them was the stench of decay. The living room was in such disarray that Wilson wondered whether it was its natural state or somebody had trashed it. 'Finlay and his team will have their work cut out with this place.'

Moira had moved to the back of the flat and returned to the living room. 'The smell is coming from the kitchen. The electric is on the meter and has probably been off for weeks. There's milk in the fridge that's over two weeks passed its use by date. I need a shower after just looking at it. The bedroom and kitchen are in as big a mess as this place.'

'Mr Carmody was not house-proud.' Wilson wasn't the neatest, although the women in his life had imparted training, but Carmody wasn't just untidy he was a dirty bugger. One thing was sure: Carmody had been gone for more than two weeks. Also, money wasn't the motivation for his disappearance.

'No blood anywhere around,' Moira said. 'Although there might be anything under this mountain of crap.'

'It wouldn't surprise me if Finlay found Shergar under that mess.' Wilson moved on to the rear of the flat. He gave the kitchen a miss. The bed looked slept in and it had been months since the sheets had last met a washing machine. He was surprised that his sergeant had been in this place. Maybe at that time it wasn't in such a state, but it was still an unpleasant thought. It showed what an almighty drive sex was. 'Let's get out of here.'

Moira was rooting around in a press in the living room. She came up with a photo album. She flicked through the pages. One person featured in many photos and she assumed she was looking at Carmody. Some might consider him good-looking. He had fair hair and a thin moustache in one large black-and-white photo. His features were regular. Nothing stood out. His eyes might be blue and were his best attribute. His mouth was small and his lips thin. He was not her type. Someone stuck the photo to the page with some gum and she wriggled it free. They would need it for a flyer. She put the album back where she found it. 'Meet Vincent Carmody.' She handed the photo to Wilson.

He dredged up the memory of the young man he had seen with Browne on Victoria Street. It was the same guy. 'I wonder where Mr Carmody is now.' People like Carmody disappear without a trace and are seldom found. The reason is simple. Nobody gives a damn whether they live or die. It was why the Yorkshire Ripper got away with murdering thirteen women before he was convicted, many of those women were prostitutes so they didn't count. You only had to look around the flat to see that Carmody's world was in the shitter. Now some bastard had taken away the only thing of value he had: his life. There were dozens of people like Carmody in every city in the world. They were just one segment of the used and abused.

'A penny for them, boss.'

'My thoughts aren't worth a penny, like Mr Carmody,' Wilson replied. 'We need to find this man though; somebody has to care what happened to him.'

CHAPTER FORTY-SIX

The team assembled at the whiteboard. Wilson had stuck the photo of Carmody beside that of Whyte. 'We have a second disappearance,' he announced without indicating the source of the information. 'This is Vincent Carmody and we haven't yet established how long he's been missing, neither do we know his movements. It might be important if we can link Carmody with the disappearance of Roger Whyte. Where are we on the CCTV?'

'We have cameras all over central Belfast,' O'Neill said. 'And there are several in Howard Street. I've already requested the footage from our cameras and I've contacted the businesses in the area to ask for their footage. I've received two disks and I've started on them. It's not helpful that the days in question were holidays with thousands of people on the streets.'

'Keep at it,' Wilson said. 'Any calls to the confidential number?'

'The usual cranks,' Graham said. 'Only one or two worth following up, which I've passed on to the uniforms for a preliminary look.'

'What do we know about Carmody?' Wilson said.

'Vincent Carmody, born to Mary Carmody on 23 March 1993, father unknown,' O'Neill said. 'Mother died when he was sixteen from an overdose. Social Services tried to house him in a shelter to help him complete his education, but he kept running away. There was a question of sexual abuse, but it was never fully investigated. He found his way to the streets. He has had a couple of jobs. He worked in a warehouse for a year and seemed to get his life on track but then quit. Three arrests for shoplifting; no convictions. His last arrest was for soliciting. The investigation is still pending.'

Wilson could have written the script of Carmody's life the minute he'd seen his flat. The poor man was on a one-way street from the day he had been born: no father, junkie mother, truant at school, lucky to have avoided reform school, abused by people and the system. 'Harry, get on to the uniforms and organise a door-to-door on Broadway. We'll interview anyone who saw Carmody or who can tell us anything about his movements. His disappearance poses more questions. Are Whyte's and Carmody's disappearances connected? Did they know each other? Did one murder the other? Where are they now? We can stand here all day developing questions, but what we really need are answers.'

Moira's phone rang. 'Sorry, boss.' She listened, spoke and put her phone away. 'Heavey's downstairs.'

'Take Harry with you.'

When they entered Interview Room 1, Moira and Graham found Charles Heavey seated and drinking a cup of tea. If being interviewed by the police bothered him, he didn't show it.

Moira did the introductions while Graham turned on the recording equipment.

'Detective Sergeant Browne not available today?' Heavey asked.

'He's busy,' Moira said.

'I saw Chief Superintendent Davis and Superintendent Wilson on the news last night,' Heavey said. 'It looks like you're finally serious about finding Roger.'

'We are very serious about finding Mr Whyte,' Moira said. 'This is a preliminary interview and there may be a follow-up.'

'Understood; anything I can do to help.'

'We're looking into Roger Whyte's life and I understand that DS Wilson has already interviewed you.'

Heavey nodded.

'Another area we've looked at involves Mr Whyte's financial affairs,' Moira said. The smile faded from Heavey's face. 'Mr Whyte was very generous to his friends, several of whom received sums ranging from tens to hundreds of pounds.'

'Yes, Roger was rather wealthy and had made some shrewd investments. He liked to share his good fortune.'

'Sharing his good fortune to the tune of twenty thousand pounds appears a little excessive.' Moira removed a bank statement from her file and put it on the table in front of Heavey. 'We have highlighted two transactions in particular. Both were made to you six months ago.'

Heavey had gone from relaxed to uncomfortable. 'I had reverses in the market and Roger agreed to bail me out. A futures contract went against me and my stockbroker called in the money.'

'Had you made arrangements to repay the loan?' Moira asked.

'Of course, we'd arranged for repayment.'

Moira took out a series of bank statements and laid them out on the table. 'Can you please show me a single repayment that you've made?' Heavey looked like he might bolt for the door. Sweat appeared on his brow, he broke eye contact and rubbed his collar. Moira reckoned rubbing the collar was his primary nervous habit. He was no longer relaxed about the interview; he'd seen where she was leading him.

'I hadn't started. Roger told me he didn't need the money and I could repay him at my discretion.'

'And now Mr Whyte has disappeared. That's rather convenient for you, isn't it?' Moira asked.

'Now look here, I was the one who informed Detective Sergeant Browne about Roger's disappearance.'

'And you think that exonerates you?'

Tears were forming in Heavey's eyes. 'I liked Roger. I wouldn't do anything to harm him.'

'Let's move on to Vincent Carmody,' Moira said. 'You also told DS Browne about his disappearance. What was your relationship with Carmody?'

'Oh God, I need to go to the toilet.'

Graham stood. 'Please come with me, sir.'

Moira turned off the recording device and closed her file. Heavey wasn't guilty of harming either Whyte or Carmody. He didn't have the balls. He was guilty, however, of abusing his friend's generosity, but there was no criminal law against that.

FIVE MINUTES later Heavey and Graham returned and retook their seats. Graham started the recorder.

'Feeling better?' Moira asked. 'Would you like water?'

'I want my solicitor,' Heavey said.

'Dr Heavey,' Moira began. 'This interview is not under caution and we have no plans to arrest you. We are simply exploring lines of inquiry. Please relax. We were discussing Vincent Carmody. What was your relationship with him?'

'I want my solicitor,' Heavey said.

'We will call your solicitor if you wish, but I assure you it is unnecessary. You may not know our procedures. If we intend to arrest someone, we must first caution them. You have not been cautioned. You are here because we need your help if we're to find out what happened to your friend.'

Heavey paused for a moment. 'I sometimes paid Vincent for sex.'

'At his flat?'

'Are you joking, I'd be afraid I'd get rabies if I took my clothes off in that dump. We had sex in different places. Sometimes at my flat, sometimes in a hotel.'

'Did Roger Whyte use Carmody for sex?'

'I don't know, but I assume so.'

'They knew each other?'

'Almost certainly.'

'Can you think of any reason they would disappear together?'

Heavey shook his head.

'Do you think that either of them was capable of violence?'

'Quite the opposite. They were both gentle people. Vincent could be a little intense, but I never felt afraid in his company.'

She made a note to see whether Heavey had ever been the victim of violence. She nodded at Graham, who switched off the recorder. 'Thank you, you've been most helpful.'

Heavey bolted from the room without replying.

'Making for the nearest pub if I'm not mistaken,' Graham said as they stood up. 'You never lost it, Moira, I wouldn't like to be in your crosshairs.'

CHAPTER FORTY-SEVEN

They were the same distance up shit creek as they were when they first got the news about Carmody, and there was still no sign of a paddle, Wilson thought. Moira had briefed him on the interview with Heavey. It was her opinion that he had nothing to do with either disappearance, and he trusted her enough to accept it as fact. The problems remained the same: no bodies, no crime scenes, no forensic evidence and no clear motive. Money had looked good as the motive, but no one was about to benefit from Whyte's death, except a brace of charities. Heavey would be obliged to repay Whyte's estate, so even he wouldn't benefit. It was all going nowhere and the clock was ticking. Wilson knew that evidence was like a pool of water sitting on earth: it seeped away as time passed until there was nothing left.

He had agreed with Davis that they wouldn't announce the disappearance of Carmody. McDevitt wouldn't be as slow as them to join the dots, and the LGBT community would soon be marching in the streets demanding police protection from a serial killer of gay men. Not that Wilson had discounted that theory; in fact, it had risen to the top of his list of possibilities. It was one thing to follow that line of enquiry, but it was another to create a panic by raising the spectre of a serial killer. Ulster had had its fair share of serial murderers, many of whom were currently walking the streets. They had declared their crimes as 'political' and been set free in the name of peace. But it took a certain mentality to, for example, stab someone twenty-three times, and it had nothing to do with peace.

Wilson's mentor, Donald Spence, had trained him in the plod theory, and that was what they were applying at the moment. Moira and O'Neill were reviewing CCTV footage. Next to them Graham was manning the phones, looking for the gem of information that might unlock the case. He had done as much as he could in relation to Whyte. If there was anyone alive out there who had information about Whyte's movements, they would have seen a news broadcast, read an article in the *Chronicle* or heard a friend speak about it by now. Somebody knew what happened to Whyte and to Carmody. Assuming they were dead, the killer knew. But it was likely that someone else knew. There was no such thing as the perfect crime. There was always a flaw and the trick was finding it.

THE THRILL of seeing his handiwork written about in the newspaper had worn off. He had taped *The News* and watched the two PSNI officers begging for help from the public. They were stumped, which only showed how smart he was. He had left no clues and that had forced them to beg the public to do their work for them. The sheriff in the US who had turned down a candidate because he was 'too smart to be a cop' had it right. Most cops were as thick as two short planks. He had gone on the Internet and looked up the two officers who appeared on the news. The male one was a macho former rugby player. Some idiot had written an article on Wikipedia saying how smart he was, and how many murderers he'd caught. You're not so smart now, Mr Macho Rugby Player, otherwise you wouldn't be out there belittling yourself by showing everyone that you know nothing. You haven't even discovered that Carmody is missing.

He'd posted a note to the journalist on the *Chronicle*. He'd used his computer and printer, and worn gloves when he touched the paper and envelope. The message was simple: 'Whyte isn't the only one.' It should have been delivered today. He looked forward to watching them on TV again, hoping for help to locate Carmody. Good luck with that. Some day he would tell Dr Rose how smart he was. He wondered if she would abide by doctor–patient confidentiality. If not, he could always kill her.

It was nearing five o'clock and McDevitt was finishing up a column for the next edition of the *Chronicle*. He hadn't made the front page in weeks. Every day there was something new about Brexit and the impact on the border between Northern Ireland and the Irish Republic. He was sick and tired of the posturing politicians on all sides. One developed red lines that couldn't be crossed and the next developed blood-red lines in a stupid game of one-upmanship. The border had the same status for the people on either side of it as the Berlin Wall had had for Germans. The old border marked by blockhouses, barriers and customs men checking cars had disappeared without a whimper and to the delight of all but the most bigoted Unionists. Now it was raising its ugly head again. Everyone in the province knew what happened the last time there was a border. Nobody wanted to go back there.

McDevitt's present concern was how to get his byline back on the front page. It might give a boost to the flagging sales of his book on the Cummerford affair. He shuffled the papers on his desk and the white envelope that had been clinging precariously to the edge finally fell off. He picked it up and looked at the postmark. 'Who put this on my desk?' he shouted above the noise of the newsroom. Nobody answered, which was what he should have expected. He felt the envelope to see if there was anything bulky inside. It was a stupid precaution. The local terrorists didn't send letter bombs, if they wanted to blow you up, they did a proper job using a couple of kilos of Semtex.

He opened the top of the envelope with a silver letter opener his wife had given him on their first anniversary. It was the only anniversary present she'd ever given him as their marriage hadn't lasted two years. He pointed the opening away from him and let the single sheet of paper tumble out. He shook the envelope but the sheet of paper was all it contained. He used the letter opener to prise the folded edges of the paper apart and pressed the paper against the desk. He read the message. He put his fingers to his lips and let out a shrill whistle. 'Get a photographer over here pronto.' The protocol was that letters like this had to be handed over to the authorities immediately. But a picture and his accompanying article would force Brexit and the border off the front page. He looked up to see one of the junior photographers rushing towards him.

He pressed a button on his mobile phone and when it was answered said, 'Ian, I think you should come over here immediately. I have something important to show you.'

CHAPTER FORTY-EIGHT

'The arrogant bastard.' Wilson sat in McDevitt's office chair, aware that half the people in the newsroom were staring at him. The single sheet of paper was on the desk, the two diagonal corners pinned down with blocks of yellow Post-it notes.

'It's genuine?' McDevitt said.

'This happens when we put out a call for information. Harry Graham once fielded a call from a woman in Glengormley who said that the aliens living in her kitchen cabinets had done it.'

'Does that mean there isn't another guy missing?'

'Not as far as we know.'

'You lie with the aplomb of a politician.'

Wilson had put on his latex gloves and picked up and folded the letter before replacing it in the envelope and dropping it into a plastic evidence bag. He popped the bag into his pocket. He watched McDevitt's lips curl as he suppressed a smile. 'I know you've taken a copy of this letter, which runs contrary to the agreement between the police and the press on evidence. If you print a story, we'll deny its veracity and you'll be embarrassed – if that's possible. If you play ball, you might have a follow-up book.' He saw the dilemma play out on McDevitt's face. 'By the end of the day, we'll have a good two-dozen decent leads to follow.' He tapped his pocket. 'The world is full of eejits who have nothing to do but screw around in something that's not their business. But we'll check it out.'

'What's the news from the Police Ombudsman's Office?'

'Nothing official yet, but I'm reliably informed that no action will be taken.'

'The boys in Castlereagh must be mighty relieved. But what about you? The person who wants you dead is still out there somewhere.'

Wilson kept his face blank. 'Probably licking his wounds; these guys don't like failure.'

'Aye. I've been asking around Ballymacarrett, and the picture that emerges is very confusing, too bloody confusing. I think there might be more chance of a follow-up book there. Keeping the letter under my hat is a big ask.'

'I'll be in touch.' He needed to get back to the station.

Moira was examining images covering Howard Street. They had already found an image of Whyte and Heavey leaving the restaurant. The two men had paused at the door for about a minute before Whyte moved off towards the City Hall and Heavey left in the opposite direction. They would have to download video from most of the cameras in central Belfast and put together a sequence following Whyte. It wouldn't be easy and it certainly would not be enjoyable, but at least this time they had a computer wizard working alongside them. She had never expected police work to be as exciting as American TV shows make it out to be, but this really was tedious work. Nobody liked checking through hundreds of hours of CCTV, listening to the ramblings of lonely people on the confidential line, knocking on doors and scrabbling around trying to find clues. But at least they were doing something.

She looked across the room at Browne. His eyes stared forward and there was a vacant look on his face. He'd screwed up, but with luck he'd get over it. She had a fair idea what was going on inside his head because she'd been there. When things hadn't worked out with her husband, she'd hit a wall of depression and hadn't been able to pull herself out. Things only got better when she took herself to the local police station and turned the abusive bastard in. She hoped that Browne had enough resilience to ride out this rough patch.

Wilson handed the letter over to FSNI to check for fingerprints. He knew it was pointless. The envelope would be covered in them but none would belong to the sender and the letter inside would be pristine. McDevitt had opened the envelope with care and swore that he hadn't handled the contents. There was a time when envelopes had to be licked and so DNA could be extracted from the seal, but modern envelopes only required the pulling of a tab to seal them.

They now knew that Whyte and Carmody were victims of the same killer. A secondary fact was that the killer wanted his handiwork recognised. He, or she, had probably been following the media coverage that Whyte had received. The letter was an attempt to push disclosure of Carmody's disappearance. Wilson would not oblige. But he judged it safe to declare Whyte's disappearance as a murder inquiry. He wondered how far the killer would go if they didn't play ball with him. McDevitt would resist the temptation to publish the story of the letter for now, but his resistance had a history of crumbling.

CHAPTER FORTY-NINE

Wilson looked at the whiteboard. A photo of Whyte and Heavey parting company on Howard Street was the only change since early morning. The team members were lounging at their desks. Like much of life, a murder investigation has a three-act structure. Act one is the crime, act two is the hustle and bustle of the investigation and act three winds the investigation up. The most important act is the middle one. It is also where all the hard work is done and where motivation drops. Moira and O'Neill were red-eyed and lethargic from staring at screens all day. Graham looked like he needed a drink and Browne sat slumped in his chair with his arms folded, staring into space. Wilson briefed them on the letter. 'It's from the killer, and I'm assuming he's trying to show us how clever he is. We must play the game a little by his rules. We have no alternative. That's what makes the CCTV and the public appeals so important.'

'We're doing our best, boss,' Moira said. 'We've interviewed all Whyte's acquaintances. It doesn't look like someone targeted him so we're probably looking for someone he met by chance. It's the kind of case that ends up going nowhere.' She knew that motiveless crimes are the hardest to solve. They teach every young police recruit about motive, means and opportunity, but the most important is motive.

'We bring it as far as we can,' Wilson said. 'I know it's hard, but we have to keep following the leads. Tomorrow a man walking his dog might stumble across the body of Whyte or Carmody or both and then the odds turn in our favour. So, let's have everybody back here nice and fresh tomorrow.' The looks on the faces of the team showed they thought he was talking bullshit but part of his job description read 'motivate staff' and experience told him the guy who had written the letter wasn't finished killing.

Wilson was in need of a little motivation himself, but Davis was attending an important meeting at HQ so he would have to look for it elsewhere. He called Reid and her assistant informed him that the professor was giving a lecture until six. Wilson texted her to meet him at the usual location as soon as possible.

THE SUN WAS STILL BEATING down and the air was hot when Wilson left the station. He'd heard that Northern Ireland was hotter than the Algarve. There has to a first time for everything. He had at least another hour before Reid would be free. There was no point in heading for the Crown because the tourists would be busy photographing every square inch of the pub and the snugs would be crammed. He wasn't ready for any of that. Instead, he walked along the Shankill towards the city centre. From North Street, he turned left onto Union Street and proceeded to his destination on Donegall Street.

Northern Ireland had come a long way in terms of respect for people's sexual orientation, but there was still a long way to go. The Scottish Plantation of Ulster in the seventeenth century had brought a strict Presbyterian brand of Protestantism that was still plain in Ulster life. Northern Ireland was the only part of the United Kingdom that forbade gay marriage, and there was a section of the population who wanted homosexuals and lesbians jailed.

Wilson stood in front of the Kremlin cocktail lounge. A set of gates constructed of vertical iron bars were open wide on each side of the entrance. Above, a statue of Lenin towered over him. He climbed the stairs and entered the bar. Thankfully there wasn't a tourist or a mobile phone in sight. Inside was gay chic; red was the dominant colour and fluorescent lighting backlit the whole expanse. It couldn't have been further from the stained wood and brass old-world look of the Crown. Wilson noted that only a few booths were occupied. He supposed it would be a different story later in the evening. He sat on a bar stool and laid his warrant card on the bar when the barman approached.

'I'll get the manager,' the barman said.

'Don't bother, it's not an unofficial visit. Pint of whatever you think I should have.'

The barman returned with a pint of fancy continental lager.

Wilson sipped. 'Not bad.'

'But you'd prefer Guinness.'

Wilson nodded. 'Did you know Roger Whyte?'

'He's one of our regulars. I saw you on the news yesterday. People are talking.'

'What are they saying?'

'That the public acceptance of the gay lifestyle is only skin deep here. That there are still many people who discriminate against gays.'

'Discrimination is a crime. They should go to the police.'

'You guys don't take gays seriously.'

'Not true; one of my officers is gay. There are a lot of gay police officers. If I remember well, they marched in the last Gay Pride parade. Was Whyte in here around the twelfth?'

'If he was and I remembered, I would have contacted you. The press conference yesterday has put people on edge.'

'We haven't established a motive yet for Whyte's disappearance.'

'When you're sure, put it on the wire, until then our regulars will go on thinking that it has to do with him being gay.'

'Was he popular?'

'He liked to splash the cash, and anyone who does that is popular. But behind the cash, I think he was quiet.'

Wilson put a five-pound note on the bar.

'That'll be six pounds fifty please.'

Wilson whistled and fished out two one-pound coins and put them on top of the five. 'Keep the change.'

'Thank you, sir, that's very generous of you.'

BROWNE HAD SPENT the day brooding at his desk. He had hoped Wilson would have felt able to flaunt convention and keep him on the Whyte and Carmody investigation. The letter to McDevitt confirmed the two disappearances were connected, and since the only thing the two men had in common was their sexual orientation, the motive was becoming clear. Except that no one wanted to admit that someone was going around Belfast murdering gays. Wilson might have taken him off the case, but he could still spend his spare time looking for the killer. He had all the information that the team had and one advantage besides, he moved easily in the gay community. There would be a lot of doors closed to the investigating team that would be open to him. He would start this evening. It would probably come to nothing, but it was worth a try.

CHAPTER FIFTY

The tourists had drifted off to have their dinner and the Crown was a more inviting place thanks to their absence. Reid was already sitting in a snug and working on a gin and tonic when he arrived.

He ordered a drink, kissed her and sat. 'I've just had a pint of some fancy lager in Kremlin.'

'It's about time you came out.'

He told her about the letter sent to McDevitt.

'Do you think it's genuine?'

'I don't know. It might be a dingbat trying to mess us around. I hope I convinced Jock to hold off publishing it.'

'Good luck with that.'

'How was work?'

'You cut up one body, you've cut up them all. I read an article about a colleague who suffered from PTSD. He reckoned he'd cut up twenty-three thousand bodies, so I did a count of my own. I stopped when I reached five thousand, and considered what was ahead of me. Another eighteen thousand might qualify me to become a basket case.'

'You do a very important job and you're good at it.' He took her hand. 'Is it possible your mood has something to do with the death of your mother?'

'I suppose there's something niggling at the back of my mind about mortality and what the hell we're doing here. It's strange that someone who has been dealing with death for half her life should be so affected by one particular death.'

'I thought I'd never get over my father's death. I still have vivid recollections of his funeral, the coffin being lowered into the grave. I had a lot to live for, but I would have joined him that day. The pain was so intense. It eases though and we find the strength to go on. We accept and that closes the cycle.'

'I'm a doctor, dickhead, you don't have to explain the cycle of grief to me. Just keep supporting me.'

He kissed her. 'Always.'

His phone rang and he looked at the caller ID. 'Good evening, chief superintendent.'

'Bad news,' Davis said. 'Another press conference tomorrow, this one to be attended by the chief constable. We're both required.'

'Whyte?'

'It looks like DS McElvaney threw the fear of God into some poor gay bastard.'

'Sounds like her.'

'You two are quite a pair, you were made for each other. Anyway, Dr Heavey contacted the LGBT Coalition and said that he didn't think the police were taking Mr Whyte's disappearance seriously. They got on the phone to the chief constable to report the feeling among the LGBT community that Whyte was targeted because of his sexual orientation. The press conference is at midday and we're due in the chief's office at a quarter to. Thought I'd give you a heads up. You've spoiled my evening so why shouldn't I spoil yours.'

'Any sign of Jack?'

The line went dead.

'Trouble?' Reid asked.

'Nothing we can't handle. If we put it out that two gay men are missing, there'll be a panic in the gay community. If we keep quiet about the second missing man and someone else goes missing, we have a problem.'

She finished her drink. 'Let's get an Indian takeaway and a bottle of red, kick off our shoes and binge on the *Bodyguard*.'

He stood. 'Sounds like a plan.'

MOIRA SWITCHED on her printer and brought up her folder of website documents mentioning Helen McCann. There wasn't a lot of room in her cramped studio, but she had found space for a whiteboard and had already tacked a picture of McCann on the top. She had reread the Carlisle file a half-dozen times. She couldn't believe that one of Ulster's leading citizens had organised a murder, but the evidence was there. What was even more frightening was that a serving officer in the Special Branch of the PSNI had murdered Carlisle at McCann's behest. McCann intrigued her and there was ninety per cent of the information iceberg yet to be uncovered. She downloaded a document and hit the print key. Her ultimate aim was to get inside the skin of Helen McCann by tracking her from birth to the present day.

BROWNE WAS out on the town. If the motive for the disappearances of Whyte and Carmody was their sexual orientation, then the answer would most likely be found in the close-knit gay community. This closeness was a legacy of having to exist in secret until relatively recently. Northern Ireland had been the last part of the United Kingdom to legalise same-sex sexual activity, and to end a lifetime ban on blood donation by men who have sex with men. The Save Ulster from Sodomy political campaign had driven the gay community further underground.

Browne was on a mission to redeem himself in the eyes of his superior, but he also saw his unofficial investigation as a test of his ability to be a police officer. He spent the evening drinking at several gay establishments. Everyone he encountered knew about Whyte's disappearance, and there was a detectable level of concern that it might be motivated by his sexual orientation. By eleven o'clock, he had hit all the major gay pubs and had drunk a good deal more than he was accustomed to. He'd been propositioned twice but he declined. It was time to head home. His first foray may not have uncovered anything relevant to the investigation, but he wasn't about to give up after just one night.

HE WAS ANNOYED that there was no mention on the TV news of the *Chronicle* having received his letter and there was also no reference to Whyte either. Why? Whyte's disappearance should be a major story; HE should be a major story. The police must have suppressed it.

Maybe he shouldn't have hidden the bodies so well. He could always dig Whyte up. The body would be nice and ripe by now, with maggots crawling out of every orifice. He'd been careful, but there would still be DNA on the body. No, Whyte can stay where he is. There's another way to keep the public interested in his activities. Someone else will have to die.

CHAPTER FIFTY-ONE

The fine weather had broken with overnight rain. The path along the Lagan was slick as Wilson pounded his way along his usual route. A cover of low grey clouds hung over the city and the air was charged with rain. The farmers' prayers were being answered. There were few joggers out and as he neared the turn, Wilson was aware of feet splashing behind him. He felt a moment's apprehension. What if there was still a price on his head? The feet behind sped up and he moved to the left in anticipation of being overtaken.

'Rotten start to the day.'

Wilson recognised the voice. 'Where the hell have you been?'

Duane pulled level and they ran together, matching strides. 'I thought it might be better if I didn't come to the station. I went to the Crown last night, but you'd already left.'

'Why did you drop off the radar?'

'I had to make some arrangements, and then I heard about the Ombudsman's investigation here. I figured it might be politic to keep a low profile and absent myself from Belfast.'

'The words Jack Duane and politic don't go together.'

'I hear they've cleared you.'

'It was tricky. The investigator, a guy called Matthews, wasn't a pushover. And let's be honest, the PSNI cover story was constructed out of gossamer. The more I had to repeat it the more I saw the flaws.'

'All's well that ends well though.'

Wilson slowed to a walk. 'It's not over, Jack. I need to see the ballistic report on Brennan.'

'No problem, the bullets taken from his body were from a Smith and Wesson 38. We've identified the gun as a weapon used in another gangland killing.'

'What the fuck are you talking about? Either you or I shot that guy.'

'I'll send you the ballistics report. Maybe that will put your mind at rest.'

Wilson looked into Duane's eyes. 'How can you live like that?'

'Someone has to deal with the shit end of the stick. Would you have preferred if it had been you on the autopsy table?'

Wilson didn't reply.

'I thought so. I'm in Belfast with someone I met at Quantico. You know the way we say things like "if you're ever in Ireland, drop in and I'll show you around" and we don't really mean it. Well this guy took me up on it and I've spent the past four days showing him Connemara and Kerry. Today we're off to the Giant's Causeway and Dunluce Castle. He's a *Game of Thrones* nut. I've taken about as much of him as I can, so I want you and Steph to join us this evening for dinner, my treat.'

'Why am I sceptical about dinner with you and some guy from Quantico?'

'No hidden agenda.'

'Why don't I believe you?'

Duane ran and Wilson joined him. They escalated their

pace until they were sprinting. People on the path moved aside as the two men ran at full tilt. After a hundred and fifty metres they slowed.

'You're not bad for an old man.' Duane bent with his hands on his knees and pulled in great gulps of air.

'Not so much of the old man.' Wilson's chest heaved.

'Seven-thirty at Deanes.' Duane turned and jogged back towards the city.

WILSON BRIEFED the team on the upcoming press conference. There was nothing new on the confidential line, the report on the house-to-house on Broadway had come in negative and a couple of new CCTV disks had arrived. Carmody was a difficult man to track. Unlike Whyte, who stuck to the same weekly agenda, Carmody was like a free electron wandering all over the city. None of his neighbours could pinpoint when they had seen him last. He came and he went, where and when were mysteries. The investigation was becoming stalled. Browne was looking even more morose than he did the previous day.

At eleven-thirty, Wilson joined Davis and they went to HQ. CC Baird was alone when they were shown to his office.

Baird shook hands with Davis and nodded at Wilson. 'Any news?'

Wilson shook his head.

'We only have a few minutes,' Baird said. 'I'll announce that the search for Roger Whyte is now a murder inquiry.' He saw that Wilson was about to interrupt and put his hand up. 'I know, we don't have a body so technically he's still missing. But we all know there's little or no chance of finding him alive.'

'If he turns up, we'll look like fools,' Wilson said.

'I'll take that risk,' Baird said. 'You're our top murder man, do you think he will turn up?'

'No, I don't,' Wilson admitted.

'Jeffrey Carrington, the President of the Northern Ireland branch of the LGBT Coalition will join us. I'll speak first, then he'll say a few words and you two will handle the questions. Understood?'

Davis and Wilson nodded.

'Then let's do it.' Baird picked up his cap from his desk and placed it on his head.

Wilson thought that Baird made an imposing figure in full uniform.

Carrington, who turned out to be a prematurely bald thirty-something-year-old with a neatly trimmed moustache and goatee, was waiting outside the office and joined the procession downstairs in Baird's wake. The female constable who had led the previous press conference opened the door to the briefing room just as Baird and his entourage reached it. The CC led the way to the podium and sat in the centre seat, facing a barrage of microphones and recording devices set on a table. Two TV cameras were filming from the rear of the room. Baird motioned for Davis to take the seat on his left, Carrington sat to his right and Wilson took the vacant seat beside Davis. The constable did her introductory patter and handed over the microphone to Baird.

'Good afternoon, ladies and gentlemen,' Baird began. 'I'll be brief. You all know that we held a press conference here two days ago expressing our concern for the safety of Roger Whyte, who has been missing for about one month. I want to announce that we are upgrading this investigation from that of a missing person to murder. Detective Superintendent Wilson will be the senior investigating officer and I can think of no more capable officer on my force. His extraordinary record speaks for itself. I want to make one further point. The PSNI treats every investigation on its merits. There is no attempt to discriminate victims by race, gender, creed or sexual orientation. I would like to hand over now to Mr Jeffrey Carrington of the LGBT Coalition.'

Carrington didn't stand but cleared his throat and leaned towards the microphone. 'Good afternoon. Many of you will not know that Roger Whyte is a gay man. Unfortunately, and contradictory to what the chief constable has just said, the PSNI does not take seriously victims of crime who are members of the LGBT community. Roger Whyte has been missing for a month and only now are we seeing some significant action from the police. This situation is not unique to the province but is paralleled on the mainland. I am here today to express the disquiet of the whole LGBT community that there may well be a sexual motivation to Roger Whyte's disappearance. Thank you.' He sat back.

'Questions?' Baird asked.

McDevitt had his arm in the air even before Baird spoke. Baird pointed at him.

'A question for the SIO,' McDevitt said. 'Does the PSNI believe that there is a sexual motive for Whyte's disappearance, and now possible homicide?'

Baird looked at Wilson.

'We are keeping an open mind regarding possible motivations for Mr Whyte's disappearance. Roger Whyte was a wealthy man and that might also be the motive behind his disappearance and possible murder,' Wilson responded.

'Are there any other related cases?' McDevitt said.

'Not at the moment.' Wilson sometimes felt like strangling Jock.

Baird pointed at a female journalist, who asked about Whyte's mother. Wilson answered and saw Baird look at his watch. The constable picked up a microphone and professionally closed the proceedings.

Baird shook hands with Carrington. 'My office,' he said to Davis and Wilson. As soon as they entered the office, Baird removed his cap and tossed it on the desk. 'What was McDevitt up to in there?'

Davis and Wilson looked at each other. Wilson knew that he was being passed the ball. He explained the situation of the letter McDevitt had received 'That's the problem with making a call to the public for help. All sorts of characters creep out from under their rocks.'

'Don't snow me,' Baird said. 'Is there someone else missing?'

'It appears so,' Wilson said. 'But we have no reason to connect the two disappearances. Whyte was wealthy, the second man was as close to a pauper as you can get.'

'Is the second man gay?' Baird asked.

'Yes,' Wilson said. 'He was reputedly a gay prostitute.'

'But he'd no arrests or convictions,' Davis added.

Baird sat behind his desk. 'How high is the possibility that someone, or some group, is targeting gay men?'

'It's a possibility,' Wilson said. 'But so far we have no clear evidence to connect Whyte and Carmody.'

'People like Carrington have made the connection. And we're not dealing with an unfortunate case of gay bashing. It looks like men are being murdered. We need to get a handle on this and quick. I do not want people out on the streets waving banners.'

'Ian and his team are doing their best,' Davis said.

'Whatever you need, you have it,' Baird said.

There was a knock on the door and Baird's PA stuck her head around the corner.

'I know,' he said. He stood, picked up his hat and turned to Davis. 'I want a daily briefing.' He led the way from the office.

'JACK'S IN TOWN,' Wilson said when they sat in the rear of Davis's car.

'I know, we spent the night together. He's squiring some American psychologist around.'

'He's invited Steph and me to dinner, but I thought the visitor was a copper from Quantico.'

'He is from Quantico, but he's not a copper. What will you do about Whyte?'

He looked her in the face. 'Pray for a break.'

'Then we must pray together.'

CHAPTER FIFTY-TWO

Wilson leaned over O'Neill's shoulder. Unlike the grainy images of yesteryear, these images on screen were clear enough to see the pimples on noses. 'Run me through what you've got.'

O'Neill's fingers flew over the keys. 'This is Whyte and Heavey leaving Deanes at three o'clock. They talk for a few minutes and then leave in opposite directions. I picked Whyte up on Royal Avenue, heading towards CastleCourt shopping centre. I've asked the security at CastleCourt for their CCTV footage. I'm also looking at the CCTV we have from our own cameras that cover the exits. It's slow, but we'll get there.'

He looked over at Moira and saw that she was watching them. 'Anything?'

Moira shook her head.

The pressure was ratcheting up and he had no idea how to push the investigation forward. Graham was on the phone. Answering calls was a waste of time for a trained detective. Wilson decided to test Baird's offer of additional help and ask for some first-year detective from one of the other stations to man the phone. He could find something more productive for Graham to do. If there really is a killer out there, he has murdered two men and hidden their bodies without leaving a trace.

He went back to his office and emailed Baird to request the additional person for the duration of the investigation.

BROWNE COULD NOT STOP THINKING about how he had screwed up. He also questioned the wisdom of his plan to involve himself in the investigation through his nocturnal manoeuvres. He was a bookworm and had read the PSNI manual from cover to cover. He knew there were severe penalties associated with launching your own private investigation. His behaviour was erratic at best and downright stupid at worst. Being found out would probably end his PSNI career. Perhaps that was his ultimate aim. Maybe it wasn't about Whyte or Carmody, maybe it was about him and the PSNI. Across the room, Graham was exploding into the phone. He imagined the idiots he had to listen to. Moira and O'Neill were watching hours of CCTV. It was mind-numbingly boring, but they hadn't flinched from their tasks. He knew everyone was feeling the pressure, but they were sticking to their jobs like good police officers; everyone except for him.

Graham slammed the phone onto the cradle and rubbed his forehead.

'Nothing stirring?' Browne walked over to Graham's desk.

'If people are lonely, they should call the Samaritans. It's always the same when we ask the public to respond. I should record the crazies and write a book about them. This last guy claims he knew for certain that Whyte's wife was responsible for his disappearance. I told him Whyte didn't have a wife, but he insisted he was a psychic and he'd had a message from her confessing. And he was a half-sensible one.'

'Tea?'

'Why not? The operator will take the calls while I'm away.'

. . .

BROWNE PUT two cups of tea on the cafeteria table and sat down. 'It's going nowhere fast.'

'We'll get a lead. It only needs someone to call about something strange that they saw, or maybe they heard a guy boasting about getting rid of Whyte.' Graham put milk and sugar in his tea and sipped. 'It's like the old days when a ship was becalmed. A wind always springs up eventually and the ship sails again. When we get a lead, the boss will be after it like a ferret down a rabbit hole.'

'Have you seen the report on the door-to-door at Carmody's place?'

Graham nodded. 'A big chunk of nothing.'

'Was there any mention of a girl having asked Carmody to buy drugs for her a few weeks ago?'

Graham's brow furrowed. 'No, and if there had been I would have been surprised. Nobody would tell something like that to a uniform.'

He supposed Graham was right. If they had found her, perhaps she would have described a man who came looking for Carmody. Then he would be in the frame.

WILSON CALLED the team together at five o'clock. He briefed them on the press conference. 'It is now officially a murder inquiry. It would be helpful to have a body and a crime scene, but we have neither.' The only change to the whiteboard was a photo of Whyte walking alone along Royal Avenue. 'I know you're all frustrated because so am I. But we can't invent evidence. We must dig harder to get it. We don't know whether we're looking for a single killer or a group. The possibilities are endless and we have to exclude them one by one. There's a hell of a lot of work ahead, so let's all go home and hope that we'll catch a break tomorrow.'

CHAPTER FIFTY-THREE

Wilson and Reid watched the evening news, then dressed and went into town. He wasn't in the humour for a dinner party, but it was a chance for Reid to get her glad rags on. She was returning to her old self. The change was barely perceptible, but it was there. The fact that she cut up dead people for a living hadn't really helped the grieving process. They rolled up fifteen minutes after the appointed time to find Duane gesticulating at them from the body of a full restaurant. As a senior officer, Wilson was sometimes obliged to host visiting senior police officers. Since most of them were men and sports fans, the evening centred on his locker-room stories. Hosting a psychologist for four days would be his equivalent of eating broken glass. He sensed how Duane felt by the frantic signals he was making to get their attention.

Duane jumped to his feet as they approached and threw his arms around Reid, planting wet kisses on both her cheeks.

Wilson smiled at Duane's obvious relief. He'd been there.

Duane's guest stood and proffered his hand to Wilson. 'Tad Mezrich.'

Wilson shook. 'Ian Wilson.'

Duane released Reid and introduced her to Mezrich, who Wilson noticed held her hand a little too long. Mezrich was in his forties and had a full head of blond hair. He would be considered attractive, with full lips, blue eyes and an oval face.

'Well. Tad,' Wilson said when they were seated. 'How are you enjoying Ireland?'

'It's been great and Jack knows so many interesting people.'

I bet he does, Wilson thought. He examined his menu.

'What do you do at Quantico?' Reid asked.

'I'm a clinical psychologist, so I work at the interface between the law and psychology. Most of the problems with building cases arise from assessing witness statements. I train police officers to interview properly and to elicit information.'

'How interesting,' Reid said. 'I've always been interested in psychology.'

Mezrich beamed. An interest from Reid had that effect on men.

'Tad is also an expert on serial killers,' Duane said. 'He'd keep you enthralled for hours with stories about Jeffrey Dahmer and John Wayne Gacy.'

'Is that so,' Wilson said.

'I spent several years as a profiler,' Mezrich said.

'I suspect Ian doesn't believe in profilers,' Duane said.

The waiter arrived and they ordered.

'I prefer old-fashioned police work,' Wilson said when the waiter departed.

'Well then, let's have some fun,' Mezrich said. 'Are you working on a murder case at the moment?'

'Yes, several as it happens,' Wilson said.

Mezrich looked at Reid. 'I hope I won't bore you?'

Reid smiled. 'Not if it's about living people.'

'Let's have the details of one.' Mezrich took a pen from his jacket pocket and spread his serviette on the table.

Wilson went through the Whyte and Carmody disappearances and Mezrich took notes.

'That's one to baffle Sherlock Holmes,' Mezrich said when Wilson finished.

The food had arrived during Wilson's story and they were all eating. Wilson wished that Mezrich had been a rugby fan, going through his repertoire of rugby stories would have been easier.

'I can see your problem,' Mezrich said. He was ignoring the plate in front of him. 'You have no hard evidence. The bodies haven't turned up and probably won't. There's no forensic and you have no suspect, so where do you go with traditional police work? You've looked at possible motives and you've struck out. Do you think the two disappearances are connected?'

'I don't believe in coincidences.'

'So, you think there's a serial killer out there,' Mezrich said. 'Any connected cases in other cities?'

Wilson shook his head. 'We've already checked with the National Crime Agency and there's nothing at the moment. Are you ready to look into your crystal ball and tell us who the killer is?'

Mezrich laughed. 'If I were able, that would be great. We can make some assumptions though. Let's say someone has murdered both men. The only factor common to both men is their homosexuality. So, it's safe to assume that's the reason someone chose them. Whyte had no known enemies, so he's a random victim, and let's assume that Carmody is as well. This means the murderer is killing for killing's sake. You've been looking into both men's lives?'

Wilson nodded as the waiter came to clear away the dishes.

'You're wasting your time,' Mezrich said. 'It's my guess that both men were targets of opportunity.'

'We've already been over this ground,' Wilson said.

'I'm sure you have. When Jack told me we were meeting you tonight, I looked you up and I know you're no beginner. But your traditional approach won't work this time.'

'Tell me about the murderer,' Wilson said.

Mezrich turned to Reid. 'I looked you up too, only your photos don't do you justice. It's a terrible waste that we have spent the evening speaking about Ian's case while ignoring a beautiful woman.'

'What about Jack?' Reid asked. 'Doesn't he count?'

'I think Jack has probably had enough of me by now,' Mezrich said. 'I understand that you're a professor as well as a practitioner. I bet when you get switched on to pathology, you can't be stopped. That's the way I am with the psychology of crime.'

'I don't feel at all left out,' Reid said.

Duane ordered the coffees.

'He's most likely a homosexual himself,' Mezrich said. 'Probably one who was abused in puberty. There's a psychological theory that suggests that people who rebel against a societal norm are pathologically predisposed to violence. That can include homosexuals, alcoholics and drug addicts. I'm not a great believer in this theory, although a number of serial killers are homosexuals and prey on homosexuals. One of the oldest questions in criminology, and for that fact in philosophy, law and theology, is whether criminals are born or made.' Three faces stared at him. 'Don't look at me for an answer. It's central to the human survival mechanism that we have this capacity to kill. Killers are holdovers whose primal instincts are not being moderated by the more intellectual parts of their brain.'

'Where are we going with this?' Wilson asked.

'I'm sorry,' Mezrich said. 'I get carried away. What I suppose I'm trying to do is dance around your problem. I can't point at him directly, but maybe I can help you recognise him when you meet him. Your murderer might well be an un-fully socialised person with the capacity to kill, and tacked on to that capacity is a sexually aggressive impulse most likely developed at puberty. Many people may exhibit these traits, but your murderer has acted on his feelings. He is a psychopath and will exhibit a lack of empathy. He needs to lie, is bored easily and is narcissistic.'

'I'm no nearer to catching him,' Wilson said.

'But you are closer to seeing who he might be,' Mezrich said. 'Has there ever been a gay serial killer in Northern Ireland before?'

'No. But we've had plenty of killers who have displayed the traits you've outlined,' Wilson said. 'But when questioned they gave the preservation of some outdated ideology as their motive. I didn't buy it.'

'There have been dozens of gay serial killers in the States,' Mezrich said. 'Mainly in the 1960s and 70s, when there was a stigma attached to being gay. In repressive societies, gay serial killers are more effective because they and their victims are living secret double lives. They are already acclimatised to clandestine behaviour and covering up what they are.'

'It's an unfortunate fact that the LGBT community is still stigmatised here,' Reid said. 'Religion may have caused that stigma.'

The waiter arrived with the bill and Duane paid.

'It's been an interesting evening.' Wilson stood.

'You ever been to Quantico, Ian?' Mezrich said.

'No. Quantico is for people like Jack.'

'I'll send you some details of our courses. And you can bring Stephanie along.'

They shook and Wilson and Reid left. He put his arm around her shoulder as they walked down Howard Street.

'Feeling possessive?' she said. 'I never considered you the jealous type.'

'He couldn't take his eyes off you.'

'Afraid I'll run away with him?'

He stopped and held her. 'No, just afraid you'll run away.'

She kissed him. 'One thing I've learned about fear is that it's pointless to be afraid about something that might happen. You get afraid when it's happening.'

'I fancy a nightcap.' They started walking again.

'Funny, so do I.'

CHAPTER FIFTY-FOUR

Less than a mile away from Wilson, the man who had murdered Roger Whyte and Vincent Carmody was drinking a Bloody Mary and watching a drag act in the Maverick Bar. He scanned the crowd searching for a likely candidate. Most of the men were accompanied. He was feeling apprehensive. The Whyte and Carmody killings were perfectly executed. He had studied forensics and was sure he hadn't left a trace. He could be putting everything in jeopardy by reacting viscerally to not receiving the credit he was due. He had beaten the police and he wanted them to admit it. He was smarter than them. Smarter than the macho rugby-playing detective they had put in charge of the case. He had watched his recording of the police press conference repeatedly and hated that there was no mention of Carmody. He scanned the crowd again. They were laughing their heads off at a man dressed like a woman telling smutty jokes, pathetic cretins.

Browne had met one of the first friends he'd made in the gay community and they were drinking and enjoying the Maverick's drag show. He almost forgot that he was supposed to be looking for a killer. There were over sixty men in the small bar. Any of them might be the man who had spirited Whyte and Carmody away. He was realising the futility of his decision to play the Lone Ranger. He burst out laughing off cue and was conscious he was getting drunk. He cast an eye over the faces in the room. None of them had been kind enough to have 'Murderer' tattooed on their forehead. He felt his hand being covered and when he looked up his friend was smiling. The evening would end with them in bed together. It was the life they led. But it was no way to search for a killer.

CHAPTER FIFTY-FIVE

Wilson looked at his bedside clock. It was five minutes to three. He'd read a statistic somewhere that said a disproportionate number of people die at three o'clock in the morning. One of his former colleagues had suffered a stroke in bed at three o'clock and had been paralysed and unable to wake his wife. Wilson slipped out of bed, put on his bathrobe and made his way to the living room. The sky outside was dark, but the streetlights cast an orange glow that lit up the room. He sat at his desk and switched on the banker's lamp. He took out a notepad and pen from the drawer and laid them in front of him. The population of Belfast city is around 300,000. Assuming an even split of men and women, there are about 150,000 men in the city. He turned on his phone and found the website of the Office for National Statistics. For the UK as a whole, 1.5 per cent of the male population self-identified as homosexual. So, if he accepted Mezrich's primary theory that the killer was homosexual, the investigation's focus should be on the roughly 2,250 men in Belfast who are gay.

The PSNI had never dealt with a serial homosexual killer. At least, Wilson hadn't come across one. He had heard about the alleged London Underground serial killer Kieran Kelly, who had pushed his victims under trains. He was an alcoholic who hated alcoholics and a closet homosexual who despised homosexuals. The murders were apparently motiveless, just like the murders of Whyte and Carmody. According to Mezrich, he was looking for a homosexual, a narcissist, a psychopath who displays no empathy and a good liar who kills out of boredom. He would have to keep Mezrich's theory within the team.

The man from Quantico and Wilson were agreed on some points: solving the disappearances was almost impossible without finding the bodies, and if the crimes were motiveless, delving into the lives of Whyte and Carmody was a waste of time. The precepts of a police investigation are based on developing hypotheses relating to the motive, forensics, taking witness statements and identifying suspects. If any of those factors is missing, the difficulty of solving the crime increases. As long as the killer stuck to his modus operandi and didn't make a silly mistake, the province stood a chance of having its first real serial killer. It wasn't in Wilson's DNA to wait for the killer to make a mistake. Somehow or other he would have to concentrate the investigation on lines that stood a chance of producing results. Otherwise more innocent men would die. The room was bathed in light and he turned to see Reid standing at the entrance.

'I think a cup of cocoa is in order.' She moved to the kitchen, filled the kettle and pressed the switch.

Wilson joined her at the breakfast bar. 'I tried not to wake you.'

'I missed you in bed. We must be getting used to each other.' She ruffled his hair. 'And you won't catch this killer if you don't get your beauty sleep.'

'I don't think I'll catch this killer period.'

'It's not like you to be so pessimistic. They all get caught in the end.'

'I suppose that's why we have over one thousand unsolved murders in the province. This killer is very careful, or very lucky; in either case, if we don't stop him, more people will die. And our friend Mezrich wasn't much help.'

'You're only saying that because he fancied me.' The kettle boiled and she poured hot water into two mugs containing a liberal measure of cocoa. She handed one to Wilson.

'I'll recognise him when I see him.' He sipped the hot chocolate. 'What crap! If Mezrich is right and our killer is gay, I've worked out there are, at a minimum, over two thousand suspects in metropolitan Belfast. Whyte has been missing for a month, Carmody for at least two weeks. For any crime, if we don't have a suspect within the first forty-eight hours, the chances of finding the culprit tumble.'

'And as your doctor, I can tell you that losing sleep won't help you find your killer. Maybe it's not Whyte and Carmody's killer that keeps you up at night.'

'What do you mean?'

'For God's sake, Ian, somebody tried to kill you. Even in your macho world, that is a traumatic event. You should see a counsellor. And okay, they failed this time, but there's a good chance that they'll try again. This province lives on a knife-edge. We all like to believe that the trouble is in the past, but in our hearts we know it isn't. If it's Belfast or Northern Ireland that's responsible for someone trying to kill you, I want out.'

He saw she was on the point of tears. 'There's a cancer in this province and it isn't just the religious divide. There are people who foster division and who profit from the ruined lives of good decent people. And they are not above murder. That's how I think I might have inadvertently stumbled across them. I can't let them win.'

'Even if it costs you your life?'

He didn't answer.

She finished her cocoa. 'I'm going back to bed, but I doubt that I'll sleep.'

He drained his cup and put it in the sink. He took her hand and they walked back together to the bedroom. He was wondering whether he was part of the solution, or part of the problem.

CHAPTER FIFTY-SIX

Moira had been up into the small hours working on her Helen McCann dossier and then had had a long call with her friend and former colleague Jamie Carmichael in Boston. Her life was turning into a series of agonising decisions and recriminations. Her parents had been harsh on her when she had split from Brendan. What did she want? Brendan had offered her what ninety-nine per cent of people would consider a 'good life'. And she had turned her nose up at it, to quote her mother. Sitting at a vintage 1960s plastic-covered table in a dingy flat, she saw where her mother was coming from. She opened the file in front of her and took out a magazine photo of McCann's pad in the south of France. The house and grounds were stunning and had to be worth several millions. There were no plastic tables on view there. The wages of sin had provided McCann with an enviable lifestyle. This woman was at least guilty of murder and Moira wanted to bring her down. That wouldn't be easy.

She finished her breakfast and washed and put away the single dish she'd used. Her meal plan had changed since living alone. It was all about easy cooking and cleaning, but at least she wasn't gaining weight. She needed to get out more. Since arriving back in Belfast, she had become a monk. Work was an obsession, but it wouldn't always be there and it wouldn't keep her warm at night. A picture of Frank Shea floated through her mind. Maybe, she thought. Then she quickly banished that idea. She put away her file on McCann. She had another day of CCTV viewing ahead, plod, plod, plod.

BROWNE WOKE up in a strange bed. Thankfully he was alone. He dressed and was almost out the door when he ran into last night's lover holding a small brown bag.

'I popped out for croissants,' he said by way of explanation.

Browne brushed past. 'Sorry, I'm late for work.' He found himself in the University area and had a faint recollection of the taxi from the club. Although he must have been drunk the previous evening, he had no headache. But he was in need of a shower. He checked his watch. There was no time to go back to his flat. He felt uncomfortable turning up at work in last night's clothes. He popped into a chemist, bought a deodorant and sprayed himself liberally. He sniffed and smiled. He smelled like a whorehouse in Istanbul.

Something was happening to him that he didn't quite understand. Maybe it had to do with Moira's return to the squad or maybe it was about Whyte and Carmody. He'd sometimes wished Vinny dead, but really he was a harmless bastard. Now that he probably was dead, Browne castigated himself for having such evil thoughts. His nocturnal exploits were a way of atoning for how he felt about Vinny. It should have been something to do with his being a police officer, but he wasn't so sure.

THE TEAM ASSEMBLED before the whiteboard and Wilson gave them a potted version of his conversation with Mezrich. He had already written the characteristics that Mezrich had specified onto the board. Browne gave himself an imaginary clap on the back. He'd already worked them out. Perhaps he had the makings of a detective after all.

'We're still as much in the dark, boss,' Moira said. 'We can't put out that kind of character sketch. Aside from the gay connection, the other attributes are shared by most of the male population.'

'You move in limited circles,' Wilson said. 'Either that or you have a very poor opinion of men. Mezrich's observations are for team consideration only. I don't want the press to get wind of this. The forensic reports of Whyte's and Carmody's flats have turned up nothing of interest. We have lots of fingerprints. None of them are in the system. We don't have either man's mobile phone. Siobhan has logged in to Whyte's phone, which apparently he hardly ever used. Carmody's not on any system so he must have a burner phone.'

'So we're left with a hundred per cent of feck all,' Graham said. 'The confidential line hasn't produced anything either. It's a bust.'

'Someone out there has murdered two men for no clear reason other than their sexual orientation,' Wilson said. 'He may have satisfied his bloodlust, but my guess is that he's only just beginning. We're up against it. But we'll keep going until we find the thread that we can pull to unravel the story. We keep working the CCTV and listening to the crap that's coming in on the confidential line. This killer is a cold, ruthless bastard who will kill again. We have to stop him.'

Wilson closed his office door and sat down at his desk. He had got back to sleep for a few hours but nightmares still disturbed him. He and Reid had clung together as shipwreck survivors cling to flotsam. He knew that she was worried for him. He wasn't as nonchalant about the attempt on his life as he seemed. Helen McCann was a ruthless and resourceful foe.

All the evidence against her was circumstantial and a decent barrister would rip their case apart in court. There was a long way to go before Helen McCann would be standing in the dock. Right now, he needed to find the man who he was sure had killed two gay men. His computer pinged and a pop-up on his screen told him that he was late for the chief super's senior officers' meeting. He wasn't sure that he'd be able take a bull-shit session, but he didn't want to undermine Davis's authority by slacking off any time he felt like it. He picked up the file containing the papers that had been circulated for the meeting. He hadn't read any of them, but it didn't matter. He rarely contributed. He was drowning in an ocean of administration.

CHAPTER FIFTY-SEVEN

Wilson returned to the office just before lunch and checked in with the team. There was nothing new. He was angry about the two hours he'd spent listening to colleagues climbing up Davis's arse. Maybe Reid was right. He was a relic, a dinosaur whose time had passed. 'Organisation man' was dominating the force now, with the strange idea that it could solve all crime using computers and technology. Orwell's *1984* would soon be a reality. They were already standing on the threshold with one hand on the doorknob. His phone beeped and he looked at the message. It was a single word and a question mark: 'Lunch?' There was no caller ID, which meant Duane. He didn't know if he wanted to do this, but what the hell, at least it would be entertaining. He messaged back: 'Where?'

Duane was already halfway through a bowl of ramen when Wilson arrived in Obento.

'Where's your American sidekick?'

'Probably taking your missus to lunch.' Duane sucked in a noodle. He looked up and saw that Wilson was taking him seriously. 'I'm only kidding, although he sure took a shine to her. Strange fish.'

'He's a strange fish because he took a shine to her?' Wilson concentrated on the menu.

'Don't be an eejit. Any man still with a breath in his body would take a shine to Steph. I recommend the ramen followed by the eel and crab sushi.'

Wilson closed the menu. 'What are we doing here? You're telling me there's another hit on me?'

Duane took a paper from his inside pocket and put it on the table. 'A present.'

Wilson took up the paper and opened it. The face of Simon Jackson was visible through the windscreen of a black SUV. 'Where was this taken?'

A waitress arrived and Wilson followed Duane's recommendation on the ramen.

'Rosslare Ferry Terminal. We've got some new facial recognition software and we've been trying it out. I asked them to look for your guy. Took about an hour to run through all the passengers in the past six months.'

'Where was he heading?'

'France.'

The waitress returned with the ramen for Wilson and sushi for Duane.

'That's a coincidence.'

'Want to tell me about it.'

Wilson explained about the Carlisle investigation and Jackson's part in the murder. He left out Helen McCann's role.

'There have been rogue policemen since the job was created,' Duane said. 'Wyatt Earp was a lawman one day and an outlaw the next. A major contract killer turned out to be a New York cop. This Jackson guy seems like a right bastard, just perfect for Special Branch.'

'I thought you were Special Branch.'

'Good God no, I wouldn't be seen dead with that crowd.'

'I'll ask HQ to put a request in to Interpol.'

'It's difficult to hunt one of your own. He was smart enough to run and he'll have been trained to have a plan that won't involve him showing his face for a while. We've had dumb criminals who've stayed on the run for years.'

Wilson had a good idea where Jackson had gone to ground. You had to admire the swine for running to the one person who would have to take him in. Jackson would come to grief someday, and Wilson wanted to get him before that happened. He had to answer for almost killing Davidson.

'Steph is subdued these days.' Duane finished his sushi and pushed his plate away.

'Her mother's death hit her a lot harder than she'd expected. She's still working her way through the grief.'

'You guys ready to do something permanent?'

'How are things going with you and Davis?'

'Do you follow Gaelic football?'

'I've been to a few games.'

Duane waved at the waitress and called for the bill. 'I have two tickets for the all-Ireland football final in September. Why don't you and Steph take a break in Dublin?'

'Sounds like a fine idea.'

CHAPTER FIFTY-EIGHT

Moira and O'Neill were bent over their computers when Wilson returned from lunch. He was glad he had accepted Duane's invitation for two reasons. The first was he now knew where Jackson had run to and who was protecting him. The second was that spending some time with Duane was the perfect antidote to the tedium generated by listening to several hours of bullshit. He and Duane had something in common: they were both dinosaurs. He stood behind Moira and O'Neill. 'Where are we?'

'The evening of the eleventh.' Moira brought up an image on her screen. 'This is Whyte entering Queen's Film Theatre. We're looking for him leaving.'

'I've got him here,' O'Neill said.

Wilson and Moira turned their attention to O'Neill's screen. There were time-stamped framed photos of the crowd leaving the theatre.

'Stay with Whyte and see where he goes,' Wilson said.

O'Neill had the images from six different cameras on her screen. 'Where the hell has he gone?' She was searching through the images.

'Check the camera on University Road,' Moira said. 'He'd have to pass there on his way back to his flat.'

O'Neill brought up CCTV from that camera. A small crowd of cinemagoers were dispersing in both directions, but there was no sign of Whyte. 'He must have gone in the other direction.'

'Check it out,' Wilson said.

O'Neill brought up another bank of cameras and played the tape forward. 'Nothing, he must have slipped down a street without a CCTV camera.'

'We need to find him,' Wilson said.

Three heads were concentrated on O'Neill's screen. They watched the images until only deserted streets appeared on the screen. 'Go back to the images of the crowd exiting the cinema.'

O'Neill hit some keys and the departing crowd appeared. The picture was jerky.

'Can you get a continuous picture?' Wilson asked.

'Old-style security cameras don't record a continuous stream,' O'Neill said. 'My guess is that we're looking at about 7.5 frames per second. The human eye can discern 150 frames per second. So you're looking at twenty still photos per second.'

'Watch the young man on Whyte's right,' Wilson said. 'Maybe I'm imagining it, but he appears to be speaking to Whyte as they exit.'

Moira stared at the picture. 'He might be, boss, but it's impossible to tell. Half the crowd have their mouths open and appear to be speaking.'

'Run it frame by frame,' Wilson said.

O'Neill moved the picture forward.

'Stop,' Wilson said. 'Can you zoom in on Whyte's face?'

O'Neill zoomed in. Whyte was smiling.

Wilson turned to Moira. 'Find out what film was playing there on the eleventh of July.'

Moira went online. 'Believe it or not, there was a talk on queer cinema.'

'Run it on again,' Wilson said. This time he concentrated on Whyte and the man at his shoulder. They didn't appear to be together, and yet. The departing crowd swallowed them up and their faces were turned away from the camera. Then they disappeared. 'Where did they go?'

'They must have turned onto Botanic Avenue, we have no coverage there,' O'Neill said.

'Keep looking,' Wilson said. 'See if you can find either Whyte or the young man again.'

Wilson went into his office. There was something there. They had exchanged a remark, Whyte had smiled. Or maybe it was wishful thinking. Perhaps no remark had been made and Whyte was smiling at the memory of some joke that had been told at the talk. At some point, O'Neill would come bounding into his office and tell him that she'd found Whyte and he was alone.

He signalled to Moira. She entered the office and closed the door. He took out the picture of Jackson and handed it to her. 'That's Simon Jackson. The photo was taken as he passed the checkpoint for the Rosslare to Cherbourg ferry. Put it in the Carlisle file. I'd bet a month's pay he's at Helen McCann's place in the south of France.'

Moira stared at the picture. 'I've seen this face somewhere in the past few days, but for the life of me I can't remember where.'

'It'll come back to you.'

'It's almost there ... '

'I know that feeling.'

'I'm building a dossier on Helen McCann. She'll be a tough nut to crack. To finish it you may have to drive a stake through her heart.'

'I might have trouble finding it.'

'I know we're building a case on the Carlisle murder, but maybe her Achilles heel is located somewhere else.'

'What do you mean?'

'Since she's been able to count, she's been involved with money. Do you know anyone who handles millions of pounds who's squeaky clean?'

'That's not our line of business. Jackson murdered Carlisle, but McCann was pulling the strings. Our business is to get Jackson and sweat him until he gives us McCann.'

'And if he doesn't?'

'I don't want to think about that possibility.'

'I've read the file. What was the motivation behind killing Carlisle? The man was dying. Carlisle knew something or was about to do something that ran contrary to McCann. What if there's a conspiracy and there are others involved?'

'Nobody said it would be easy.' He'd already come to the same conclusion as Moira. People like Carlisle weren't removed without a bloody good reason. The road would be long and hard and he was glad Moira would be on it with him.

'When I was a little girl, I didn't play with dolls. I was addicted to puzzle books. Look where my misspent youth has landed me.'

CHAPTER FIFTY-NINE

O'Neill didn't bound into his office, and the news she brought wasn't what he expected.

'The departing crowd from the Queen's Film Theatre is the last sighting of Whyte I can find.'

'Print some copies of two frames: one of Whyte and the man at his shoulder leaving the cinema and a separate close-up of the young man's face. If that was the last sighting of Whyte, that young man was possibly the last person to see him alive.'

O'Neill left the office and returned five minutes later with the photographs.

'Put this last sighting photo on the whiteboard, and well done.'

O'Neill smiled and nodded.

She's bloody good, he thought as he watched her leave. Too bloody good for this place. Someday she'll wake up and discover that there's a lot more to her than being a DC in the PSNI. But for the moment she was his DC and he would get every ounce of value out of her.

He picked up the phone and called Davis. 'We need to talk.'

'You were already on my agenda.'

. . .

BROWNE WATCHED the activity involving Wilson, Moira and O'Neill. In the other corner of the room, Graham appeared to be having difficulty keeping his eyes open. Browne had given up on the Helen's Bay inquiry. Several of the drone clubs had reported back that none of their members were flying in that area on the day in question. His only interest was the Whyte and Carmody investigation and he was annoyed at his exclusion. He watched the boss leave, carrying what looked like photos.

O'Neill returned from the coffee machine, blowing on the liquid in the cardboard cup. She put the cup on her desk, picked up a photo and stuck it on the whiteboard. Browne couldn't contain his curiosity. He stood, stretched and walked around the room. He felt Moira's eyes on him. He was no actor, so trying to appear nonchalant was out of the question. He stood at the whiteboard and studied the photo O'Neill had put up. He recognised the background as Queen's Film Theatre because he often went there. Roger Whyte was in the middle of a group of people leaving the theatre. He stared at the people around him. There were several people he had seen before. Belfast was a small city and the gay community was tight-knit. O'Neill had written 'The last sighting of Whyte' on the board. He continued to stare at the faces around Whyte.

DAVIS SIGHED AS WILSON ENTERED, closed the tome she had been reading and tossed it on a stack of reports. 'They talk about the paperless office and then they drown you in paper.'

Wilson dropped into the visitor's chair. 'I'd run a thousand miles if I ever had to do your job.'

Davis's jacket was over the back of her chair and the heat had obliged her to remove her black bow tie and open the top two buttons of her shirt. 'I think that is a very unlikely occurrence. I assume you're here to brief me on the Whyte investigation.' Her tone was more business-like than usual.

Things must not be going well with Jack, Wilson thought. He'd tried to warn her. He put the photo on her desk. 'The last sighting of Roger Whyte.'

She picked up the photo and looked at it. 'Queen's Film Theatre. Nothing after this?'

Wilson shook his head.

'Where do we go from here?'

'I'm interested in the young man at his shoulder. Don't ask me why, but I want to find him and ask him a few questions. And there's only one way to do that, which is why I'm here.'

'I thought you were media shy.'

'I am, so no personal appearances this time. Get this photo on the news and say that we're interested in talking to anyone in this photo. We'll crop it so only three or four people other than Whyte are in the photo.'

'Do you think the guy you want will respond?'

'If he doesn't, we'll increase the pressure by putting out a request for him alone. According to Duane's friend from Quantico, we're looking for a narcissist who is a consummate liar and likes to manipulate people. It's an invitation a guy with a profile like that won't be able to refuse.'

'What do you want?'

'The TV news this evening and tomorrow morning and the *Chronicle*, online and print versions.'

'The media people will be pleased. Get the electronic versions ready.'

'Did someone kick your dog today?'

'Need to know.'

'Don't let them grind you down just when we're getting used to each other.'

'My eldest son has been doing drugs and my ex is full on with the blame game. I should have stayed home and done my duty as a wife instead of being the main provider for our family. Some days I'd like to wring that bastard's neck.'

'That can be arranged.' Wilson saw that she was not in the mood for humour. 'It's a phase. With luck, he'll come out the other end and put it down to experience.'

'We might have a junkie on our hands.'

'Do you want me to have a word with him?'

'Do you have a lot of experience of being a parent?'

Wilson didn't speak.

'I'm sorry, that was uncalled for,' she said. 'There's enough stress in this job without having the ex on the phone bending my ear.'

'I understand. The offer still stands.'

'Thanks, and it's appreciated.'

'Don't forget, meet the problem head on.'

'I'm going for a family meal this evening. Funny, I feel on edge about it.'

'It's a problem that needs solving. Just don't let it turn into a slagging match.' He stood. 'If I can help.'

'I know. I'll call Media Affairs and ask them to get the photo on the wire straight away.'

CHAPTER SIXTY

Wilson walked through the door of the Crown and saw only a few tourists snapping away with their mobile phones. He concluded that summer was coming to an end. He received a nod from the barman and pushed open the door of the snug that was normally reserved for his use. The photo from Queen's Film Theatre would be on the six o'clock news and O'Neill had confirmed that it was already on the online version of the *Chronicle*. She had cropped the photo so that only Whyte and three other men appeared in it.

'Who's been a naughty boy then?' McDevitt sat in the corner with a half-drunk pint of Guinness on the table.

Wilson feigned surprise and sat. 'What's on your mind, Jock?'

McDevitt took an iPad out of his satchel, turned it on and put it on the table. The photograph of Whyte leaving the film theatre stared up at them. 'Friends don't stab their friends in the back. They give their friends scoops.'

'There was a question of time.' A pint of Guinness arrived for Wilson and he ordered a fresh one for McDevitt. 'But you'll be there at the finish line.'

'Tell old Jock all about it.'

'Not now.' Wilson had never met a journalist he fully trusted and that included McDevitt. 'But you'll have the scoop.'

A smile lit up McDevitt's face. 'I have your word on it? The summer's been light on crime.'

'Burglaries are up.' Wilson sipped his pint.

'Burglaries don't make the populace's pulses race. Murders do.'

'I'd hate to have a job like yours. Wishing people dead by violence.'

'I hear the Police Ombudsman's Office has more or less cleared you.'

'I have no idea what you're talking about.'

'I've been down the Ballymacarrett Road talking with some residents. Following in the Ombudsman's investigator's footsteps, you might say.' He took a business card from his pocket and tossed it on the table. It was one of Matthews' cards. 'Everyone I talked to had one of those. You'd swear he was up for election to the City Council.'

'Nothing to do with me.'

'You're a devious bastard. I want to know what you did that was so bad someone wanted you dead. There's got to be a hell of a story in that.'

Reid stuck her head in the snug before entering. She air-kissed McDevitt and kissed Wilson hard on the lips. 'Gin and tonic.'

Wilson ordered. 'Why the furtive look around the snug before entering?'

'I wanted to make sure that Mezrich wasn't here.'

'I thought he was leaving today,' Wilson said.

'So did I, but he called me this afternoon about a forensic pathology session that was starting in Quantico in three weeks' time and would I be interested in attending. He invited me to stay with him.'

'The hell,' Wilson said. 'What did you say?'

Reid's gin and tonic arrived, and she sipped. 'I told him my agenda for the month was already full. But I'd think about it.'

'Who the hell is Mezrich?' McDevitt asked.

Wilson ignored the question. 'That guy has some gall, I have a good mind to sort him out.' He looked at Reid's face and saw that she was smiling. In the snug's corner, McDevitt was chuckling to himself.

'Got you,' Reid said. 'But I appreciate your reaction.'

Wilson laughed along with them. This was what Belfast was about, a fantastic pub, good company, a few pints of the black stuff and the craic.

Howard Timoney was sitting in the Student's Union bar at Queen's University when he looked up at the television in the corner of the room and saw a picture of himself. The shock almost made him spill his drink and wasn't lost on his companions.

'Seen a ghost?' one of them said.

Timoney smiled. He thought about Whyte. 'You might say that.' He quickly composed himself by breathing deeply. It was inevitable that the police would search every bit of CCTV that contained Whyte and it was equally inevitable that they would come upon him somewhere. He had been super-careful, but he knew that sooner or later he would be interviewed about either Whyte or Carmody. Both men were dead and buried and would never be found. He had nothing to worry about. He'd check the recording of the news when he returned to his flat, but it was clear that the police were asking for the people in the photograph to come forward and help with their inquiries. And that was what he would do. He was composed. They had nothing on him and he would give them nothing, and neither would the other men in the photo. He would be a helpful citizen. 'Another round?' he asked, and his companions nodded. He walked to the bar with a spring in his step. He was about to inflict the ultimate indignity on them. They would interview the killer of Whyte and Carmody and set him free to kill again.

Moira had been outside the Europa Hotel and fancied a drink. She had been about to cross the street when she'd seen Reid enter the Crown. She'd done a swift turnaround. Instead, she picked up a one-person rogan josh from M&S and headed home, where she ate her microwaved curry and drank a half-bottle of red. It was a poor substitute for the gourmet food she'd enjoyed on Frank Shea's balcony in Boston. Perhaps her mother was right. She'd promised her parents that she would visit at the weekend, but she didn't fancy another lecture from her mother on what a silly bitch she'd been. She dumped the remnants of her meal into the bin. Would it be an evening of TV or would she delve further into the life of Helen McCann? Maybe she was a silly bitch. She pulled out her laptop and fired it and her printer up. She checked the *Chronicle*'s website and saw that the photo of Whyte had been uploaded. There was something about the Jackson guy trying to force itself to the front of her brain, but it wasn't quite there yet. She got on with her background reading on McCann.

Browne was standing at the bar in Kremlin. It was after eleven, and the place was heaving. Before leaving the squad room, he'd raided O'Neill's desk and took a copy of the photo of Whyte's last sighting. At home, he'd engraved the faces of the men on his mind. He had seen one or all of them previously but couldn't remember where. The bar was heaving and the jam-packed bodies made it difficult to concentrate on individual faces. Somehow or other he would locate the killer and beat Moira and Wilson to the punch. He'd prove that he was just as good a detective as anyone else in the PSNI. He waved at the barman and ordered another drink.

CHAPTER SIXTY-ONE

Wilson arrived at the station feeling invigorated. There was a point in every case where the balance swung in favour of the police. It might take days, weeks, months or even years, but if you tease the problem enough, and you don't become disheartened, the nugget of information finally appears that springs the lock. He prayed that the final photo of Whyte was that nugget.

'We've gone the distance on this one,' Wilson said to the assembled team. 'We've gone by the book, but the deck was stacked against us from the start. No corpse, no crime scene to process and no forensic put us at a disadvantage that is difficult to overcome. There were no witnesses to interview, the door-to-door on Whyte and Carmody came up with nothing, and the confidential phoneline was a bust. We've hypothesised a motive, and we hit a dry well. Now, our options are limited.' He tapped the photo on the whiteboard. 'This is the last sighting of Roger Whyte, and it's all we've got. We caught one break on this case, and that was Whyte's character. We could trace his movements on what we believe was the last day of his life. Beyond this point we have nothing.'

'So we go back to our desks and pray?' Moira said.

'We don't have that luxury,' Wilson said. 'And do you know why. Because there's someone out there who has killed twice, and who will kill again if we don't stop him. That's the reason we don't just sit with our thumbs up our collective arses. We look at what little evidence we have from 360 degrees. We keep looking at it until it's ingrained in our minds. And we also pray. We do anything and everything that gets us one inch further ahead.' He wanted to see hope on the faces of the team. It was there, but only in small quantities.

THE FIRST CALL came an hour later. Graham was manning the confidential number and he raised his hand to signal to the team. He jotted down the name Michael Fenton. Moira joined him and he put the call on speaker-phone.

'Mr Fenton,' Graham said. 'Detective Sergeant Moira McElvaney has joined me on the line.'

'Mr Fenton,' Moira said. 'We'd like to thank you for coming forward so quickly. You probably heard on the radio or television that we are searching for Roger Whyte. The last image we have of him on CCTV is leaving the Queen's Film Theatre on the eleventh of July.'

'Aye,' Fenton said. 'I was there that night with some friends. But I know nothing about Mr Whyte. I see myself in the photo, but he's only a face in the crowd.'

'We'd still like to talk to you,' Moira said. 'Maybe we can jog your memory. We can interview you at your home or you can drop into the station.'

There was a pause on the line. 'I'm at work at the minute. I'll drop by Tennent Street during my lunch break.'

'We'd be very grateful,' Moira said. 'Ask for DS McElvaney or DC Graham at the reception. It won't take long, and you'll soon be on your way.'

'I get off at one and I'm not far away.'

'We'll expect you after one then, and thanks again for responding.'

The line went dead.

'Siobhan,' Moira said. 'Michael Fenton, everything you've got on him.'

O'Neill got busy.

Moira gave a thumbs-up sign to Wilson.

THE SECOND CALL came half an hour later. Graham and Moira did the same double act and Kevin McBurney was scheduled for a visit to the station at five o'clock.

THE THIRD, and last, call came just before midday. Howard Timoney would be available to visit the station at two o'clock.

AT TWELVE-THIRTY, Wilson sat behind his desk with three dossiers in front of him. O'Neill had worked her usual magic and had assembled all that was publicly known about the three men who had called.

'They all contacted us,' Moira said. 'Does that mean they have nothing to hide?'

'Possibly,' Wilson said. 'Or perhaps one of them has something to hide, but he's confident we won't discover it.' He'd read the three dossiers. 'On the surface, all three are law-abiding citizens, and that's pretty much what I expected. They attended a talk on queer cinema but in itself that meant nothing. All three are most probably film buffs.' He would have to wait to see them in the flesh. 'You and Harry handle the interviews. No rough stuff. I never told you, but Heavey complained about the way you handled him.'

'Me, rough? You've got to be kidding. I'm a pussycat.'

'So is a mountain lion. Use the kid gloves until we find out whether I'm right or not. This case has stretched my intuition to the limit, and I might just have overdone it.'

'Fenton is due first,' Moira said. 'I'll let Harry handle him. We can watch in the TV room and if I need to go in, I will.'

Graham walked into Interview Room 1 and put the thin dossier on Fenton on the table. One look at the man across the table was enough to convince him that Fenton was not a murderer. Then he remembered the number of killers who had been interviewed in the early stages of inquiries and dismissed only to kill again. Mass murderers seldom look as evil as they should. In fact, most look innocuous. He wouldn't like to make the mistake of misjudging a killer.

He extended his hand to Fenton. 'DC Graham, we spoke on the phone.'

Fenton smiled, stood and shook hands before retaking his seat.

Graham opened the dossier. Fenton looked every bit of his fifty-two years. He was overweight, had smokers' lines around his mouth and his breath came like rushes of wind. Graham concluded that there were some hard years in Fenton's life. He placed the photo of the crowd leaving the theatre on the table in front of him. He put his finger on Whyte. 'Do you know this man?'

Fenton leaned forward until his head was over the photo. 'Never saw him in my life. Looks like a nice kind of fella.'

'You said that you attended the talk with some friends. Can you point them out?'

Fenton pointed to three men exiting the theatre in a group.

Graham pushed a pen and paper across the table. 'Would you please write down their names and phone numbers?'

Fenton wrote the names and numbers and pushed the paper back to Graham.

'What's your interest in gay cinema?' Graham asked.

Fenton's face reddened. 'My friends and I have an interest in independent films. I run a video equipment rental business.'

'So, you make your own films?'

'No, I rent equipment. What has my business got to do with this missing man?'

'Sorry. I'm a bit of a film fan myself and I thought I might have met a kindred spirit. So you don't know Roger Whyte and you didn't speak to him at the theatre?'

'No, I didn't.'

'Did you see anyone else speaking to him?'

'There was a lot of noise as the crowd was leaving the theatre. But I didn't take much notice.'

'What did you and your friends do after the theatre?'

'We went for a drink at the Parlour.'

Graham had never been there, but he'd heard the young university types patronised it. He wouldn't associate Fenton with that particular pub. 'Is that your regular haunt?'

'We go there sometimes after a film.'

'So, they would know you there?'

'They know me to see.'

Graham stood. 'Thank you, Mr Fenton, and I hope we didn't spoil your lunch break.'

'Just trying to do my duty and help.'

'You have been very helpful.'

GRAHAM LED Fenton to reception and waved him away before making his own way to the viewing room. Wilson and Moira sat in front of a large monitor.

'What do you think, boss?' Graham asked.

'You did good, Harry. We'll check out the story with the friends, and it might be worth dropping by the Parlour. Get

Siobhan to run off a still from the recording and take it along. There's no hurry. I don't think Fenton is our guy.'

'Let's grab a sandwich and a coffee,' Wilson said. 'Our next arrival is at two o'clock and I think we should give Moira a chance.'

CHAPTER SIXTY-TWO

Graham knocked on Wilson's door. 'Timoney's here, he signed in at ten minutes to two. He's a keen one. He didn't look best pleased when he was told that the officers weren't ready for him and he'd have to wait in the interview room. I don't think Tennent Street is a part of the city he normally frequents.'

Wilson closed the file he was working on. 'Get Moira and let's take a look at him.'

Wilson, Moira and Graham gathered around the monitor in the viewing room. 'Young, handsome and quietly confident.' Wilson turned to Moira. 'Just the way you like them. Better get started.'

Moira gathered her dossier and left the room.

As soon as the door closed, Graham laughed. 'This should be fun.'

Moira breezed into the interview room. 'Good afternoon, Mr Timoney, sorry for the slight delay.' She put her dossier on the table and sat facing Timoney. 'Thank you for coming forward, we'll get you out of here as soon as possible as I'm sure you have other things to do. I'm Detective Sergeant Moira McElvaney.' A smile flitted across his lips. She assumed it had something to do with her being a lowly sergeant. She was willing to dislike Timoney, and she'd only just met him. She took out the picture of the crowd exiting the film theatre and put it on the table. 'This is you.' She put her finger on his face.

'Yes.'

'Perhaps over the past few days you have heard that we are searching for Roger Whyte, who hasn't been seen since the eleventh of July, the date when this photo was taken.'

'I think I have seen something on the TV.'

'The man exiting in front of you in this photo is Roger Whyte. You didn't know him?'

Timoney stared at the photo. 'No, I don't think so.'

'Then you might know him?'

'No, I mean I don't know him.'

'You didn't speak to him as you left the theatre.'

'There was a lot of pushing and shoving. I may have said something, but I'm not sure.'

'Were you alone at the theatre that night?'

'Yes.'

'And you're interested in gay cinema.'

'I'm interested in all kinds of cinema.'

'Is that what you're studying?'

'No, I'm doing a PhD in philosophy.'

She looked at him without speaking.

'It's about Bentham's utility theory,' he added.

'Highbrow stuff no doubt.' Moira smiled. 'So you may have said something to Mr Whyte. Any idea what that might have been?'

'I didn't say I had spoken to him. I said I might have.'

'And what might you have said?'

'I'm not even sure I said anything. Maybe I remarked on the talk. But I don't think I said anything.'

'But why would you have made any remark if you didn't know Roger Whyte?'

'Let's go back to the beginning. I didn't speak to this chap Whyte.'

Moira removed a series of photos from the file and laid them out on the table. 'These are stills from the CCTV footage. We've examined them closely. It looks like you said something and he smiled.'

'I don't remember saying anything. Perhaps someone on the other side of him said something.'

'What did you do after you left the cinema?'

'I went back to my flat.'

'Alone?'

'Yes, alone.'

'Where is your flat?'

'In India Street.'

'That's a fashionable address.'

'My parents are rather well-off. I'm afraid I know nothing about Mr Whyte. We just so happened to be exiting the film theatre together. You asked for the men in the photo to come forward and that's what I've done.'

Moira collected up the photos and put them back in her file. 'You've been very helpful, sir.' She took a business card from her pocket. 'If you remember anything else that happened as you left the film theatre, you can contact me any time. It looks like you're possibly the last person to have seen Mr Whyte before he disappeared.'

Timoney slid Moira's card towards him and put it in his pocket.

Moira led him to the door and opened it for him. She wanted to say 'we'll be seeing you' but forewarned was forearmed and she didn't want Howard Timoney on his guard. She watched him disappear in the direction of the reception.

She turned towards the ladies toilet. She needed to wash her hands.

THAT SNOTTY LITTLE GINGER BITCH, Timoney thought as he headed down the Shankill Road. He was eager to get away from this dump. A fucking sergeant, that's how little they thought of him. He'd expected the big guy who had appeared on the news. Treating him like a pipsqueak. He'd bloody teach them. He was disappointed that he'd let the bitch annoy him. They had nothing on him. So what if he'd attended a talk on gay cinema? So what if they thought he'd spoken to Whyte? They had vision but no sound and as long as he maintained that he didn't speak to Whyte they couldn't prove he did. He was sucking in deep breaths when he turned the corner and headed towards CastleCourt shopping centre. There was a Starbucks there and he badly needed a coffee. He replayed the whole interview in his mind as he remembered it. The bitch had tried to trap him, but he had evaded her.

WILSON, Moira and Graham watched a rerun of the interview with Timoney.

'What do you think, boss?' Moira asked.

'I think you just about had him by the short and curlies,' Wilson said.

'I didn't want to follow through until I heard what you thought. There's no loss in letting him think he's away free. And I think he would have been shouting for his solicitor if I had pushed any harder.'

Graham smiled at Moira. 'And she looks so bloody sweet.'

'He's a suspect,' Wilson said. 'For the moment he's all we've got. Although I'm ashamed to say it, he fits most of Mezrich's profile. That doesn't mean that he's guilty, but we have to take a closer look at him.' He turned to Moira and held up the file on Timoney. 'Get Siobhan on the job. She has to dig a lot deeper than this. I want to know everything there is to know about that boy. Harry, I want you to go down to India Street and have a nose around. See if there are any CCTV cameras in the vicinity. Look for shop cameras, security cameras, whatever.' They were making progress at last. It may all end up in the dustbin along with his theory on Whyte's money, but it may not. If it didn't pan out, they would just have to keep plodding. But somewhere in his head there was a ticking clock, which meant that they needed to move fast.

Browne waited until Wilson, Moira and Harry left the viewing room. He begged the key from the duty sergeant and then watched the two interviews. Fenton was a non-starter. He was the kind of man who took photographs up a girl's skirt. He stopped the tape on Fenton's face and was sure he had never seen the man before. The second interview was much more promising. Maybe it had something to do with the way Moira had handled it, but she made Timoney a likely candidate. He was sure that he'd seen him before, but he didn't remember where. It would come to him.

CHAPTER SIXTY-THREE

Moira went through with the scheduled interview with Kevin McBurney, but she was sure from the first few minutes that he wasn't their man. This was borne out when McBurney produced details of his revels on the evening of July 11th, following the talk, which had ended with him in triage in the Royal Victoria Hospital. He'd been drunk, fallen and split his skull. The scar was still visible. He'd spent the night and most of the twelfth on a trolley in A&E. It was as good as you could get in the way of an alibi.

Wilson was shaking his head when she met him in the corridor. 'He's not our man,' he said. He didn't bother with a rerun of the tape and he saw from Moira's expression that she felt the same.

'I agree. All our bets are on Timoney,' Moira said.

'Maybe we're jumping into the first passing lifeboat,' Wilson wondered.

'If it's not him, we're back at square one. Sometime, I'd love it to be like TV. Gather all the possible suspects in the drawing room and pull a rabbit out of a hat.'

'That's the difference between real life and fiction. If Timoney is our man, we need to prove it. We have nothing in terms of evidence, and he doesn't look like the kind of guy who'll fold as soon as he's confronted.'

'We can only do what we can do, boss.'

'Let's see what Siobhan and Harry have come up with.'

O'Neill had put a photo of Timoney on the whiteboard and had written some salient points underneath. Wilson assembled the team and looked at O'Neill.

'Howard Timoney,' she began. 'Born 28 September 1996, the only child of Sir William Timoney and Lady Victoria. The Timoneys were one of Lloyd's' "Names" for generations until the *Prestige* oil spill almost wiped them out. Sir William still holds several directorships, but the Timoneys now live in what they might call reduced circumstances in a five-bed detached house in Hillsborough. They enrolled young Timoney in Eton, but he had to leave after the family encountered financial difficulties. He attended various private schools here before enrolling in Queen's University. We have nothing in our database on him. He appears to be squeaky clean, but I've only scratched the surface.'

Wilson looked at Graham.

'Swish place on India Street, owner-occupier, the lease is in Howard Timoney's name. Little in the way of CCTV; there are few shops around, and it's a very upmarket area so I wouldn't say the residents appreciate their privacy being invaded.'

'I suppose you might say the same of the Hillsborough property,' Wilson said.

'I'd guess so,' Graham said. 'But I'll give it a once-over tomorrow just in case.'

'I'm considering surveillance.' Wilson looked at Graham. 'Don't get your hopes up about overtime until we build a better picture. He's in the frame, but I've already called it wrong with Heavey. We'll check the Hillsborough house out and Siobhan will keep churning out information. See you lot tomorrow, bright and early.'

Wilson would have preferred to continue working, but his team needed to recharge their batteries for what might be their last shot at finding out what happened to Whyte and Carmody. In the meantime, he would have to brief Davis and see how the land lay on the overtime budget.

Davis sat back in her chair. 'Do you like him for it?'

'He's young and fit. He would handle someone like Whyte, and Carmody was young but lightweight.'

'You didn't answer my question?'

'I think he's involved. But I don't know how he got Whyte off the street without being seen, and we still don't know how or where Carmody disappeared.'

'But surveillance will help?'

'He's gone off thinking he's free. Moira took a good shot at him. She didn't want him going to ground, so she didn't push him as hard as she might have. I think she did a good job.'

'How long are we talking about?'

'How long is a piece of string? In the past month, two gay men have disappeared. We must confirm Carmody's disappearance soon, maybe even tomorrow. McDevitt is desperate to make the letter public. If all that happens, there's a strong possibility that the gay community will pressure the CC, and if that happens, there won't be a budgetary problem. The killer might be out there planning his next murder, or he might lie low for a year, or even ten years. We've been playing catch-up since we launched the investigation. Now we've caught a lead, it's a slender one, but it's all we've got.'

'I'll look at the figures and see what I can do.'

Moira hadn't gone directly home. She had arranged to meet McDevitt in McHugh's after work. The sun was still shining and the evening was hot. All the tables outside the bar were taken. Across the road, children were running around in circles trying to avoid the jets of water shooting up from the holes set in the pavement. She took a table inside and ordered a pint of cider. The drink arrived as McDevitt settled himself into the seat opposite her.

'Mine's a pint of Guinness,' McDevitt said before the waitress departed. 'What's the occasion? Pretty women don't invite ugly old buggers like me out for after-work drinks unless they want something.'

Moira was about to take a step she knew she should have consulted Wilson about. She could still pull back and tell McDevitt it was only a social drink, but that wasn't her style. She took two pages from a magazine out of her pocket. 'This is an article I took out of one of those society magazines that pay celebrities millions of pounds for their wedding photos.' She handed the article to McDevitt.

He scanned the pages. 'It's a profile of Helen McCann.' He admonished himself for stating the obvious. 'So, what should I be looking for?'

'Do you have any contacts with the magazine?'

'If I don't, I'll know somebody who does.'

'The photos used in the magazine aren't the only ones. The photographer would have taken a lot more.'

McDevitt's drink arrived. They touched glasses and drank. 'That would be the case. They could take a hundred or more photos on a shoot.'

'Do you think you might get me copies of those photos in electronic form?'

'What sort of mischief are you up to? Does Ian know about this?'

'There's something I'm following up on.'

'And it concerns Helen McCann. Are you fucking mad? That woman eats people like you for breakfast.' He looked round to see if anyone was listening. 'What's the something you're following up on?'

'I can't tell you.'

'Did you ever hear of that record label that had a dog on it, it was called "His Master's Voice", well that's what I feel I'm listening to. He's trained you so well.'

'The boss doesn't know I'm talking to you.'

McDevitt signalled to the waitress for another round of drinks. 'Don't you think he should know?'

McDevitt was right, but she'd already put her foot into the water. 'It might be nothing.' But then again it might be important.

'I've had my eye on Helen McCann long before she became involved with Ian. She doesn't take prisoners. I won't put my neck on the line unless I know what I'm dealing with. It depends how badly you need those photos.'

'Okay. It involves the attack on Peter Davidson.'

'I'm listening.'

She showed McDevitt one photo. 'See this man in the background.'

McDevitt looked at the photo. 'It's hard to make out his face.' He took a pair of spectacles from his shirt pocket, put them on and stared at the photo. 'The glasses don't help, he's still a blur.'

Moira had never seen McDevitt wearing glasses before. She supposed it was a vanity thing. 'I think it might be the man who tortured and beat Peter. I need the photo files so I can confirm it.'

The drinks arrived and Moira took out a twenty-pound note. McDevitt grabbed her hand. 'The drinks are on me.' He took the receipt from the waitress. He would claim the drinks as an expense later. 'And what if you're right?'

'Then we'd know where to find him.'

'You're a right wee minx. The real question is what is the man who beat up Peter Davidson doing in a photo taken at Helen McCann's house in France?' He looked at her.

Moira tried to keep her face blank.

'Is this the first time you've dealt one-on-one with a journalist?'

Moira started on her second pint of cider. She was regretting her decision to contact McDevitt. 'Yes.'

'Moira, I think you and I will get along famously. Just like your boss and I. But you see there are a couple of rules that govern our relationship. And the greatest of those rules is reciprocity. That means that when I do something for you, you have to do something for me in return. It'll cost me a big favour to get those photos for you. We'll have to think of a piece of information you can give me in exchange.'

'Like what for example?'

'Like what the hell are you up to.'

'I can't say right now.'

McDevitt tipped his glass to Moira's. 'I'm going to trust you, Moira, and I'll get you your photos. Somewhere in the future, you'll pay me back.'

They both drank. Moira couldn't dispel the feeling she'd just made a pact with the devil.

CHAPTER SIXTY-FOUR

The evening was kicking into full gear at Kremlin. Although he was a regular, Browne had to flash his warrant card to gain entry. It was high summer, the city was awash with tourists and Kremlin was the mecca for any gay or lesbian visitor to town or indeed anyone who wanted a good time. The music was pounding and the dance floor was packed. He bought a bottle of lager and scanned the sea of faces as he moved to the edge of the dance floor; some he recognised, some he'd had sex with, but most were unknowns. He chose a spot with a good view of the entire bar. He wasn't there long when he saw Timoney, up on the balcony looking down over the mass of dancers. The intensity with which Timoney was examining the patrons made Browne wonder if he was scoping the crowd for his next victim.

Browne had already made the jump that Wilson wasn't quite prepared to make. He was certain Timoney had lifted Whyte and Carmody and killed them. He climbed the stairs to the gallery. Timoney was in the middle of a group. There was a gap on one side and Browne slipped into it. Every face was concentrated on the gyrating dancers. Slowly, by taking the place of people who left, Browne edged closer to Timoney. He was playing a dangerous game, putting his career and perhaps his life at risk, but it might be his only chance to redeem himself.

Howard Timoney had drunk more than usual, but what the hell, he was celebrating. He'd spent the afternoon replaying the interview in Tennent Street over and over in his mind, and he was sure he had acquitted himself pretty well. The little ginger bitch was clearly a man-hater. He hadn't seen a ring on her finger, and she was past marriageable age. He smiled at the writhing mass of men and women below. Maybe she was down there somewhere, she could easily pass as a tough butch. He had handled her. He wished the rugby guy, the guy they were presenting as some kind of stud duck detective, had been the one to interview him. Pulling the wool over that guy's eyes would be a real coup. Still, he'd shown them he was smarter than them and the feeling was heady. It was like snorting cocaine: he felt omnipotent, he was a god. There was nothing they could do to stop him and he intended to send them a reminder of that very soon. He looked to his right and saw a good-looking guy in a pink shirt. He must have just arrived because he hadn't been there the last time he looked.

'Pretty jammed,' Browne said, not speaking to anyone in particular.

Timoney was about to let the remark go, but the guy sounded like he was from the sticks. It was a miracle they'd let him in. 'It's summer, it's almost midnight and it's Kremlin, that all adds up to a night of craziness.'

'Is it always like this?'

'Your first time?'

'Yeah, I just moved here from Enniskillen. You have a great scene going on.'

Timoney smiled and remembered childhood stories of

country mice visiting the big city. 'My name is Howard, but my friends call me Howie.'

'I'm Rory.' Browne extended his hand and they shook.

'Well, Rory, now we're acquainted, you can call me Howie. Can I buy you a drink? I'm celebrating.'

Browne held up his bottle. 'No thanks, I just got one. What are you celebrating? Is it your birthday?'

'Not quite, but something like that.'

Browne touched his bottle to Timoney's glass. 'Well, congratulations whatever it is.'

'Do you know many people in Belfast, Rory?'

'Not really. I've only been here a few weeks though. I'm work for an Internet start-up, and would you believe I'm the only man in the office.' He laughed.

'I think that you and I will be firm friends.' Timoney felt Browne's shirt and allowed his fingers to touch his skin.

Browne smiled, despite the icicle that ran down his spine. 'That would be great.'

Timoney finished his drink. He took a small notebook from his pocket. 'I'm a little in my cups tonight, Rory. Write your name and phone number in this book.' He thrust the book at Browne. 'Let's get together tomorrow night, maybe somewhere a bit less noisy so we can chat.'

Browne wrote his mobile number in the book and returned it to Timoney, who was a little unsteady on his feet.

'Until tomorrow.' He ran his hand along Browne's cheekbone. 'You're pretty. I promise it'll be an interesting evening.' Timoney deposited his glass on the nearest table and made his way to the stairs.

Browne's hands were shaking. He started deep breathing as soon as Timoney was out of sight. He watched Timoney make his way through the throng below and waved when he turned to look up at him. Now he knew how a snake charmer felt. You watch them as carefully as you can because you know at any moment they can turn on you and strike. His bottle of lager was finished. He wanted to get away from the music and the dancing. He had either made a move that would make his career, or he had made the biggest mistake of his life.

TIMONEY SKIPPED past the bouncers and the queue. Life was beautiful. You think you'll have to search for a suitable candidate, and then one drops right into your lap. Naivety will undo dear Rory, just like Whyte's desperation and Carmody's greed had done for them.

CHAPTER SIXTY-FIVE

The day had started off badly. Wilson had secured a junior detective to answer the phone, but Davis's request for an overtime budget to cover surveillance of Timoney had been refused. There was not sufficient evidence to justify the manpower involved. He knew that it wasn't really about evidence, or manpower, it was about money. Somewhere along the line the politicians had become complacent about crime and there would be hell to pay as a result. Graham was already on his way to Hillsborough to spy on the Timoney family residence. Moira and O'Neill were busy developing the life and times of Howard Timoney, and Browne looked like he had the kind of night Wilson's wished he had had. Life with Reid was evolving into that pattern that every couple recognises. Great sex – when it was on they went at each other like cats in a bag – but they mostly derived pleasure just by being in each other's company. And as much as he missed the hard nights, he didn't miss the hangovers.

Somehow he would have to convince HQ that Timoney was a viable prime suspect. He reviewed the tape of Timoney's interview. The guy wasn't stupid. He would know they faced insurmountable odds in putting him away. It would be difficult to get him to confess. He would call his solicitor, keep his mouth shut and they would be obliged to set him free. The only way they would bring Timoney down would be with evidence, and there was precious little of that. The case might go cold for the next ten years waiting for Whyte's or Carmody's body to surface. That might never even happen. In the meantime, without some break soon, he was sure that someone else would be joining them.

Browne had got to sleep at five o'clock in the morning. His mind had been busy mulling over the situation he had created for himself. He was handing himself on a plate to a man he believed had already murdered two people. It was a crazy manoeuvre. Somehow, Timoney had got the jump on both Whyte and Carmody. Browne was bigger and stronger than both of them and he was well able to handle himself. So, what did he have to worry about? Still, he was only human, and he was in fear for his life. He might be living his last few days. That thought had a sobering effect. How had his life been? Was he happy? Were all his decisions the right ones? Was this the ultimate demonstration that he wasn't cut out to be a police officer? Or was it the opposite? What the hell was he trying to prove? What was his plan for a meeting with Timoney? He needed to discuss his situation with someone else, but who? Wilson would never allow him to meet with Timoney alone. Moira was Wilson's 'mini-me' so if the boss was out of the question, so was she. That left Graham and O'Neill. Harry would never put his job, and his family's future, on the line. Did Siobhan have what it takes to cover his back and keep his secret?

Timoney woke with an unaccustomed hangover. The beauty of being a PhD student was that he was able lie in bed all day and there was no one to scold him. He remembered how he had felt the previous night: strong and purposeful. It was the same feeling he'd had when he raped and killed Whyte and Carmody. The same feeling he'd had when he buried them. He climbed out of bed and stood naked in front of a full-length mirror. The hours he had spent in the gym had certainly given him the body of a god. He picked up his notebook and saw where Browne had written his name and phone number, the poor little country mouse. He would have to choose the meeting place carefully, somewhere well out of the way of CCTV cameras.

It had surprised O'Neill when DS Browne invited her for a coffee in the cafeteria. Her first reaction was to refuse, but she didn't want to offend a superior. So she'd followed him down the stairs and ordered a coffee.

Browne arrived at the table with a coffee and a tea. 'Finding out lots of interesting things about Timoney?'

'He's a strange one.' She relaxed. It would be a chat about the investigation. 'His IQ is off the charts, but every school he attended was in a hurry to get rid of him. I rang around and the reaction to my inquiries was consistently peculiar. Nobody was willing to explain why they were so eager to see the back of him. One of his former teachers suggested that I should speak to his psychiatrist. But I can find no record of him visiting a psychiatrist.'

'If I asked you to do something for me, would you?'

O'Neill shifted on her seat. 'What are we talking about?'

'I've done something without authorisation from the boss.' He waited for a reaction that never came. 'He knows Timoney is responsible for the disappearances of Whyte and Carmody, but there's nothing he can do about it. He wants to find evidence, but, given Timoney's IQ, he hasn't left any lying around for us to find. If we don't stop him, Timoney will kill again. And he'll get better at it, which will make him harder to catch. Sometimes we have to give justice a helping hand.'

She stopped drinking and looked at him with her mouth open. Did the phrase 'give justice a helping hand' mean he knew about her role in getting Noel Armstrong killed?

'I spent the last few nights hitting the gay bars in town, doing some unofficial undercover work,' Browne continued.

O'Neill wasn't at all happy with the direction the conversation was taking.

'I ran into Timoney last night in a bar. We talked, but at one point the way he looked at me made my blood run cold.'

'I really think you should be talking to the boss or DS McElvaney about this.'

'Hear me out. The only way we'll bring Timoney down is to catch him in the act.'

'This is insane. You'd be risking your life. If you want to do that, at least get official approval.'

'Have you never done something without official approval?'

O'Neill stared back. That was the second pointed remark. He either knew or had guessed about her indiscretion.

'I gave him my number and I think he'll call me today,' Browne said. 'At least, I got that impression last night. I might be wrong. Maybe he's just out for a bit of partying. If that's the case, this conversation is just so much bullshit.'

'But if he is the one who disappeared Whyte and Carmody?'

'Then he might attempt to disappear me.'

O'Neill looked into her empty cup. After what she had done, she had no right to judge her colleagues. What business was it of hers if Browne wanted to risk his life? 'What do you have in mind?'

CHAPTER SIXTY-SIX

Wilson flopped into his office chair. He did a quick scan of his emails, dumped fifty per cent and started on those marked with the red star indicating urgency. He surfaced from the email morass half an hour later and went into the squad room. O'Neill was busy writing on the whiteboard and he joined her. She jumped when she realised he was standing behind her. 'You're a little skittish today, Siobhan.'

'You gave me a start, boss.'

Wilson looked at the latest information on Timoney. He was a member of Mensa, had a chequered career in school but a stellar one in Queen's, never worked a day in his life and had no social media presence. 'That's odd,' Wilson said when he had finished reading. 'He's not on any social media platform?'

'Nothing, he doesn't even have a LinkedIn profile.'

'What do we make of that, a twenty-four-year-old male who is not media savvy? I didn't think such a person existed.'

O'Neill shrugged her shoulders. 'He could have a profile under a different name. If he has, it'll take time to find it.'

Graham joined them at the whiteboard. 'I've just been out looking at the Hillsborough pile and it's clear that old man

Timoney didn't lose all his money. I also checked in with the neighbours.' He saw the look on Wilson's face. 'Don't worry, boss, I was just a copper looking into robberies in the neighbourhood, and who didn't like the look of the empty house. Well, the Timoneys are six weeks into a three-month world cruise. How the other half lives; the wife and I haven't been on a family holiday for three years.'

'Don't worry, Harry, put your faith in the Brexiteers. They say the working man will soon be rolling in dosh.'

'So, dreaming of a world cruise with the missus and three kids isn't foolish?'

'We'll see.'

'One point to note,' Graham said. 'Although the son lives in the city, he's been a regular visitor to Hillsborough while his parents are on holiday.'

'Good work, Harry,' Wilson said, reading O'Neill's record of Timoney's school attendance on the board. 'Where was he from 2011 to 2012?'

O'Neill searched through her papers. 'I found nothing.'

'A year in Switzerland perhaps?' Graham said. 'Or being home-schooled, or maybe following the sun with mother and father?'

Wilson looked at him. 'We're not sending you to Hillsborough again. If we do, you'll come back a raving socialist.' He turned to O'Neill. 'We need to fill that gap.'

'I'm working on it.'

'Anything new on the CCTV?'

'DS McElvaney is still going through the discs,' O'Neill said.

'What's next, boss?' Graham asked.

'If I knew, you wouldn't be asking that question because we'd be doing it. Let's keep building up the picture of Timoney and keep looking at the CCTV.'

'Any news on the overtime?' Graham asked.

Wilson gave the thumbs-down sign.

'No world cruise this year then,' Graham muttered and headed back to his desk.

Wilson stopped at Browne's desk. 'How is the Helen's Bay investigation going?'

Browne looked up from the report he was studying, revealing two red-rimmed eyes with black bags beneath. It was clear he was having trouble sleeping.

'I'm following up the lines of inquiry that Moira identified. Most of the drone clubs have reported back negatively. I've been over Hills' life from birth to the present day and found no connection to Helen's Bay, but we don't have records on family holidays or picnics.'

A picture of Ronald McIver jumped into Wilson's mind. Few people make it out the other end of police work unscathed. The injuries to the body usually heal. The effect on the mind is another issue. McIver had disintegrated on his watch. The signs had been there, but he had been so wrapped up in his own problems that he had failed to recognise them. The result of his neglect had been catastrophic for McIver and his wife. When he looked into Browne's eyes, he wondered was he looking at a repeat of McIver. 'Is everything all right?'

'I'm having a bit of insomnia, but otherwise I'm okay.'

'There'll be other investigations. Take time off and go see the doctor. Get some pills. I know you're pissed at being taken off the Whyte and Carmody investigation, but you gave me no choice. If we get somebody for the murders, your connection with Carmody would present serious difficulties for the prosecution.'

'I accept that.'

'No hard feelings?'

'Absolutely none, boss.'

THE DETRITUS of Wilson's half-eaten lunch was still on his

desk when Moira walked into his office and shut the door behind her. 'What's going down, boss?'

'What are we talking about?'

'You haven't noticed the atmosphere in the squad room?'

'I was only there for a few minutes. Tell me about it.'

'There's something going on with Rory and Siobhan. Rory has been like a lost soul since you took him off the case, and Siobhan is as jumpy as a scalded cat.'

'I've talked to Rory already, and he understands he was a liability on the Carmody investigation.' In reality, there was no separate Carmody investigation. Since learning of Carmody's disappearance, he had made a connection between Whyte and Carmody that might not exist. The whole investigation was a shambles. The lack of evidence was forcing him to make all kinds of mental jumps that had no basis in fact.

'I tell you, boss, something is up and it involves both of them. He's gay and she's straight, yet there are a lot of eye signals passing between them.'

'What do you think?'

'I don't know, and that worries me. Rory is quiet and Siobhan is young and a bit naive. If it's not about sex, what is it about?'

'Keep an eye on them. We don't want a recurrence of the McIver business.'

CHAPTER SIXTY-SEVEN

Browne reread the text. It had arrived after lunch and his stomach hadn't been the same since. He was exchanging messages with the prime suspect in a double-murder case. It was so against the rules that it was ridiculous. The prime suspect wanted to meet with him and gave specific instructions as to the meeting place and how to get there. The instructions were a little too precise. Browne had no doubt now that he'd put his head into the lion's mouth, the only question was when the lion would close its jaws. Probably sooner rather than later. He wasn't a brave man, neither was he a coward. He was a man who had embarked on a plan of action that had graver consequences than he had first envisaged. There was a way out. He could ignore the text and forget that he had ever met the man. But he had studied the whiteboard and it was obvious to him that the man responsible for the disappearance of Whyte and Carmody was going to get away with it. There was no evidence against him. All they had was a photo of a crowd leaving a film theatre. The case would go cold. They would move on to other investigations and Timoney would have slipped the net. He didn't want that to happen, but did he want to risk his life to prevent it? And then there was the fact that Timoney would probably try to kill again. Wasn't it better if the next target was him rather than some unsuspecting member of the public? At least he would be prepared. He didn't have to guess what Wilson's reaction to his plan would be. There was no way he would approve it. The days of using police officers as bait for murderous criminals were long gone. The decision to go undercover had to be his alone. It's also a possibility that Timoney isn't a killer. In that case, he will be making a complete fool of himself. But only O'Neill would know, and she wouldn't talk because she'd look as foolish as him.

O'Neill wasn't able to concentrate on anything. Why had she agreed to Browne's crazy plan? What the hell had she been thinking? If Browne ended up being injured, or God forbid killed, then she could kiss her career in the PSNI goodbye. She worked for a hierarchical organisation with rules and procedures. If the shit hit the fan in a big way, she could claim that Browne had instructed her as her superior and that he told her he had Wilson's approval. That thought did not console her. Whatever way she looked at it, she'd made a mistake, and unlike the shopping of Noel Armstrong, it was a mistake that she instantly regretted. But she'd agreed to be Browne's backup and that wasn't something she felt she could walk away from now.

Moira watched Browne and O'Neill. The sense of apprehension in the squad room was palpable. O'Neill was fidgeting with every item on her desk and Browne had stood up and walked around the room aimlessly several times. Something was up and she could feel the fear. One of the amazing qualities of fear is that it is transferable. She didn't know how the process worked, but it did, and she needed to know what they were afraid of. Identifying a problem wasn't the end point for Moira, she was all about finding solutions. There was no apparent reason for Browne and O'Neill to share fear. They were working on separate cases. But she had seen the looks that passed between them. It was nearing the end of the afternoon and she knew that she couldn't let the situation wait. She would have to confront one of them. Browne would be the more difficult prospect. They were the same rank and he could tell her to piss off and mind her own business. Also a confrontation would only bring to the surface the resentment he felt about her return to the squad. O'Neill was an easier target. Moira could pull rank although she wouldn't like to.

Browne left on the stroke of five o'clock, closely followed by Graham. Wilson was still in his office. Moira judged the time was right for a chat with O'Neill.

'What's going on?' Moira stood beside O'Neill's desk.

O'Neill turned off her computer. 'Nothing.'

'I don't like bullshit, so don't give me any. I felt your fear from across the room. What have you got yourself into? What are you and Rory up to?'

'I told you, nothing.'

Moira could hear the quiver in O'Neill's voice. 'Have it your way, but I'll find out and when I do, you'll find yourself filling a Xerox box with your personal effects. Use that big brain of yours. Tell me what's going on and we'll sort it out.' She could see that O'Neill was struggling to keep her composure.

'If there was anything to tell, I'd tell you.'

Moira knew that O'Neill had been on the point of spilling, but the young woman's resolve had held and was now stronger than before. She took out one of her business cards and wrote her mobile number on the back. 'Call me night or day, but do not screw up whatever you're involved in.'

O'Neill took the card, dropped it in her bag and stood up. 'I'm away home.'

. . .

WILSON WATCHED the scene in the squad room. As soon as O'Neill left, he motioned Moira to join him. 'What's up?'

'We definitely have a problem, boss. Rory and Siobhan have cooked up something between them. I tried to get her to open up and I think that she might have been on the point of telling me, but it passed.'

'I don't like it. Rory has been off-colour since this whole business began. Carmody and he were lovers. It's always bad news when the job collides with your personal life, especially in our business. I hoped that Rory wouldn't have a personal stake in finding what happened to Carmody. That's why I took him off the case. But maybe Rory hasn't been as "off" the case as I imagined.'

'He's been spending a lot of time staring at the whiteboard.'

'He knows about Timoney.' The thought was becoming more concrete. 'He couldn't be that stupid?'

Moira was on the same wavelength. 'He could screw up the entire investigation.'

'Think of it another way. Ever since this case began, we've had a great big handful of nothing. Maybe when Rory looked at the whiteboard, he drew the same conclusion that I have; we won't find Whyte or Carmody. Even if Timoney is a murderer, we don't have a shred of evidence against him. Whatever Rory has in mind will probably end up in shit. But what exactly has he in mind and how would it involve Siobhan?'

'She's his back-up plan.' The idea had just struck Moira. 'He's recognised the risk he's running and he's using her as his back-up. If everything is cool, they walk away without a word. But if things go tits-up, O'Neill is the cavalry.'

'So, whatever he has planned is outside the rule book.'

'Way outside the rule book.'

'Do you think he's approached Timoney?'

'Could have.'

'We'll have to stop whatever they have planned.'

Moira stared at him. 'I don't like what you're thinking. It's too bloody dangerous.'

'How do you know what I'm thinking?'

'Because I'm thinking the same thing. You don't want Timoney to go free.'

'Maybe it's not him, and even if it is, this isn't the way to do it. What the hell does Rory think he can do?'

'He wants to get evidence.'

'You've been in the room with Timoney, do you think he'll bare his soul to a stranger?'

'Maybe that not what's on the cards.'

'What do you mean?'

'What if Rory is setting himself up?'

The suggestion hit Wilson like a hammer blow. 'I don't even want to contemplate that.'

'It's a possibility.'

'Rory is a smart guy, he wouldn't do something that stupid.'

'Let's say that someone you'd loved had disappeared, and you felt guilty, what might you do?'

She was right. Rory wasn't thinking with his brain. 'And you think it's going down now.'

'It may be going down as we speak.'

'Then what the hell are we doing sitting here talking about it. If Howard Timoney is our man, and Rory is playing the tethered goat. We need to find out where he is.'

Moira took out her phone and called Browne. There was no answer.

'Get on to technical. Find out what tower Rory's phone is pinging.'

Wilson called Reid and told her not to expect him home. Then he called O'Neill's mobile. There was no answer. 'Shit.'

CHAPTER SIXTY-EIGHT

Timoney had been delighted when Rory Browne accepted his invitation for a drink and dinner. He'd chosen a nice rural location, Wally's Bar in the townland of Culcavy, and sent instructions on how to get there. His sense of excitement was so great that he had already installed himself in the shaded corner of the outside garden. It was strange, but he never felt more alive than when he was about to take a life. Whyte and Carmody had flitted into his life without a thought in their heads. They died without knowing how or why, and in effect, there was no why, other than his desire to rape and kill. Some of the best shrinks had examined his head, but despite their efforts to peer into the real him, he kept such important information to himself. How could one explain to a rational person that the first thought that crossed his mind upon meeting someone was that he would like to kill them? How could they understand a feeling so outside their experience? The air in the garden was balmy and there was a sweet scent from the flowers that hung over the walls enclosing the space. It was a wonderful day to die.

. . .

Browne had taken the bus from Belfast and alighted at the stop closest to Wally's Bar. He contemplated crossing the road and taking the next bus back to the city rather than walking the two hundred yards that separated him from a callous murderer. He started to walk in case his resolve failed him.

Wally's Bar was in a thatched cottage that had probably been operating as a shebeen since King Billy's pikemen marched through County Down. He made his way through the single room that was the pub to the beer-garden at the rear. The evening was perfect, and the sun was flooding the outside drinking area. Timoney sat at a table under an awning advertising Jameson whiskey. He waved a hand to acknowledge Browne's arrival.

'Hi,' Browne couldn't get the nervousness out of his voice, but he hoped that Timoney would judge it as first-date jitters. He sat on the wooden bench.

Timoney beamed. 'Have any trouble finding the place?'

'Not really, your instructions were clear. What's the plan?'

'A few drinks here and then move on to a restaurant I know for a nice meal. This round is on you.'

'What would you like?'

'Let's see if they know how to make a decent vodka martini.'

'Shaken not stirred.'

Timoney smiled. 'Another Bond fan.'

Browne rose and went inside to the bar. It was early evening and there were only three other patrons. He looked around for a CCTV camera but saw none. If he were to disappear, nobody would come to the middle of nowhere looking for CCTV footage. He ordered the martini and a pint of lager. He checked his mobile and saw the missed call from Moira. He ignored it and sent the 'all OK' code to O'Neill. His hands shook as he paid the barman. He composed himself before taking the drinks outside.

He handed Timoney his martini and sat down. 'Cheers.'

'Cheers,' Timoney raised his drink and they touched glasses.

'Tell me about yourself?' Browne asked.

'Not much to tell. I was born quite close to here. After school, I went to Queen's. When I got my degree, I decided work wasn't for me so I stayed on for a PhD. That's it.'

'And when did you realise you were gay?'

Timoney was surprised. He hadn't expected the question. 'I suppose I always knew, but I came out to my parents when I was fourteen or fifteen. What about you?'

'Somewhat the same. Except after school, I bummed around Australia and New Zealand before coming home and doing an IT degree.' The truth was so different.

'You're what, thirty or thirty-two, no boyfriends?' Timoney asked.

'A few along the way but nothing that lasted.' Browne had been struggling all day with the development of his new character. He'd decided that simple was best.

'I have great travel plans.' Timoney drained his drink. 'As soon as I complete my PhD. Hurry up and finish that pint, it's my round.' He held his hand out to take Browne's empty glass.

Browne waited until Timoney disappeared inside before sending another 'all OK' message to O'Neill. He was wondering if they all had called this one wrong. Timoney was charming and appeared to be well-adjusted. He relaxed. Maybe he should try to enjoy the rest of the evening.

TIMONEY ENTERED the bar with a wide grin on his face. It was looking good. Rory Browne appeared to be a bit of a waif. He probably wouldn't be missed for a while and by the time he was, the trail would be as cold as it was for Whyte and Carmody. He went to the bar and ordered a soda water for himself and another pint of lager for his victim. He rejected the barman's offer to deliver the drinks to their table and instead hung around at the bar waiting. When the drinks were ready, he asked for them on a tray. While the barman searched for one, he shook the contents of a small sachet into the pint of lager. He'd given Whyte a dose that would have stunned a horse, but he had been experimenting and was sure that the quantity he was giving Rory Browne was just the right amount to paralyse him. He carried the tray to the table and placed the fresh pint in front of his next victim.

'Drink up, Rory, our reservation is for fifteen minutes.'

CHAPTER SIXTY-NINE

Wilson had been calling O'Neill every five minutes while Moira was dealing with the technicians trying to use Browne's mobile signal to locate the tower closest to his position. O'Neill wasn't responding and Wilson guessed why. Moira was pacing the squad room, waiting for information from the technicians. Wilson's mobile rang. He turned it on without looking at the caller ID.

'Boss, you're trying to reach me,' O'Neill's voice was an octave higher than normal.

'Moira and I have worked out what you and Rory are up to. If this goes pear-shaped, both of you have spent your last day working for the PSNI. Now tell me where Rory is.'

'I don't know.' O'Neill was sobbing. 'I was his back-up. If things went wrong, I was to call you. But it's okay, we have an all-right code and a problem code. He's already sent two of the former.'

'Do you have any idea what you've done?'

The sobbing on the line intensified. 'I'm sorry, boss.'

'No, you only think you're sorry. I'd start praying if I were you.' He cut the line.

'They just got a ping,' Moira shouted from the other side of the room. 'It's the tower at Hillsborough.'

Wilson hadn't yet been formally cleared by the Police Ombudsman's Office, which meant his weapon was still with Matthews. 'Moira, bring your gun and get the address of the Timoneys' house.'

Moira looked at the whiteboard. There was no address. She rushed back to her desk, unlocked the bottom drawer and removed her service pistol. 'I'll call Harry from the car.' They rushed out the door.

BROWNE SHOOK his head to clear his senses. The scene in front of him appeared to have fuzzy edges. It usually took well over two pints for him to get a buzz on. But this was different. He was slurring his words and his tongue felt like it was wrapped in a fur coat. His brain told his hand to pick up his almost empty glass, but his hand wasn't obeying. He wondered whether he was having a stroke. There was something he urgently had to do, something to do with Siobhan O'Neill, but he had no idea what it was. He tried his best to concentrate. His eyes fluttered, he wanted so much to close them and sleep.

TIMONEY LIFTED Browne out of his seat and started to half-lead half-carry him towards the car park. As he left the bar, he made the sign to the barman that his friend had had too much to drink. He put Browne into the passenger seat. There was an attempt at resistance, but he overcame it. He logged the resistance though as an input to developing future dosages. He put on Browne's safety belt, it wouldn't do to be stopped by the police for a minor infringement. He tapped Browne's pockets and found his mobile phone. He removed the battery and tossed it and the phone into the bushes. Then he sat into his parents' Mercedes and drove the short distance to Hillsborough.

Moira called Graham as soon as they left the station and got the Timoneys' address. She put the address into Google maps. Their ETA was thirty minutes. A lot could happen in thirty minutes.

Timoney used the remote to close the electric gate behind him. He drove into the garage and closed the garage doors. Rory Browne was now a dead weight, and it was an effort to pull him out of the seat before standing him up and grasping him under the shoulder blades. He dragged him through the side door of the house and into the living area.

Wilson hit the A1 and sped south towards Hillsborough. The business with McIver had been a monumental cock-up, but it paled into insignificance when compared with what they were facing now. Despite any extenuating circumstances, the buck stopped with him. If it hadn't been for Moira, he would be at home enjoying a meal with Reid. Unaware that one of his sergeants was in a life-threatening situation and that his own career would be heading for the toilet with DCC Jennings' hand on the flush. Maybe management was his Achilles heel. He knew he was a good detective, he could plod through the evidence with the best of them, but was that enough for someone in his position? If he had so little awareness of what was going on with his team members, maybe he shouldn't be their leader.

Wilson went so close to the car in front that Moira jumped. There wasn't the width of a small coin between the two cars as Wilson flew by.

'Take it easy, boss. We won't be much use to Rory if we're lying in a ditch on the side of the road.'

'I want to skin the stupid bastard.'

'He had his motives and we should try to understand them.'

That was the kind of empathy he lacked. Browne was doing something so untypical of the man. He'd proved that he is clever and now he's being stupid, and probably a little heroic, and it could get him killed.

Moira's mobile rang and she answered immediately. She listened for a moment and then turned to Wilson. 'Rory's phone signal has disappeared.'

Wilson floored the accelerator.

TIMONEY MOPPED his brow and flopped into a chair. He had manhandled Rory Browne into his parents' living room and dumped him on the floor. He looked down. Rory's eyes were still open, staring back into his own. He knew that he could see everything and his brain was still operational at some level, but the drug had left his body paralysed. He went to the kitchen and poured a glass of water. He needed to get on with business. He had a lot of digging to do. The heat had gone out of the sun but planting Rory Browne would be heavy work. He drank the water and left the glass in the sink.

BROWNE SAW Timoney leave the room. He fought to clear his mind, but he was battling a fog that just wouldn't lift. None of his limbs were responding. He lay awaiting his fate. Fearing his life was about to end.

WILSON WAS HITTING the outskirts of Hillsborough. What if Browne wasn't at the Timoney house? The phrase 'more haste less speed' occurred to him. No, if the rendezvous with Timoney was set for the Hillsborough area, surely his parents' house was where he would have brought Browne.

TIMONEY CLIMBED off and pulled up his zip. He looked down at the bare buttocks of another pathetic bastard. Now that he had established his power it was time to get on with erasing his victim. He picked up his mobile phone from the coffee table where he had placed it to record the performance.

A small tear crept out of Browne's left eye.

Timoney pulled up Browne's trousers and dragged him to the rear of the house. The wheelbarrow was waiting on the patio and he struggled to dump Browne into it. When he succeeded, he hummed to himself as he pushed the wheelbarrow down the lawn towards his mother's rose garden.

WILSON PULLED up at the electric gate. The house beyond appeared to be empty. They would have to enter the property without a warrant. But they had every right to do so since they believed that a serious crime was about to be committed. The gate was only five feet high and Wilson and Moira scaled it with ease and ran up the driveway.

'You take the front,' Wilson said. 'And I'll take the rear.'

Moira pushed the doorbell while Wilson went through a small gate at the side of the house into a large back garden. There was a patio outside the back door, which was open. Wilson entered the house and heard the bell ringing. 'PSNI, anyone here?' he shouted. There was no answer, so he went to the front door and opened it for Moira. 'Check the house. I'll take the garden.'

Moira took out her pistol and disappeared into the living room.

Wilson went back to the patio. The garden was the size of

a football field. There was a large lawn area in the centre and the boundaries consisted of trees and dense foliage. He walked straight down the centre of the lawn, listening carefully as he went. As he approached the back boundary, he heard the sounds of digging and what he took to be bees humming. He walked towards the noise. Through some foliage he could see Timoney digging a hole. Then he spotted Browne lying prone in a wheelbarrow. They were too late, the stupid young bastard. Anger welled in him and he rushed forward.

Timoney tensed when he heard the bushes rustling behind him. He pivoted and saw the famous rugby guy from the press conference rushing at him. He swung the spade at his head.

Wilson went low in a perfect rugby tackle. He felt the rush of air above his head and the swish of the shovel as it flew past him. He caught Timoney around the middle and drove him into a tree at the boundary wall. The spade flew out of Timoney's hand and Wilson didn't let go until he heard Timoney's ribs crack. The adrenaline was coursing through his body. He stood over the prostrate man. His instinct was to kick Timoney in the head and inflict a serious wound. He drew back his foot, and heard a noise behind him.

'Don't, boss, it's over.'

'Why don't you turn your back for a few minutes?'

'That's not you. We need to take care of Rory.' She rushed to the wheelbarrow and put her fingers on Browne's neck. 'He's alive. That bastard must have drugged him.' She pulled out her mobile and called for an ambulance.

Wilson looked down at Timoney, who was struggling for breath. 'You piece of shit! You would have buried him alive?'

'I can't breathe,' Timoney gasped. 'I think you've punctured my lung.'

'Good,' Wilson said.

'We need to get Rory to the patio.' Moira turned the wheelbarrow around. 'The ambulance should be here soon.'

Wilson went to assist.

'No, boss, you handle that arsehole. Are you okay?'

'Yes. Don't worry, I won't kill him.'

'You know Rory?' Timoney wheezed.

'Yes, he's one of mine.'

'A police officer?'

'One of my police officers.'

Moira reached the patio. She took out her phone and called McDevitt, gave him the address in Hillsborough and told him to get there immediately. She heard a commotion at the front and went around to see an ambulance parked outside the electric gate. She waved at them. 'Do what you have to do to get in. There's a sick man on the patio.' She didn't care about Timoney or the damage that might have to be done to the gate.

One of the ambulance men vaulted over the gate with a steel handle in his hand. He inserted it in a hole at the bottom and used it to free the gate. Two paramedics rushed in carrying heavy bags. Moira flashed her warrant card and led them to the rear, where Browne was still lying in the wheelbarrow.

'He's been drugged,' Moira said.

She looked down the garden and saw Wilson coming towards the house, pulling Timoney behind him.

A paramedic looked up from attending Browne. 'His vitals are good, but the outcome will depend on what he was given and how much of it he was given.' He saw Wilson tugging Timoney, who appeared injured. 'You have another injury?'

'You can deal with him later,' Moira said.

Wilson handed Timoney over to Moira. 'Keep an eye on this lowlife. If he's off to the hospital, you go with him. Don't leave him for a moment. He takes a piss, you stand beside him. You have my approval to restrain him by force if you deem it necessary. I've got some calls to make. It's going to be a long night.'

Two uniforms came around the corner of the house.

Wilson showed his warrant card and instructed them to man the gate. A few onlookers were already assembling and a second ambulance had arrived.

Davis was still at the station when Wilson called. He told her where he was and that they had a man in custody who he was sure was responsible for the killing of Roger Whyte and Vincent Carmody. He was also certain he knew where the bodies were buried. There were elements of the arrest that she wouldn't be happy with, which they could discuss later. She tried to push him for more information, but he wasn't up to discussing it. They had prevented another homicide. In the meantime, he would be grateful if she would stay at the station because Harry Graham would be there for a warrant to search the house and grounds. He also needed Forensics to be informed that a major operation would be required, probably involving the disinterment of more than one body.

Two police vehicles had arrived while Wilson was speaking. The crowd was being moved back from the gate and crime scene tape was being strung in front of the property. A paramedic was wheeling a gurney up the drive.

Wilson called Graham and told him to go to the station to prepare a search warrant for the Timoneys' house and then to present it for Davis's signature immediately.

The paramedics came back with the still body of Rory Browne on the gurney. Wilson caught one of them by the arm. 'How is he?'

'He'll survive, but he won't be feeling so good tomorrow.'

'I want a full tox screen done. I'm making you responsible it happens.'

The paramedic nodded. 'Understood.' He hurried towards the ambulance.

Wilson went back to the patio, where another paramedic was treating Timoney. 'Moira, do the necessary with our friend.'

Moira pulled Timoney to his feet.

'Take it easy, you bitch. Can't you see I'm injured?'

'Howard Timoney, I am arresting you on suspicion of kidnap and murder, you do not have to say anything but it may harm your defence if you do not mention when questioned something you later rely on in court. Anything you do say may be used in evidence.'

'Take this down,' Timoney gave her the middle finger.

'What's that over there?' Wilson said.

Moira, Timoney and the paramedic all turned away. Wilson punched Timoney hard in the stomach. Timoney sucked in air then vomited on the patio.

'That's what comes of insulting a police officer doing her duty,' Wilson said.

The paramedic smiled. 'That's possibly a condition.'

A second gurney had arrived.

'I suppose he should go to the hospital,' Wilson said.

'It would be best,' the paramedic said.

He turned to Moira. 'Stay in touch and as soon as he's discharged, I want him in a cell in Tennent Street.'

Wilson sat on a chair in a quiet corner of the patio. He phoned Reid and told her of the happenings in Hillsborough. 'I'd bet a month's pay that the forensic boys will dig up a couple of bodies tomorrow.'

'How are you, Ian?'

'The bastard almost gave me a new haircut. If I hadn't been a rugby player accustomed to tackling low, I might well have lost my head.'

'Come home, you sound tired.'

'I have to hand the scene over to the uniforms, and I need to go to the hospital to make sure Rory is okay. I'm realising that I'm not as young as I used to be.'

'There's always Santa Monica.'

'Right now Santa Monica sounds like heaven.' He knew the reply would please her, but he hadn't meant it.

A young uniform inspector arrived and Wilson ended the call. He briefed the inspector and then decided there was nothing more he could do at the scene tonight. He'd parked outside the gate and the road leading to the house was blocked at both ends by police vehicles. He was about to climb into his car when he heard a familiar voice shouting his name from beyond the crime scene tape. He closed the car door and walked to where McDevitt was standing.

'What the story?' McDevitt said.

'We've arrested a man in connection with the disappearances of Roger Whyte and Vincent Carmody. He has sustained a slight rib injury and, after medical treatment, he will be transferred to Tennent Street, where he will help the police with their inquiries. That's as much copy as I'm going to write for you. How the hell did you get here so quickly? I didn't think this was on the scanner.'

McDevitt touched his index finger to the side of his nose. 'Jock has contacts everywhere. I have an intern looking into the owner of the house and we'll have a name before morning. I need a bit of grisly stuff for the readers. Did you find any bodies inside?'

'There will be a forensic investigation of the house and grounds beginning tomorrow. Now, piss off.'

'There'll probably be some grisly news tomorrow then?'

'Don't you have any feelings for the dead?'

'I do, they sell papers, which keeps me employed. I remember the days when the newsroom was crammed with reporters. I've watched those desks empty one after another. You can hear yourself think in the newsroom these days. The only thing on Jock's mind is making sure that his desk stays occupied.'

'See you around.' Wilson walked back to his car. He understood Jock's point. He might lose two officers from his team over this fiasco. Some bean counter at HQ will probably attempt to cut the posts altogether and he will have to fight back. He climbed into his car and drove away.

CHAPTER SEVENTY

It was quiet in the waiting room of Lagan Valley Hospital. Wilson sat alone, drinking a cup of coffee. Browne was still in triage, but a nurse had informed him that he would recover. Meanwhile Timoney's ribs had been strapped, and he was now sitting in a police car on his way to Tennent Street with Moira. Wilson had contemplated starting the interrogation immediately but decided to wait until the forensic team reported. The good news was a murderer had been taken off the streets. The bad news was that there would be an inquiry and he doubted that either Browne or O'Neill would come out of it well. When you decide on a course of action, it's important to know that there will always be a price to pay.

After a couple of hours, a doctor in a hijab, who looked about eighteen years old, told Wilson that he should go home. Browne was asleep and would stay in overnight for observation. He'd be discharged in the morning. Wilson said he'd return then.

Reid was sitting in the living room reading when Wilson

entered the apartment. She immediately put her book away and hugged him.

'I need a drink,' he whispered in her ear.

'I'll bet you do.' She broke off the hug.

He poured himself a whiskey. 'Anything for you?'

Reid shook her head. 'It's a hell of a result.'

'Aye, but the cost will be heavy.' He sat on the sofa. 'There's a good chance I'll lose Browne and O'Neill.'

'HQ will understand.' She sat beside him and held his hand. He looked all-in.

'They don't like coppers running around trying to get themselves killed. The only exception they make is when THEY tell you to run around and try to get yourself killed. I'm afraid Rory is for the high jump, and there's a good chance that O'Neill will be joining him.'

'Maybe you'll sleep now.'

'I'm not so sure. At least that bastard won't be planting any more bodies in the rose garden.'

'Finish your whiskey and let's go to bed. I need to be held and I think you do as well.'

'What did I do to deserve you?'

'You are one lucky man.' She kissed him and they sat clinging to each other on the sofa.

CHAPTER SEVENTY-ONE

Wilson was back in Lagan Valley. He needed to speak to Browne and the hospital had informed him that Browne's discharge papers had been prepared and he would soon be ready to leave. He stood up from his chair in the reception area when he saw his sergeant coming out of the lift.

'I'm sorry, boss.' Browne was as white as a ghost.

'Not here.' Wilson took his arm and led him out into the sunshine.

'He raped me.' Tears were running down Browne's face.

Wilson stopped in his tracks. 'What!'

'I wasn't able to move, and he raped me. I told the doctor, and they used the rape kit. God, boss, I feel terrible.'

Wilson's plan to get involved in the blame game was now off the table. Browne might not have a future in the PSNI, but there was no way he would kick a man when he was down. 'It's okay, Rory. They'll give you counselling. You'll get over it in time.' He knew it was a lie. He'd had counselling after his injuries caused by the bomb, but he still woke up some nights bathed in sweat. That would be Browne's future.

'I've been an idiot, boss.'

Wilson steered him to his car and opened the passenger

door. 'You did what you thought was right.' He examined his own conscience and couldn't declare himself innocent.

'I screwed everything up.' Browne sat in the car and Wilson closed the door.

Wilson walked to the driver's side and sat behind the wheel. 'You stopped a killer from killing again.'

'It was you who did that. Are we going to the station?'

'No, I'll drop you at home. You need to rest and I need a chance to sort things out with the chief super.'

Browne slumped back into his seat. 'I'm done. They'll throw me out.'

'You must have seen it as a possibility.'

'I suppose so.'

'But one of the things I learned as a rugby player was that it's not over until it's over. And you're not over.'

'TELL ME IT'S NOT TRUE.' Davis did her nervous tell of flicking a loose strand of hair that wasn't there.

'It's not true.'

'Don't be an arsehole, Ian.'

Wilson didn't want the meeting to turn into a slanging match. He'd already noticed the absence of tea and biscuits, always a bad sign. 'What's not true?'

'That Browne went off half-cocked without your approval and put himself in danger.'

'DS Browne was discharged from hospital this morning. He was drugged and nearly lost his life. However, he exposed a man that we believe had already murdered two men and planned to murder many more. Yesterday, we had no evidence against this man; today, we probably have enough to put him away.' He knew that the forensic team had been in Hillsborough since first light and that they had already discovered two burial sites. 'Timoney is in the cells and I'm delaying his interrogation until I take a look at what Forensics come up with.'

'We need to report all this to HQ.' Davis sat back. 'We can emphasise the positive result, but my guess is they will want their pound of flesh. I think you know that too.'

'Like you said, we got a positive result. We hadn't a shred of evidence against Timoney.'

'Browne may have given up his career in a good cause.'

'He needs friends. Timoney raped him. They used a rape kit at the hospital so we'll have Timoney's DNA.'

'Holy God.' Davis held her head in her hands. 'Look, I'll do what I can for the poor man. You write it up and we'll work on it together.'

Wilson stood. 'I'll keep you informed.'

WILSON HAD COLLECTED Moira from the squad room and they had retraced their journey of the previous evening. Two TV trucks were stationed at either end of the road leading to the Timoneys' house. The uniform on duty at the tape lifted it to allow Wilson's car to pass. Moira signed them in. At the house, they put latex booties over their shoes and donned gloves before walking to where the forensic team was excavating the graves.

Wilson recognised Michael Finlay among the group of white-suited technicians. 'Good morning, Mick.'

'Good to see you, Ian.'

'This is DS Moira McElvaney,' Wilson said. 'I don't think you've met.'

'I would have remembered if we had,' Finlay said.

Another admirer Moira could add to the list, Wilson thought.

'We've got the first one partly exposed.' Finlay led them to the makeshift grave.

Wilson recognised the jacket Roger Whyte had been wearing when he disappeared. He took out his mobile phone and took a picture. 'I want photos as soon as possible.'

'You got it,' Finlay said. 'The graves are still fairly fresh so we're making good progress. We should have the bodies disinterred by early afternoon. There are a couple of other sites but the ground radar shows them as animal remains.'

'Perhaps Timoney was practising,' Moira said.

'Have the corpses sent to the Royal,' Wilson said. 'I want Professor Reid to do the autopsies.'

'There's something inside that I want to show you.' Finlay led the way back up the garden and into the house, where he retrieved a clear plastic evidence bag with a mobile phone inside. He took the phone from the bag and pressed some buttons before handing it to Wilson. 'It's been dusted. Look at the video.'

Wilson pressed the arrow on the centre of the screen and watched Browne being raped in vivid colour. He hit pause and handed the phone back to Finlay. Timoney was one sick puppy. He would have to review the video later and, down the line, the prosecution would probably insist that it be played in court. He could only imagine the effect it would have on Rory.

'We'll send it along with the rest of the physical evidence,' Finlay said.

'Good job,' Wilson slapped the young man on the back. He walked through the house and out the front door. Two men had ended their lives in that house. He didn't believe in ghosts, but if they existed that's where they'd be.

CHAPTER SEVENTY-TWO

They drove back to the station in silence. Watching a video of someone you know being raped can have that effect.

'I think young Finlay took a shine to you,' Wilson said as they entered the station.

'I didn't notice,' Moira replied.

'Let's take a run at this gobshite.'

Wilson instructed the duty sergeant to have Timoney brought up and deposited in an interview room. And he wanted him handcuffed. Then he and Moira went to the TV room to watch Timoney as he was brought in and put sitting at the table. A uniformed officer stood at the door. Timoney looked up at the camera in the corner of the room and yawned.

'Spence told me that in the old days an arrogant bastard like that might have a bad fall down the stairs on his way to the cells.'

'Bring back the old days,' Moira muttered under her breath.

'I need a coffee. Let him stew.'

. . .

THEY RETURNED to the TV room half an hour later. Timoney had his head resting on the table. Wilson turned to Moira. 'I should have taken Mezrich more seriously. He's a narcissist, and you don't kill two people and bury them in your parents' back garden if you're not psychotic. I think we're looking at our first psychopathic serial killer not fuelled by religious hatred or political ideology.'

'I only did psychology for two years. We didn't get on to psychopaths.'

'I think we may spend some time with this boy. Let's see what bullshit he wants to feed us.'

They walked into the interview room and sat at the table. Wilson nodded and the uniform left. Timoney ignored their arrival.

Moira switched on the recording device.

'Mr Timoney,' Wilson began. 'My name is Detective Superintendent Ian Wilson, and this is Detective Sergeant Moira McElvaney. She has already cautioned you. You are accused of kidnapping and murdering Roger Whyte and Vincent Carmody and the kidnapping and attempted murder of Detective Sergeant Rory Browne. Are you ready to tell us why you murdered two men and buried them in your parents' back garden?'

Timoney's head came up slowly. He looked at Moira. 'Last time the monkey interviewed me. This time they've sent the organ grinder as well.' He turned towards Wilson. 'You broke my ribs. I will sue you and the PSNI for police brutality.'

'Please go ahead,' Wilson said.

'I want my solicitor.'

Wilson pushed a pen and paper across the table. 'Write your solicitor's name and address or phone number.'

Timoney took the pen, wrote down the details and pushed the paper back.

Wilson looked at the name on the paper. 'DS McElvaney

will you please contact Mr Cave and tell him his client wishes to see him.'

Moira took the paper and left. Graham entered and took Moira's place.

'DS McElvaney has left the room and DC Graham is now present,' Wilson said. 'Why did you kill Roger Whyte?'

'No comment.'

'Vincent Carmody was a helpless poor devil, why in God's name did you kill him?'

'No comment.'

Wilson stood up. 'Interview terminated at twelve forty-one.' He and Graham left together.

'It's a pity you didn't break his fucking skull instead of his ribs,' Graham said just before Wilson closed himself off in his office.

Sometimes Harry made the salient comment, even if it wasn't the politically correct one, Wilson thought. He dreaded what was ahead. He knew there would be a trial, and Timoney would ensure that the audience was entertained. There would be Timoney's home movies and Wilson hoped the clerk of the court had plenty of sick bags handy for the jury. Yes, Harry was right, it would have saved a lot of time, effort and expense if he had broken Timoney's skull.

Moira knocked on Wilson's door before opening it. 'Mr Cave will be here soon. When he arrives, he wants to speak with his client, and he wants all recording equipment turned off while he and his client consult.'

'What do good solicitors and sharks have in common?' Wilson asked.

Moira shook her head. 'Tell me.'

'They can both smell blood in the water. The trial of Howard Timoney will attract as much publicity as the recent rugby rape trial. Cave and whatever barrister he engages will be in front of the TV cameras daily. It's the kind of publicity money can't buy.'

THE DESK SERGEANT had informed Wilson of Dermot Cave's arrival, and asked if someone from Wilson's squad could please do the honours. Wilson had sent Moira to introduce him to his client.

Minutes later, she returned and stopped at Wilson's open door. 'What an arrogant prick.'

'Did he treat you like something he found on the sole of his shoe?'

'Something like that.' She went back to her desk.

Wilson wouldn't like to be Cave if Moira ever got her nails into him. He continued working on his account of the events of the previous evening. He had written many such reports. Normally they involved a simple reiteration of the facts. Sometimes he tried to put a spin on how events evolved, as he had done for the happenings at the warehouse in Ballymacarrett. The facts were there, but it didn't happen exactly in the way he wrote it in the report. He was trying to save Browne's career, but even with the most positive spin, he wasn't optimistic. The trolls in HQ would look for his blood. The DPP would crap all over them about his unauthorised activity. And although Davis would help with the final draft, there was no way she would jeopardise her own career.

He declined Moira and Harry's invitation to a cafeteria lunch and worked through. The photos arrived from the forensic team and he sent them to Moira for printing. Finlay had included an MP4 file containing the rapes of Whyte, Carmody and Browne. He asked Moira to put the file on a USB stick.

Just before three o'clock, the word came from the desk that Mr Cave and his client were ready for an interview.

Wilson continued working on his report until the desk

sergeant made a second call. He motioned to Moira, and she met him at the squad room door. She handed him a file with the photos from the gravesites and a USB stick.

CHAPTER SEVENTY-THREE

Wilson and Moira sat opposite Timoney and Cave. The solicitor had his pad and gold pen at the ready. He was wearing an expensive suit and his briefcase had a Gucci logo on it. Dermot Cave didn't do poor.

'Mr Cave, good to see you again,' Wilson lied. 'I understand that you've already met DS McElvaney.'

Cave didn't look at Moira but nodded.

Wilson opened the file and laid four photos from the gravesite on the table. He stared at Timoney. 'As I told you already, you are still under caution.'

Timoney looked at Cave, who nodded. 'I understand.'

'Good. Is there anything you'd like to tell me about the scene shown in these photographs?'

'Yes. I killed those two men, and I buried them in my parents' back garden.'

'And why did you kill them?'

'I suppose because I could. Have you ever tried drugs?'

Wilson didn't answer.

'The first time gives you an incredible high. That's what killing does for me. As you can see from the photos, my actions were not those of a rational person. I have a serious psychological condition, which has led me to commit these terrible crimes. I've been receiving treatment for my condition since the age of sixteen.'

'So, you admit that you murdered both Roger Whyte and Vincent Carmody and buried their bodies.'

'Yes.'

'Just like that.'

'Yes. What would you like me to say?'

'You've just admitted that you took the life of two men with the same level of emotion that you might have exhibited if I'd asked what you thought of the weather.'

'I don't understand.'

Wilson shook his head. He'd take an old-time criminal any day of the week. 'How did you choose Mr Whyte?' Wilson took a photo of Whyte from the file and pushed it across the table.

Timoney looked at the photo. 'I'd seen him around and knew he liked young flesh. When I noticed him at the Queen's Film Theatre, I caught him with three words: "Like a date?" I was parked around the corner and I drove him to Hillsborough.'

'You don't have a car.'

'My parents have three.'

'You drugged him. What did you use?' The tox screen on Browne was in the file.

'GHB.'

'Gamma-hydroxybutyric acid.'

Timoney smiled and nodded. 'Yes.'

'And what about Mr Carmody?' Wilson put a photo of Carmody on the table.

Timoney looked at it. 'Everybody knew Vinny was a whore. I offered him money for sex and he almost came with excitement.'

'Did you use GHB on him as well?'

'Yes.'

'Were you aware that both men were alive when you buried them?'

'I thought Whyte had died from an overdose. Burying him was a buzz. I knew Vinny was alive when he went in the hole.'

Wilson gathered his photos and replaced them in the file. Looking at Cave, he said, 'I think we're done for the moment. We'll be returning your client to the cells. We need to review the forensic evidence and discuss the future action with the DPP. In the meantime, we'll be requesting an extension for the full ninety-six hours to facilitate additional questioning.' Wilson and Moira stood.

'You think you have me,' Timoney said.

Cave put his hand on his client's arm, but Timoney shook him off. 'With a psychological record like mine, they'll never convict me of murder; even manslaughter will be difficult to get past a jury. The evidence of the psychiatrists will bamboozle them.'

Wilson ignored him and opened the door. The uniformed officer was standing outside. 'Bring the prisoner back to the cells.' He and Moira started back towards the squad room.

'Detective superintendent.'

Wilson turned. Cave was walking towards them.

'He'll never serve a day,' Cave said when he came level.

'That's your opinion,' Wilson said. 'I happen to have a little more faith in the justice system.'

'He's a very disturbed young man. He is more in need of help than incarceration.'

'We're in agreement on the fact that he's disturbed. But if it were up to me, I'd turn the lock and throw away the key. If he gets out, he'll kill again and either me or some other poor copper will have to pick up the pieces. And you'll be nowhere around. But at least I won't be responsible for the death of another innocent person.'

'Are you intimating that perhaps I should feel responsible?'

'I'm intimating nothing. I've done my job, and it's your turn to do yours. Your conscience is your business. See you in court.' Wilson turned and continued walking.

'He can't slide, boss,' Moira said. 'We have him bang to rights.'

'We've done our job. Now it's up to the DPP.'

'Oh shit, you think he's right.'

'One of the first cases I worked on as a DC was Susan Christie. Did you ever hear of her?'

'No.'

'Christie befriended her lover's wife, Penny McAllister, and the two women went for a walk in Drumkerragh National Park in County Down. During that walk, Christie cut Penny's throat. A woman named Eileen Rice saw Christie coming out of the woods alone. Christie babbled incoherently about an attack by a man in the forest and pleaded with the woman to "help Penny". An ambulance took Christie to Downe Hospital in Downpatrick, where she repeated her story that a wild bearded man had jumped out of the undergrowth and attacked them with a large knife. He had lunged at Penny and Christie had managed to escape when one of Penny's dogs began barking and, much more effectively, she'd kneed the stranger in the testicles. It was all bullshit. The husband came forward and we built a watertight case against Christie. When it went to court, Christie claimed that her mind was a total blank about Penny's death. The jury deliberated for three hours before declaring that they couldn't reach a verdict. The judge said he would accept a majority verdict, and when the jury returned for the second time they found her not guilty of murder. The judge imposed a five-year sentence, which would have seen Christie serve eighteen months. The sentence was increased to nine years on appeal. Christie was out in six. She changed her name, but I still keep an eye on her.'

'That sucks.'

'We're only one branch of the justice system. We do our

jobs and we hope the others do their jobs. I need to get out of here. Fancy a trip?'

'Why not?'

WILSON PULLED into the car park at Sunny Days. He and Moira stood and looked across Belfast Lough to Carrickfergus in the distance. It was a beautiful day, not the kind of day on which to tell a mother that her son had been murdered. They stood for several minutes admiring the scene. Wilson turned abruptly and pushed the front door.

The same receptionist was on duty and Wilson showed his warrant card. 'Mrs. Whyte, please.'

The receptionist was about to raise an objection when she saw the look on his face. She came from behind her desk and led them to the old lady's room.

Norma Whyte was sitting in her wheelchair facing the window. She was enjoying the view of Belfast Lough.

'You have visitors,' the receptionist said and left.

Whyte turned her wheelchair to face her visitors. 'Detective Superintendent, I've been expecting you.'

'This is Detective Sergeant Moira McElvaney,' Wilson said. He looked at the old woman's face. It had only been days since he'd last seen her, but the signs of impending death were already more pronounced.

'It's all right, superintendent, I've known for some time that my son is dead.' She looked at Moira. 'Thank you for coming, dear, but I've already cried all my tears for Roger.'

Wilson moved towards her and offered her his hand. 'I'm sorry and I'd like to offer you condolences on behalf of the PSNI and myself. We found him yesterday. I'd prefer not to go into the details, but he was simply the target of an opportunist. He did nothing wrong. At least now he can have a Christian burial.'

She took his hand and held it in hers. 'I'll be seeing him

soon. My belief in God and the afterlife is strong. I'm very grateful to you and your colleague for taking the time to come and tell me personally.'

'It was the least we could do. And if you need any help ... '

'The staff here are adept at handling funeral arrangements. They have had plenty of experience.' She released Wilson's hand. 'I appreciate your consideration. Now, if you don't mind, I'd like to be alone.'

They went back to the entrance and informed the receptionist of the purpose of their visit. She assured them she would take care of all the arrangements. Wilson left his card and said he would advise when the body was ready for collection.

He didn't want to go back to the station so they drove to the High Street, where they picked up two ice creams. He parked on Seacliff Road, across from the traditional cottage that serves as the tourist information centre. They walked towards the sea and sat on a bench. The water was alive with children learning to sail small boats. It was the perfect antidote to interviewing an evil monster. He licked his cone and watched the children scream when they tacked and fell into the water. He thought of Reid and wondered.

'Have you any regrets about what happened with Brendan?' he asked.

'No. We liked each other well enough, but it just didn't work out. He'll make some woman a fine husband someday.'

'There was someone else, wasn't there?' He could see the wheel of her mind turning and he knew he was right.

'Maybe.'

'Only maybe?'

'For the moment.'

'Take my advice, Moira, if you find something good, hold on to it. Life goes fast, years pass like months and months pass in instants.' He wondered whether he was talking to himself or to her. He stood up. 'I don't know if I told you, but I'm happy you returned.'

'I'm glad to be back where I belong.' She wasn't totally convincing.

As soon as he arrived back at the station, Wilson went into his office and sat behind his desk. He knew just how Moira felt about the justice system because he'd been feeling like that for twenty years. Sammy Rice was still missing, one of David Grant's killers was still at large and whoever killed Mad Mickey was also out there. But at least, for him, this one was almost over. Another interview or two with that sick fucker down in the cells, a few months on the documentation and interviews with the DPP and he would move on.

He opened up his emails. The latest was from Davis and the subject line read 'Rory Browne'. He opened the mail. HQ had put Browne on suspension pending an inquiry. He'd expected that outcome but still felt like he'd failed another colleague. His phone rang and he answered, 'Wilson.'

'Hi Wilson, it's Reid. It's a beautiful day outside and you're sounding like the grinch.'

'Rory is on suspension.'

'Oh no, what will that mean?'

'He'll have a lot of questions to answer. He may not think it worth his while.'

'What about O'Neill?'

'The jury's still out. It depends whether HQ think being naive is against the rules.'

'Your two clients arrive this afternoon. Anything special you want me to look for?'

'He says he drugged them with GHB. Check that. And see if there's any semen in their rectums. You can get DNA from it, right?'

'If the sperm is there, we'll get the DNA.'

'I'll be buying drinks in the Crown this evening. I don't think we'll be the jolliest bunch, but we got a result and there's a tradition to uphold.'

'I'll be there.'

CHAPTER SEVENTY-FOUR

The small padded envelope was sitting on Moira's keyboard. Her name was written on one side. She felt it and concluded it was a USB stick. She opened the packet and the small stick slipped out. She threw the envelope into the trash and put the USB into her computer. Dozens of thumbnail photos came up on the screen. They were the photos from the shoot at Helen McCann's house in Antibes. She brought them up one by one until she found the one she'd seen in the magazine article. He was standing in the garden. She zoomed in on his face. The photos were in high resolution, but he was standing far behind the subject of the photo and his face broke up into pixels. She zoomed out until the features became clear. She was looking at Simon Jackson. McDevitt had come through. She was about to take this new piece of evidence to Wilson's attention but changed her mind. He had enough on his plate.

Wilson, Moira and Graham sat facing the whiteboard. 'We would probably never have got Timoney without Rory,' Wilson said.

'Do you think he'll get through this?' Moira asked.

'I don't know. Before anything else happens, I'm going to make sure he gets counselling,' Wilson said.

'What about Siobhan?' Moira asked.

'I tried to convince her to come and have a drink with us this evening, but she just broke down in tears.'

'I thought she was made a sterner stuff, boss,' Graham said. 'We all screw up now and then. It's the human condition.'

'I've left her out of the report with Davis's agreement. The chief super is the kind that forgives but doesn't forget. I don't think Siobhan should look for promotion any time soon.'

Graham looked at Wilson and Moira. 'We're a bit of a motley crew when you think of the old gang.'

'We have to get ourselves together and get on with things. I've booked a snug at the Crown for half five. I suppose we should be on our way.' Wilson glanced at Rory's desk as he passed. He'd grown fond of his sergeant. They'd had some good times together.

A FEW MINUTES LATER, the office was empty and Browne's computer pinged indicating an email. A member of the East Antrim Drone Club had been flying his drone in Helen's Bay on the day the BMW had caught fire and had some footage of the event.

THE MOOD in the snug was sombre. Even Reid was dragged down by the general torpor. Davis had wanted to buy the drinks, but Wilson had insisted on paying. The steady flow of alcohol wasn't having the desired effect.

McDevitt stuck his head around the door. 'Is this wake private or can anyone join?'

Wilson waved him inside and ordered him a drink.

McDevitt put a copy of the street edition of the *Chronicle* on the table. Timoney's arrest was the lead story. There was praise for the efforts of the PSNI.

'The job's safe for another few months,' Wilson said. He noticed smiles on the faces of Reid and Davis. McDevitt was a bit of a pain in the arse at times, but he had a way of lightening the atmosphere.

McDevitt sat beside Moira and they toasted each other when McDevitt's drink arrived. 'Now I have two new best friends.'

'Can you take a holiday the week after next?' Wilson asked Reid.

'I can rearrange my schedule, why?'

Wilson handed her an envelope. She opened it and took out two plane tickets.

'There's someone in Nova Scotia I think you should meet.'

She hugged and kissed him. 'I've always wanted to visit Nova Scotia.'

His phone beeped and he looked at the message: 'We need to talk. Michael Gowan'.

Wilson had to think for a moment. Then he remembered Carlisle's coded notebook. Not right now, dear God, not right now, he thought.

AUTHOR'S PLEA

I hope that you enjoyed this book. As an indie author, I very much depend on your feedback to see where my writing is going. I would be very grateful if you would take the time to pen a short review. This will not only help me but will also indicate to others your feelings, positive or negative, on the work. Writing is a lonely profession, and this is especially true for indie authors who don't have the backup of traditional publishers.

Please check out my other books , and if you have time visit my web site (derekfee.com) and sign up to receive additional materials, competitions for signed books and announcements of new book launches.

You can contact me at derekfee.com.

ABOUT THE AUTHOR

Derek Fee is a former oil company executive and EU Ambassador. He is the author of seven non-fiction books and sixteen novels. Derek can be contacted at http://derekfee.com.

ALSO BY DEREK FEE

The Wilson Series

Nothing But Memories

Shadow Sins

Death To Pay

Deadly Circles

Box Full of Darkness

Yield Up the Dead

Death on the Line

A Licence to Murder

Dead Rat

Cold in the Soul

Border Badlands

Moira McElvaney Books

The Marlboro Man

A Convenient Death

Made in the USA
Monee, IL
15 May 2022

96478056R00177